Praise for *Bui*

"Young adult romance author Hahn dazzles in her adult rom-com debut set to a circa 2010 teen-pop beat and featuring two child stars from the Midwest who left L.A. and celebrity behind. . . . Home renovation was never this sexy, and readers who enjoy small-town ambiance will get their fill with scenes of market festivals, karaoke at the local brewery, and long drives."

—*Booklist* (starred review)

"In her adult debut, Hahn (*Never Saw You Coming*) successfully brings likable protagonists to life in this character-driven second-chance romance, perfect for fans of Tessa Bailey."

—*Library Journal*

"Plenty of charm."

—*Publishers Weekly*

"Hahn proves one novel after another that she's no slouch when it comes to writing. Each new book seems to be a love letter to her craft. They are filled with beautifully balanced prose and dialogue, and layered with creativity."

—*CSM Times*

"Erin Hahn's YA contemporaries have long been favorites, and this all-too-welcome branch into the adult sphere of romance joins that tradition."

—*BuzzFeed Books*

"If Hallmark movies are your favorite thing about fall, you will want to be sure to check out *Built to Last* by Erin Hahn."
—*Franklin County Times*

"*Built to Last* is the hilarious, romantic celebrity gossip/house-flipping mashup I didn't know I needed! Thank you, Erin Hahn, for making me laugh and swoon and cry sweet, happy tears. I want to move to Michigan, become best friends with Shelby and Cameron, and have them renovate my house, which is to say . . . Can I live in this book?"
—Jen Doll, author of *Save the Date* and *Unclaimed Baggage*

"I loved this delightful romance about makeovers of old homes, old personas, and relationships that never had a chance to launch. A sweet, charming reminder of what you can build with a strong foundation."
—Jodi Picoult, #1 *New York Times* bestselling author of *The Book of Two Ways*

"'If Taylor Swift retired and decided to restore furniture instead' is the best way I can describe Erin Hahn's magnificent adult romance debut."
—Mike Lasagna, bookseller, Barnes & Noble

Friends Don't Fall in Love

a novel

ERIN HAHN

ST. MARTIN'S GRIFFIN
NEW YORK

First published in the United States by St. Martin's Griffin,
an imprint of St. Martin's Publishing Group

FRIENDS DON'T FALL IN LOVE. Copyright © 2023 by Erin Hahn.
All rights reserved. Printed in the United States of America.
For information, address St. Martin's Publishing Group,
120 Broadway, New York, NY 10271.

www.stmartins.com

Library of Congress Cataloging-in-Publication Data

Names: Hahn, Erin, author.
Title: Friends don't fall in love : a novel / Erin Hahn.
Other titles: Friends do not fall in love
Description: First Edition. | New York : St. Martin's Griffin, 2023.
Identifiers: LCCN 2023016830 | ISBN 9781250827111 (trade paperback) |
    ISBN 9781250827128 (ebook)
Subjects: LCGFT: Romance fiction. | Novels.
Classification: LCC PS3608.A444 F75 2023 | DDC 813/.6—dc23/
    eng/20230421
LC record available at https://lccn.loc.gov/2023016830

Our books may be purchased in bulk for promotional, educational,
or business use. Please contact your local bookseller or the
Macmillan Corporate and Premium Sales Department at
1-800-221-7945, extension 5442, or by email at
MacmillanSpecialMarkets@macmillan.com.

First Edition: 2023

10 9 8 7 6 5 4 3 2 1

For everyone who was told they couldn't:
Just because they wouldn't doesn't mean you shouldn't.
Which is why I just did.

NOTE TO READER

Some of the thematic content in *Friends Don't Fall in Love*
contains discussions of school shootings and gun violence.
Neither event occurs on the page.

For more information, please visit the author's website.

JONESIN'
(as sung by Drake Colter)

Asleep, she's mine
Eyes closed, lips chase and pin me
Pin me down
I'm overcome and trembling, searing alive
Heart open, unspoken words chase and pin me
Pin me down
When I wake, she's gone

I reach and I'll keep reaching
I wish and I'll keep wishing
Wrestle with my inconstancies
       Worthless and regretting
I miss and I'll keep missing
Craving her, I'm jonesin'

Intoxicated, she's mine
Fists closed, memories chase and pin me
Pin me down
I'm spinning and breathless, burning alive
Regrets open, opportunities wasted chase me and pin
    me
Pin me down
Sober, she's gone

I reach and I'll keep reaching
I wish and I'll keep wishing
Wrestle with my inconstancies

Worthless and regretting
I'll miss and I'll keep missing
Craving her, I'm jonesin'

So many things I should have said
(I'm jonesin')
The times I should have begged you to stay
(I'm jonesin')
The empty half of my bed
(I'm jonesin')
Why did I push you away?
(I'm jonesin')

I reach and I'll keep reaching
I wish and I'll keep wishing
Wrestle with my own inconstancies
      Worthless and regretting
I miss you and I'll keep missing
Craving her, I'm jonesin'

1

CRAIG

TAKE YOUR TIME

(SIX YEARS EARLIER)

It takes me approximately five minutes to find Lorelai Jones, recently spurned country music princess, let loose in Nashville. She's perched effortlessly at the end of a shiny bar top and appears to be up to her gorgeous eyeballs in tequila and righteous fury. As expected. And as the Good Lord intended, really. Nothing will make a man take a full step back, clutching his chest, like the sight of a stunning woman, indignant, haughty, hot as hell, and ready to throat-punch the next asshole who has the nerve to tell her to shut up and sing.

She's a goddamn vision.

I pause at the entrance to Georgie's, the seediest of seedy dive bars off Broadway, to give my eyes time to adjust. The contrast inside to the glowing neon outside is almost poetic, if not most certainly ironic as fuck. Everyone, and I mean everyone, is looking for Lorelai: her cowardly sycophant agent, her second-rate bandmates, every country music news outlet from CMT to Square to Sirius to TMZ . . . everyone except the one fucker who ought to be hunting her down on his hands and knees, her ex-fiancé, Drake Colter.

But since my partner is off being a supreme dickhead, rejecting his almost-wife as publicly and soundly as possible in the barely eighteen hours since she bravely played Crosby, Stills, Nash & Young's "Ohio" to a sold-out stadium crowd, calling out legislators to challenge the Second Amendment after yet another devastating mass shooting . . . well. Since all that happened, I'm here. At Georgie's.

I rub my hand against my face, catching on stubble, and grimace. I'm not the one who should be here, but somehow I always am. Can't help it. It's what friends do, and if there's anything I am, it's one hell of a friend.

Lorelai still hasn't noticed me, so I take a deep breath, straighten my shoulders, and wipe the exhaustion from my features, replacing it with good old-fashioned shit-eating charm. Because that's me. Irreverent goofball. Backup bass player. Best-friend trope in the flesh.

(What? I've read romance. Well, I've read the "aliens fucking" ones, anyway.)

Lorelai's head is thrown back in a loud cackle, her long slender throat exposed and the Jose Cuervo fumes rolling off her smooth skin in those wavy little heat waves. She's shimmying to some Halsey, which is the first clue that something's really wrong (as if I needed confirmation). Halsey is for bottles of overpriced Cabernet on my loft balcony while the stars wink overhead; she's for deep conversations and sarcastic avoidance.

She's not for bar-top shimmying and forced hilarity in a dingy dive where the clientele is ninety percent bikers.

I make my way to the electronic jukebox and swipe my debit card, picking Tom Petty's "Mary Jane's Last Dance" as well as loading a bunch of Willie Nelson, Merle Haggard, and George Strait in case we're here for a while. The familiar opening guitar riff kicks in and it's as if Lorelai's been struck by lightning. She freezes in place comically, spinning her head around, searching, until she locks eyes with who she's looking for.

Me.

I ignore the sharp pang in the region of my long-dead heart and hitch a half-cocked grin before making my way to her side and, forgoing the stool, hopping straight onto the bar top next to her.

"Had to be 'Ohio,' huh? Should have just gone for the full-frontal assault and pulled out 'Southern Man' to really do the thing properly."

She snorts into her glass, making the ice cubes clink. "Might as well have done. I was going for subtle."

"Fun fact: *subtle* and *stadium* aren't as synonymous as you think."

She makes a face. "Where were you with that wisdom two days ago?"

I accept my beer from a harried Georgie with a nod and raise my brow to my friend. "Would it have made a difference?"

She doesn't respond. Doesn't need to. It is what it is. Lorelai can't change, and I wouldn't ask her to. Before she became famous for country crooning, she was a schoolteacher.

She'll never be able to shed the trauma of hiding twenty-five eight-year-olds in a tiny bathroom during active shooter drills every other month all while knowing if someone ever threatened her students with a gun, she would place her own tiny body between that person and them without hesitation.

That shit doesn't fade just because you sing to arenas full of people and accept gold statues. It imprints on your DNA and bleeds out in every interaction. Lorelai Jones couldn't hold on to that mic night after night and stay silent about her biggest heartache.

And I love her for it.

So instead of criticizing, I take a long draw from my beer and say, "'A Boy Named Sue.'"

A relieved pretty smile spreads across Lorelai's flushed face and she immediately picks up on our favorite game of Best Song Ever Written. She thinks a minute and says, "'Blue Eyes Crying in the Rain.'"

"Hell," I mutter. "I handed you that one." I concede that round and start another. "'Night Moves.'"

"'Tennessee Whiskey,'" she counters.

"'Jolene,'" I fire back. This time, she concedes my win with a tilt of her head, her dark waves falling over her shoulder. There might be better songs than "Jolene." Arguably, Dolly Parton's "Coat of Many Colors" or even "9 to 5" are mighty contenders. That Lorelai doesn't even try is plenty telling. That's not what we're about tonight.

"Next round's on me," she offers, tipping back the rest of her drink. I work to catch up, gulping my beer down. If Lorelai wants to sit in this bar and get drunk, then that's what we'll do.

4

. . .

An hour later, Georgie's is packed to the rafters with inebriated bodies and the off-kilter soundtrack of a cover band that is quite literally ruining the originals. Not that Lorelai cares about the travesty that is Lynyrd Skynyrd being played with a calypso backbeat. She pulled me to the suffocating dance floor three songs ago and hasn't let up.

If I'm being honest, I'm an excellent dancer, so I don't mind much. Typically, when we're back in town and hitting up the local bar scene, I'm too beat down with exhaustion and jet lag to hold cohesive conversations with pretty girls, so I'll cheat and head straight for the dance floor. What I lack in physique, I more than make up for in rhythm. Many a hookup was born out of my ability to two-step. Which is a good thing, because otherwise, I completely missed out on the three tenets good old southern boys are supposed to excel at: hunting, football, and/or rodeo. I'm an embarrassment to my hometown. A proud vegetarian who couldn't catch a fucking yoga ball if you threw it directly at my head.

But I can roll my hips like the devil himself blessed me. And according to my older sister, he has.

It's not a lot, but it's what I have, and you can be damn sure I've learned to use it to my advantage. Except with my current partner, who is at least two drinks ahead of me while also weighing seventy pounds less. I twirl Lorelai out and drag her back in. Her entire body accidentally on purpose brushes against me before she grabs my hips with her small hands, steadying herself on wobbly legs, and lets out a breathless giggle.

"Do it again, Huckleberry."

Yep, proof in the pudding right there. We're at least four shots in when "Huckleberry" comes out. Back when I first met Lorelai Jones, I told her my name was Craig Boseman, and she immediately shut that down, saying, "No way. I can do Boseman. Bose, even, but definitely not Craig. My first singing coach was a Craig, and he was a dick."

Eventually she found out my middle name was Huckleberry. (Yes, like Finn. Yeah, I know, I can't believe I can't catch a football, either. All the key elements are *right fucking there*.) Whenever she's feeling really good, she calls me Huck, and when she's feeling really, really good, like "three sheets to the wind" good, she calls me Huckleberry. Consequently, Drake has always hated the name. Because Drake hates fun.

I wink, rolling my hips in an exaggerated effort, and she throws her head back, smoky peals of laughter erupting from her golden vocal cords before she starts singing along to the band, outshining them from the middle of a crowded bar where no one cares she's someone trending on Twitter.

Damn, she's fun.

The band transitions into the next tune, and it's something sultry, sexy, and way too familiar. Lorelai freezes in place as the singer breathes into the mic, doing a terrible imitation of Drake Colter's signature raspy tenor.

Even in the dim glow of the bar, I can see the color leach out of Lorelai's flushed face. Her eyes grow wide and her pulse flutters against her long throat. I immediately take action, stepping into her space, my hands grasping hers, still fisted against my hips, and I lean close to her ear. She's mostly drunk, so what I'm about to tell her probably doesn't matter.

She's likely to forget this in the morning. I'm counting on it, actually. But for the moment . . . it's the one thing I can think of that might snap her out of her heartache.

"Want to know a secret no one else knows?"

I have to imagine it takes all the strength she possesses to jerk her head even the tiny bit she gives me, but it's enough and I press even closer, my lips a hairsbreadth from the delicate shell of her ear.

"Drake didn't even write this stupid song. I did."

She pulls back as though electrocuted and blinks, absorbing my dead-serious expression.

I lift a shoulder, still clasping her hands. "I wrote all of them, actually."

Her lips form around the words *all of them,* and I nod.

Her dark brown eyes dart back and forth between mine, searching for the truth, and I let her. After a beat, she presses herself against me, her slender arms wrapping possessively around my neck. "You wrote this beautiful song. You wrote all of them."

I feel myself heat at her reaction, but it feels good. To be honest for once. To admit the truth, even if she won't remember it in the morning and even if no one else will ever know.

"Yeah. Don't tell anyone. I have a rep to protect." Because I'm the good time and Drake Colter is the serious musician. I'm just your average country boy with average looks and average style and average stage presence. You'd never in a million years suspect I was the words behind Drake Colter's star.

Which is why our arrangement works so well.

Lorelai snorts against my neck but doesn't move back to

place space between us. Which she should do. Or I should. There should be space between us, is all I'm saying.

But she doesn't and I don't. In fact, she bucks against me, and reflexively I tighten my hold, wrapping her in both my arms, one slipping into the mythically soft hair at her nape and the other dipping to brush just under the waistband of her jeans.

And it feels fucking amazing. *Don't think. Whatever you do, don't think.*

Her whispered "Thank you" caresses the heated skin under my collar.

I'm not sure what she's thanking me for exactly. Thanks for finding her? For getting drunk with her? For practically dry humping her in the middle of a dive bar?

"Take me home, Huckleberry."

I freeze in place, head to toe, because she's not asking me. That was a declarative sentence. A softly spoken demand. But she can't possibly mean what I think she means. Lorelai Jones and I have been friends for years. Close friends. Best friends, even. We've never crossed that line.

Have I thought about crossing the proverbial line? Hell yes. Have you seen Lorelai? She's gorgeous and funny and sweet and talented, and for sure my dickish partner can't come close to deserving her. Not that I ever said anything, but the fact remains. Still, we've never been like that.

We go out and dance and drink and let loose and then she leaves with Drake and I leave with someone else, and that's how it's always been.

Lorelai's hand slips from my neck, her fingers dancing along that same feverish skin of my open collar and down my front until she stops, cupping me through my suddenly tight denim, making her intent crystal clear.

A hiss mixes with a surprised moan somewhere in the back of my throat and I work to keep my body still, my thoughts battling wildly against booze and hormones.

"Please, Huck?"

"We're pretty drunk, Lorelai."

She grips me harder and I press against her hot hand, feeling dizzy.

"We'll sober up on the way."

"Yeah, but will you even want to, sober? Let's just stay here and dance," I suggest, and it's not even halfhearted. It's quarterhearted at best.

She pauses, seeming to consider. Then she removes her hand from my cock and tugs my head down to hers, ever so slightly, offering me an out.

I don't take it. I don't want to, and anyway, it's only one night. Just one time, and then we'll never talk about any of this. Not about my secret and not about what's about to happen between us.

I drag my mouth against hers once before opening up to taste her completely. Tequila sparks on her tongue as it tangles with mine, and her fingers tug on the ends of my hair. My hips roll against her all over again, but this time it's for real. No more games between friends. We exchange breaths and I swallow her tiny gasps. Even as buzzed as I am, I know we're getting too public, so I take her hand and pull out my phone, calling us a ride.

"You're sure?" I ask once we're outside the bar. "I can always drop you off."

"Haven't you always wondered?"

I don't ask her to clarify. Instead, I hesitate, rapidly sobering up. I mean, hell yeah, I've wondered. Not only that, I'm pretty fucking sure we'd be great together. But once we know for sure . . . once I know for sure . . .

Don't think, don't think.

Eventually I give her a half nod, half shrug.

"What if you and Drake get back togeth—"

She presses her fingertip to my lips. "Fuck him. This ain't nothing to do with him. Just us. Huck and Lorelai. One night. I . . ." She trails off, contemplating her next words. "I would like . . . I want to have this with you. Before I leave."

"Where are you—" but I don't finish because I don't want to know and I'm trying not to think. Not right now. I get one chance and I'm not gonna waste it.

. . .

(THREE YEARS EARLIER)

"That kid deserves everything he's got coming to him. This industry isn't for pus—" Drake cuts off at my glare over the top of my phone screen. He huffs and continues with his tirade. "Weaklings," he amends, as if that's any better. "If you can't hack a little criticism and weather the ups and downs of fame . . ."

He's still talking, but I've stopped listening. If there's another human alive more hypocritical than Drake Colter . . . well. Never mind. There isn't. Lately it's been his obsessive ranting about the meteoric rise and fall of Clay Coolidge. The small-town kid from Indiana came on the scene with

the force of a rifle blast, filling stadiums and winning acco-
lades, including Best New Artist right from under Drake. Ever
since, my partner has held the mother of all grudges. When
the news broke that Coolidge had to cancel several shows
due to a "rumored substance abuse problem," Drake could
hardly contain his glee.

Never mind that the kid is barely twenty.

"Country music will chew you up and spit you out, man,"
Drake finishes in a tone I'm sure he thinks sounds sage.

On that front, I agree. This industry is brutal. But it's not
the fault of kids like Clay Coolidge or even socially conscious
starlets like Lorelai Jones. It's because of fuckers like Drake.
Guys that soak up fame and fortune and all the privilege life
has afforded them and refuse to reach behind them to help
the next guy. Instead, they kick them in the teeth and laugh
as they fall to the bottom of the canyon.

Without effort, my thumb finds the email icon on my
phone, pulling up the message I'd received that morning. My
great-uncle Huckleberry Boseman, the very guy my parents
named me after, died two months ago. I was on tour at the
time and couldn't make it home to Tennessee for the ser-
vices. Another thing Drake sucks at. Empathy. *He was old,
Craig. You know I can't find a decent replacement on such short
notice. Not to mention, this is Daytona. The sickest show of the
year. Besides, when was the last time you even talked to the guy?*

Two years ago, actually. Two whole years since I'd been
home and had been able to swing on my uncle Huck's porch,
drinking Manhattans and talking shit with one of the wisest
men I'd ever known.

He left me his fortune. The whole fucking thing. The

guy lived on the same thirty acres his entire life, fishing the crick, driving his patched-together John Deere, rocking on his porch, and the entire time he was sitting on a ceramics empire worth millions. You read that right. My uncle with his tiny shack in the middle of the Smokies, complete with his own kiln, produced millions of dollars' worth of art-museum-quality pottery.

And none of us had the first damn clue. I knew about the pottery. He taught me all he knew, and of course I thought he was the shit, but . . .

To my grandnephew and namesake, Craig Huckleberry Boseman, I leave the entirety of my estate and all of its holdings. Give 'em hell, Huck.

I've been reeling all day. One phone call to the lawyer outside Memphis confirmed it. I was a multimillionaire. Multi, multi. And to be clear, outside of Uncle Huckleberry, I haven't done too badly for myself, touring with Drake Colter. My expenses are low, since I'm away ten months out of the year and I've managed to carefully tuck savings away for my future.

But as of this morning? My future is suddenly within reach.

"Listen, Drake," I interrupt, with zero fucks left to give, "I quit."

The silence is deafening as Drake processes my out-of-the-blue resignation. But I'm already getting to my feet, not interested in being in his presence a second longer than I have to.

"The fuck, are you serious?"

I start to gather up my papers, random song lyrics and

notations, but at the last minute, offer them to him. "Here. So you're not in a lurch. They're mostly half-written, but I'm sure you can manage."

Which is a lie, he's never written a damn song in his life, but the deer-in-headlights expression on his face is making me feel weird. Like guilty or . . . well, just guilty.

But not guilty enough to stay.

. . .

(TWO YEARS EARLIER)

"Fucking a, Colter, are you kidding me right now? Tell me I didn't just hear what I think I heard on the radio. It's been two years, and you know damn well I did not hand-deliver you an *entire song* on purpose. Your ethics are shady as fuck." I exhale in a huff. "'Jonesin'? Seriously? After the way you . . ." I bite off the rest of that thought and take a deep breath. "My lawyers will be in touch, you plagiarizing motherfucker." I chuck my phone across the studio, where it bounces off the sound-insulated wall and lands with a muffled thud on the thick carpet.

Forking my hands through my wavy hair, I growl in frustration before retrieving the device. My next appointment will be here any minute and I need to pull it together. I slip on my glasses and flick on the overhead lights, collecting discarded water bottles and various clutter left behind from the folk trio who stayed way past their allotted time late yesterday. They'd finally hit their stride near midnight, creatively speaking, and I wasn't about to cut them off as the magic was hitting. Even if it means I'll need an IV of espresso to get me through this morning's session with a former pop princess looking to rebrand herself as a country starlet.

Besides, late nights and early mornings in my studio aren't the problem. There's no place I'd rather be. After cashing in my inheritance from Uncle Huckleberry, I found this decrepit factory building a few blocks off downtown Nashville for a steal and had it renovated into a state-of-the-art recording studio. I named it On the Floor Records. It's my fucking happy place.

No, the problem is that while I stood in line at Charlotte's Coffee Brewery too early this morning, groggy and feeling hungover (without the bonus of actually consuming alcohol recently, which is a new thing I like to call *hitting my mid-thirties*), I heard something familiar over the loudspeakers. Which in and of itself isn't that unusual. Lately, it feels like, when it comes to country music, if I didn't write it, produce it, or turn it down, I don't know it.

But this was different. I *knew* this song in my bones because I wrote it in the privacy of my shitty studio apartment three years ago after Lorelai left town. After our one night together. *The* night. It wasn't for airplay and it certainly wasn't for my former partner and bandmate Drake Colter to use for his comeback.

Fucking "Jonesin'" was *mine*.

Clearly when I threw down that pile of scrap lyrics and half-thought-out melodies, I'd included at least one real song. A song I never meant for anyone else to hear, let alone that fucker. I was in such a hurry to quit, I didn't look through what I'd handed him.

I hadn't given it a second thought until this morning.

My phone vibrates in my pocket and I tug it out right as the security doorbell buzzes. I check the camera and let in the client and her team, settling behind the booth and reading my text. I think it's going to be Colter with some bullshit excuse, but instead it's an unknown number with an area code I don't recognize.

UNKNOWN: Heard the new song.
CRAIG: Who is this? Which song?
UNKNOWN: Lorelai. Sorry. New phone.

My coffee does an uncomfortable swirl in my gut. Shit. This is why . . . I quickly respond, my fingers flying over the keys.

CRAIG: Long time no talk. I didn't recognize the area code.
CRAIG: Sorry.
LORELAI: That would be because I live in Michigan these days.
LORELAI: I heard Drake's new song. *Your* new song. Why is that dickhead still taking credit for your work?

The door opens and I gesture for the clients to get set up in the studio. I press the speaker. "Be right with you guys. Go ahead and get comfortable." Then I slump back in my chair, the momentum rolling me back a few inches, my thoughts whirling like a drunk girl at her engagement party. Lorelai knows the song is mine. She knows *the* song is mine. She's *heard* the song.

Not only that, she *remembers* that I told her I wrote all the songs.

She remembers that night and she's heard the song and she knows I wrote it.

Well. That's . . . *fuck*. I knew when that email showed up, informing me I was inheriting a boatload of money and all my dreams were coming true, that shit was just gonna nip me in the ass cheek one day.

My thumbs hover over a response, coming up empty, all while in front of me, the studio fills with the muffled rumblings of music waiting to be made. I decide to respond like any normal person would, who was just a really good friend and who definitely did *not* still wake up at least twice a week hard as an I beam at the memory of her coming apart on his tongue.

> CRAIG: Long story short, I walked away from touring and opened my own recording studio, On the Floor Records in Nashville. Small. Indie. Probably smells too much like coffee and grilled cheese. But it's mine.
> LORELAI: Holy hell, Huck. That's incredible. I'm so proud of you!

My chest squeezes at the nickname. It's been too long since anyone's called me that.

> CRAIG: And you? What're you doing in Michigan? Still playing music?
> LORELAI: Teaching third grade. In fact, I've got students coming in minutes.

I release my breath. Saved by the bell. Literally.

LORELAI: But now you have my number. Don't be a stranger, okay?

As if I could resist.

CRAIG: Wild horses, Jones. Have a great day with your students.

I drop my phone to my desk and lean back in my new fancy ergonomic chair, linking my hands behind my head.

What are the chances? Years of nothing. Nada. Didn't even know she was in Michigan, teaching. She didn't even know I broke off on my own. My phone buzzes.

LORELAI: Your name wasn't on the credits, but I know your lyrics when I hear them, and I'll bet there's a story there. Anyway . . . I like the song. Hit me up if you ever find yourself in Michigan.

I release a long slow breath and my thumbs hover to respond. With what?

No, that wasn't me. That was Drake. Your ex. Obviously. Not me secretly pining after a girl who was always way out of my reach, and who I slept with one glorious night years ago, and who ruined me for all other women.

Nope. Definitely someone else.

The denial is right there at my fingertips, but what the hell. She lives in Michigan.

Thanks. You might be on to something, there. My studio is always open to old friends, even ones who live in the northern tundra and teach third grade.

. . .

(ONE YEAR EARLIER)

Lorelai and I texted pretty much constantly from that day forward. A steady conversation featuring song lyrics, stupid internet videos, and dirty jokes. What we don't do is talk about "Jonesin'" ever again. I watch as Lorelai slowly slips back into the spotlight via the *HomeMade* drama featuring her new best friend Shelby Springfield and costar Cameron Riggs. I notice how Drake makes less and less subtle plays for Lorelai on social media. Publicly, he starts dodging questions about how things ended between them. He begins playing a new roll: the jilted heartthrob for cameras and fans.

And none of it matters because she and I both know he won't *actually* try to win her back while she's an elementary school teacher. There's nothing in it for him or his career, and if there's one thing I've learned about Drake Colter, it's that he loves using others close to him to advance his career.

Until tonight, that is.

It's a warm evening and there's a nice breeze, so I've decided to enjoy it and walk the six long blocks home to my loft.

My phone rings as I'm locking up the studio to leave, and her name flashes on the screen. I answer, a grin already in place. "Hey, Lore."

"Hey, Huckleberry," she drawls out in a singsong voice,

sounding unusually nervous. "I'm sending you something I've been working on."

That gets my attention and I freeze right in the middle of the sidewalk. "No shit?"

She huffs a chuckle into the phone. "No shit. It might be garbage, but . . . no. It's not. Can you just, um, listen and then call me back? Let me know what you think?"

"Of course. Send it right now. I have a good walk home ahead of me."

We hang up and she must have been sitting at her laptop with the mouse hovering over the send button because the file is already in my inbox. I stuff my AirPods into my ears and cue the file.

From the very first lyric, my eyes slip shut of their own volition and I have to find a bench and sit down. It's been so long since I've heard her sing, and no one, *no one* sounds like Lorelai Jones. And I know a lot of singers. She has this quality to her vocals. Richer than sweet. Almost smoky in the lower registers but clarified. Like it's been filtered of all the gunk and what's left is pure sunshine. Bonnie Raitt spliced with Regina Spektor, rolled in Miranda Lambert, and smoked with Maren Morris.

And the writing. God, the writing is . . . brutally, refreshingly, cuttingly honest.

I listen through once on the bench and twice more on the way to my loft. I hit my door and lock it behind me, tossing my keys on the counter and shrugging off my leather jacket. I drape it over a barstool and pull up her number to hit call.

"So? What do you think?"

"How fast can you get here?"

"Really? You aren't bullshitting me because we're friends?"

I roll my eyes, even though she can't see them. "I don't bullshit about music, Jones. Not anymore, anyway. Give me a little credit here."

"I have more. A lot more," she says, sounding a little breathless. "I'll need a few days, but I can come up this weekend? Do you have the studio space?"

"I'll make it," I say, already mentally reconfiguring my clients.

"Okay! Wow! Um, great!"

"I have some thoughts, but I'm not organized yet. You've fucking rattled me here. So send me what you have as you go, unless you'd rather polish first?"

"No! I mean. Um, I'm not worried about polish. We can polish together. I'd love your thoughts. I miss working with you, honestly. So I'll send as I go this week, so you do your magical brainstorming thing and I'll call you when I'm in town."

"Do you need a place to stay?" I ask before cringing. God. Did I make it awkward? "I mean, I'll have to shuffle some of my girlfriends around, obviously. Toss a few over to Arlo's place, but . . . Clarissa already knows she's on the outs. I'm about over my rebellious Yankee vegan stage." Which is only a half-truth. Clarissa was six months ago at least. It's been a bit of a dry patch since I became the big boss. It's a lot of fucking work and stupid long hours to be me these days. My hips barely leave the sound booth.

"Clarissa the Yankee vegan, huh?" Sea-salt-dry amusement filters through the phone speakers. "I think I'll just get a hotel for now. It's not fair to put out *all* your girlfriends on such short notice. But thanks. Really." Her voice goes soft, and I can hear the smile. "See you this weekend, Huck."

I say goodbye and hang up and an hour later, I'm still grinning like an idiot.

Lorelai Jones is coming back to Nashville.

2
....

LORELAI

BETTER MAN

(PRESENT DAY)

"I'm not going to miss my flight," I tell Shelby, my voice raised to be heard clearly over speakerphone as I pack. "I signed up for TSA PreCheck."

"You mean Craig signed you up for PreCheck."

I zip my suitcase with a flare and flop down on my bed, bouncing my phone as it buzzes with another notification like it's been doing all morning. I continue to ignore it. "*I mean* Huckleberry McSmartass showed me how to sign up for PreCheck after lecturing me about living in the dark ages for a solid thirty minutes. The man inherits one measly fortune and all of a sudden he's Mr. Professional."

I can practically hear the smirk in Shelby's tone. "At least you'll listen to him. I've been trying to get you to do it for over a year. There's no reason for you to be waiting in lines when you fly back and forth as much as you've been doing, something your agent should have advised months ago."

I pick up the phone and turn off the speaker, holding it up to my ear, and ignore my best friend's tone. It's no secret she thinks my agent is useless. I might not disagree, but beggars can't be choosers. "I like to people-watch," I tell her. "Anyway, I should get going. My ride'll be here any minute. I'm all packed and I'm . . ."—I scrunch my face up, considering—"eighty-five percent sure I haven't forgotten anything."

Shelby's tone is arid. "The wedding's in Michigan, not Antarctica. I'm pretty sure we have three Targets within a ten-mile radius if you need to run out for self-tanner."

I snort. "Please. I haven't voluntarily used self-tanner since high school." I flip on my belly. "Gut check. How're you feeling? Nervous? Excited?"

Shelby releases a long breath. "Starry-eyed and ready. I've been waiting for this day since I was ten years old. I just want to be married to him."

My lips spread in a wide smile, knowing that's not an exaggeration. Shelby and Cameron first met when they costarred on a popular kids' show as tweens, and while the road has been long and windy, my friend has long insisted she fell ass over chin for him on the very first day. Seeing them together, I believe it. Everyone believes it. It's like watching a miracle come to life. Baby kittens, unicorns, Mitch McConnell voting in the interest of climate change . . . that kind of thing. "I can't wait to see it, babe. I miss the fuck out of you guys."

I hear the front door and hop up from the bed. "My ride's here. I gotta go."

"Okay! Be safe! See you tonight!" Shelby chirps. I end the call, dragging my suitcase off the bed with a heavy thud. Passing my vanity, I grab a pair of Ray-Bans to stick on my head before stuffing a tube of lip balm in my jeans pocket.

I realize belatedly that the commotion at the front door is knocking, which is weird considering I'm expecting Huck and he could just use his key.

"Coming!" I yell, for no good reason since the outer walls of the duplex are old brick and extra dense. They look cool as hell and insulate perfectly so the neighbors aren't treated to any private concerts when I can't sleep. Which is admittedly often. Fortunately, my landlord slash upstairs neighbor is a night owl as well as a music fan because I swear I can hear when the man so much as sneezes.

I take one last quick look around to make sure I haven't forgotten anything obvious, and fling open the door. "Sorry, I'm rea—Drake?"

Damn. I knew I shouldn't have ignored his texts all morning, but to be honest, I'm extra not in the mood for his special brand of bullshit today.

My ex-fiancé—as well as the current pain in my ass—Drake Colter is standing at the door, hand raised and ready to bang again. The midmorning sun glows behind him, painting him in a laughably ethereal light. Time has been too kind to him. His formerly round cheeks are artfully stubbled, and his designer T-shirt hugs his tattooed biceps. He removes his sunglasses and flashes a winning grin.

"Hey, Lore."

My glasses slip down my forehead and I drop my luggage with a clunk in order to free my hand to nudge them in place before crossing my arms over my chest. "What do you want?"

His brows furrow, creating a little crease. If I didn't know better, I'd say he's hurt at my sharp tone. Luckily, I know better. I lean a hip on the jamb, waiting. "I'm on my way out, Drake."

"To Shelby and Cam's wedding." His casual use of my best friends' names raises my hackles. "I know," he says eagerly. "That's why I'm here."

I blink, wondering if I have enough time to brew a third cup of coffee. Clearly I'm undercaffeinated after staying up too late working through a tricky stanza. "Elaborate." Behind him, I see a familiar dark Subaru pull up and amend, "Quickly."

I'm aware Drake's lips are moving, but I can't hear any words over the buzzing in my ears once I realize he's not even trying to hide the designer label weekender bag at his side.

"Wait," I interrupt, holding up a hand, my dark red nails glinting in the sun and a dull ache starting to form behind my eyes. "Jesus fuck, Drake. Do you think you're coming with me?"

He flashes a half-cocked, wholly smarmy grin. "Well, yeah. I got us two first-class tickets to Michigan."

My eyes slip closed, and I bite back a groan. "Whatever gave you the idea you were invited?"

To his credit, or maybe not, he seems genuinely confused. "Your best friends are getting married. I'm trying to be supportive here. Making amends. All the garbage I should have done before. I told you this already in my texts. And I left a voice mail. And made a post on Instagram."

I ignore the whole "garbage" comment, as if being a wedding date for someone who you supposedly love is the same as disposable. "And you thought *now* was the time?"

"What d'you mean, *now*? Hell, Lore, I've been at this for months. Years even."

I scoff and roll my eyes. "Oh, sorry, were those vague social media posts that your publicist wrote supposed to be for my benefit or the benefit of your legions of rabid Colter fans?"

To his credit, he doesn't hesitate—much. "Obviously yours. If you'd let me near you, I'd tell you to your face, but clearly"—he gestures at my crossed arms—"you're still shutting me out."

He takes a step closer, his scent all too familiar, and for a habanero-hot second, I'm tempted to suck more of him into my lungs to savor. Just one more hit for the road. But just as quickly, I catch a whiff of the familiar eau de heartache, disappointment, and *Sorry, baby I would return the favor, but I've got an early morning in the studio. Can you maybe get yourself off tonight?* I shake my head, pushing him away with my palm to his (unfortunately) firm chest. "I told you, Drake. It's too late."

"It's never too late. I still love you. You still love me. This is real."

I exhale in an irritated rush. "Well, that's entirely debatable, but we'll leave it for another time when I'm not at risk of missing my flight. Kindly fuck off, Drake."

"Hey, Lorelai. Everything good? Ready to go?"

Huck.

Craig Boseman, or Huck, Huckleberry, Huck Finn, Huckleberry McSmartass, or whatever other derivative I can come up with, stands a few inches taller than his former partner. He's long and lean, in well-worn jeans, classic Vans, and a black Johnny Cash tee, covered by a faded dove-gray corduroy blazer. Not a bulging bicep or flexed ab to be seen, but he still manages to make me breathless when he catches me off guard.

In my defense, he writes erotic poetry and wears reading glasses. You just know he's the kind of man who excels at the art of cunnilingus. Well, okay, maybe *you* don't know that from the blazer and Vans, but let me tell you, from one particularly memorable experience too many years ago . . . he is, and he *does*.

My inner thighs clench and I shake off the inappropriate thought. Friends—especially friends who have recently taken up sharing a duplex with thin walls—don't think of other friends' talented tongues curling along their—

I clear my throat and reach for my suitcase, closing the purple door behind me with a click, double-checking the lock. "Yep. I'm all set." I look at Drake and sigh, steeling myself against the attractively wounded expression on his face.

"Look. I really *don't* love you anymore and you're delusional if you think you ever loved me." I lift a shoulder, resigned. "If you had, you wouldn't have walked away like you did when shit hit the fan." Craig reaches for my suitcase handle and I let him have it.

I give Drake one last glance and take a deep breath before delivering the final blow. "There was a time when I couldn't wait to go to a wedding with you. *Our* wedding, in case you've forgotten. But you backed out. Without bothering to tell me first. Instead, you ignored me and chose to air our business all over social media. That's how little you thought of me and my feelings back then. You asked me to marry you, Drake, and didn't even care enough to tell me you changed your mind." I shake my head and swallow against the threat of emotion. He doesn't deserve my tears. "I've moved on. Please let me go."

We make it to Craig's Outback and I'm pulling open the passenger door while he drops my suitcase in the trunk before Drake calls out. "Wait! Does this mean *Boseman's* going with you?"

I meet Craig's light blue eyes over the top of his car, and they crinkle kindly, as if to say "up to you," and he ducks into the seat. I pause, contemplating the space where he used to be. That's Craig for you. Never pushing, never forcing, never asking for more than I can give, never taking what isn't his. If he and Drake were opposite each other in a Venn diagram, there would be zero overlap.

Except for that time they were the power duo of country music.

A movement behind me reminds me of where I'm at. "Go home, Drake," I say over my shoulder. "You're too late." And I climb into the car, not willing to let him ruin this.

I have a wedding to get to.

3

LORELAI

MY BEST FRIEND'S WEDDINGS

Seven hours later, I'm inhaling a bone-deep breath of fresh late-summer North Woods air before pulling open the door at Lake Front Distillery in Le Croix, Michigan.

I'm met with the booming baritone of Kevin VonHause and a rush of cool, air-conditioned air the moment the door closes behind me. "Lorelai Jones in the house!" Kevin's the towering owner of this fine establishment and the groom-to-be's best man.

Conveniently, he's also one hell of a bartender.

I clip along on high-heeled booties toward the gleaming bar that extends the length of the broad open space, headed for where Kevin is standing. I step up and have to perch on the footrail to reach him for a quick hug and a peck on his bristly cheek. We pull apart and he looks over his shoulder. "Aren't you missing someone?"

Flashes of the men I left in Nashville burn behind my

eyeballs. "Hell no," I tell him. "These days I need a man like I need a burr in my ass."

He barks out a laugh, raising two beefy hands, and without another word, he gets to work making me a cocktail. It's easy to like this mountain of a man.

Truthfully, I've been too busy to worry about things like dating. I've gone so far as to download a dating app onto my phone, but not far enough to register and come up with a password. I've got a music career to reinvent after abject humiliation and unanimous public outcry. Do you realize how impossible it is to become a famous country starlet one time, let alone *twice*? I'd have better odds inhabiting Mars on some billionaire's dick rocket.

I don't say any of this to my bartender, though. I can't. Everyone here is solidly Team Boseman and they haven't even tried to be subtle about it. Especially after he came to my rescue with the whole rental thing. Truthfully, I get it. The man's so fucking perfect he's ruining my edgy comeback vibes and making me all soft and mushy in the middle. Thank Jesus for Drake and his complete lack of self-awareness or I'd be stuck writing sappy ballads (as it stands, this morning's debacle proved just the thing).

Reading my mind like the stellar bartender he is, Kevin passes me a blackberry gin fizz and motions toward the private back room. "I'm ducking out in a few, but we're locking the doors and Beth will be on the bar the rest of the night if you ladies need anything else." Everyone in Le Croix, Michigan, has always treated Cam and Shelby well, rarely making a thing out of their celebrity. But the increase of attention around us in the last few years means we're extra careful with our privacy, especially leading up to the wedding. Thus the extra exclusive bachelorette party.

"Thanks, Kev."

Half a moment later, I'm being lovingly strangled and smothered by my two closest female friends in the entire world: Shelby Springfield and Maren Laughlin. Shelby and I met outside a therapist's office more than five years ago. She was nursing a Hollywood pop princess meltdown and I was grieving the abrupt cancellation of my country music career.

The therapist didn't last, but our friendship did. Maren grew up with Shelby and is the seductive mythological mix of park ranger meets beauty queen. Her fame is limited to a since-retired YouTube channel where she paid her way through college with endorsements earned off footage from her guided musky fishing tours. Honestly, if we went off recognition, Maren might have Shelb and me beat. Not a day went by back when I lived near them that some frat boy or another wasn't stopping Mare and asking for her autograph. We all want to think those boys were learning about jigging techniques, but the honest truth is Mare's a babe and fishing was her very memorable brand of "hot girl shit."

I choke on Shelby's shoulder-length blond waves and step back, dislodging myself from their arms. Kevin's wife, Beth, interrupts our squealing, carrying in a tray of tapas. She looks to me, points to the dishes, and says, "Designated fryer," before turning to Shelby, pointing to the pitcher of iced lemonade and assuring her it's nonalcoholic. We shuffle to the table to help her and then we all settle in. My understanding was that Cameron was having a whole backyard barbecue at his and Shelby's place tonight, but because the press can be dicks in their portrayal of women, Shelby decided to keep her "bachelorette party" to the four of us.

She spends the next hour filling us in on wedding details and last-minute Lyle drama (her idiot showrunner/ ex-boyfriend wanted *HomeMade* cameras there to capture the ceremony; Cam told him to fuck off), and Ada Mae drama (Shelby's attention-seeking mom told some gossip rag that she hadn't been invited, when obviously she had, but declined the invite on her own), and honeymoon details (of which Shelby had none because Cameron used to work as a documentarian with National Geographic and has planned their month-long getaway in secret).

I knew I liked that man.

Beth makes me another gin fizz and it's even better than her husband's. And by better, I mean stronger. All this talk about how amazing Cameron is has me sucking my drink through a straw, which everyone knows is the quickest, most polite way to get sauced. It's not that I'm jealous. At least not in a negative kind of way. I'm so fucking happy for my friends, I could burst. No one on earth deserves more than those two. I just wish my own love life wasn't such a disaster. God, was it only this morning my ex-fiancé was at my door all eager and buffed up and ready for a weekend as my wedding date?

A pained groan escapes the back of my throat at the memory. Shelby arches a recently shaped brow in my direction. "Something to share with the class, Ms. Jones?"

I make a face. "Ugh. I really don't want to put the bad vibes out into the universe or whatever, but Drake showed up at my front door this morning, all packed and ready to be my date for this weekend." Shelby splutters and Maren tsks in sympathy.

"Wait. Drake as in Drake Colter?" Beth asks, her hand frozen midway to dipping a still-warm-from-the-fryer tortilla chip into a bowl of freshly made guacamole. "As in your ex?"

"That's the one." I drop my forehead to the table with a soft thud. "The self-absorbed jackhole assumed I wouldn't have a date and figured now was as good a time as any to re-unite. Even booked two first-class tickets. Clearly for show, because it's not like I wouldn't have already gotten my own ticket."

"Unreal," Maren says softly. "The idiot."

"Total idiot."

"He just . . . showed up with tickets? That's bold, even for him."

I grimaced. "He may have spent the morning texting me and posting shit on social media, but I've been busy pretending he doesn't exist."

Maren pulls out her phone and after a second, flips it around to where Drake's post about going to a wedding this weekend is still up. "Guess he doesn't actually have to go as long as he says he went on his Instagram. Kind of a 'tree falling in the forest' sitch," Maren points out.

"But you asked Craig to be your date, right?" Shelby asks, butting in.

I blink at her, bemused and, let's face it, a little sluggish from the gin fizz. "I did not."

"Wait, why? You mean he's really not here?"

I narrow my eyes at her whiny tone. Like I said, every-one loves Huck. "He's really not here. He drove me to the airport. Which threw Drake for one hell of a loop when Huck walked right past where he was standing on my stoop declaring his love and grabbed my luggage to throw it in the back of his Subaru."

Beth gasped, her short blond ponytail bobbing adorably. "Drake said he loved you?"

"Did Craig hear that part?" Shelby sounds more alarmed than the situation calls for, if you ask me.

I blink at her again. "Um, maybe? But it's not true. Obviously. He said something like"—I drop into my best dude bro voice—"'I still love you and you still love me' . . . but I told him I definitely don't love him anymore and I don't think he ever could have left me the way he did if he loved me."

"Good for you," Maren says, approving.

"What did Craig say?" Shelby presses.

I stare at her. "Nothing." I gesture to my disgruntled female anatomy. "Thoroughly friend zoned on that front."

"Yeah, but, like, what about your one-night stand?"

I glance at the door behind me, to reassure myself it's still closed. It is, and more than that, the entire restaurant is dark aside from our cozy room. "Well, Shelb, darlin'," I drawl, "I suppose that was it. One night. Like, a bunch of years ago. And it only happened because I was leaving town." I take another long draw from my straw, feeling my frown when I suck up gin-flavored air.

"I find that hard to believe. Have you tried to make a move on him recently?"

Slouching back in my chair, I grab a tortilla chip, dunking it in the salsa and stuffing it in my mouth, petulantly chewing. After swallowing, I say, "Definitely not. He's my landlord and also sort of my boss. That's got to be illegal or at the very least ethically shady."

Shelby shakes her head. "Never thought I'd see the day Lorelai Jones is worried about ethics."

"I'm not!" I insist to their knowing faces. "I'm just . . . I'm completely fucking over it, okay? I was engaged to be married once. I planned an actual wedding with flower arrangements and bridesmaid dresses and themed cocktails. I spent the first half of my twenties thinking I was in love and we were going to be together forever. That we would have babies and gold albums and share a tour bus . . . but then Drake just . . . took it all away. One song and poof! Gone. He couldn't love me anymore."

I press forward, my fingers splayed across the table in front of me. "But here's the kicker. Did you know that day when everything blew up, I called Drake at least a hundred times with no answer. Turns out the whole band was in New Orleans holed up in a studio, working on a new record, and their manager *forbade* them from having contact with me. Drake didn't even break up with me himself. He made an artsy Instagram post showing him canceling the wedding. So basically, it was implied. Fuck you, Lorelai Jones, looks like I have May tenth open now."

Shelby hisses under her breath while Beth and Maren wear matching gaping expressions.

I grin darkly and continue. "Yeah, it was bad. But *then*, apparently while this was happening, Huck hops on the first plane out of Louisiana and finds me in a dive bar in Nashville, drinking my feelings. He was there for me when no one else was, literally risking everything when my fiancé—the man who was *supposed* to be my husband—wouldn't. That's . . ." I shake my head and tap the tabletop in front of me with my painted nails. "That's a mindfuck right there. We've never discussed it since. So what am I supposed to do about it now? Because he's the first person I call when I finish a new song. I know his takeout order by heart. He smells like clean laundry and he writes like a fucking daydream, and lately I'm kind of desperate to stick my hand down his pants just to see what he'd do, but then what if it scares him off and he kicks me out and tells me to find another producer?"

"Oh," Maren says.

"Jesus, Jones," Shelby says with a soft snort.

Beth clears her throat. "I feel like I need to point out that no man in their right mind would leave if you, Lorelai Jones, stuck your hand down his pants." She smirks. "Just putting that out there."

"Especially not a guy as nice as Craig Boseman."

I laugh, because I'm really not upset. I'm resigned. It's different. "Maybe so. But I'm not that altruistic. I'd want him to put his hand down my pants and he might not do that."

"Fair enough."

I sigh. "Besides. I can't go there right now. I really, really need to focus on my career and my music, and Huck is an enormous part of that. I can't fuck this up with gratuitous handies just because I'm horny. I'm okay. I know that made me sound all angsty, but it's not like that. I love the way things are right now and I don't want to mess them up. I think the whole Drake thing from this morning messed with my head. Churned up all those gross feelings and memories." I shake my hands out and flick away the bad vibes. "I should probably call my therapist and schedule an appointment to see her when I get back to Tennessee."

"You're sure?" Shelby checks, still looking worried. Well, we can't have that. She's getting married tomorrow. Way to drag down the mood, Jones.

"Positive," I tell her. "A thousand percent. But another gin fizz wouldn't go amiss."

"Already on it," says Beth, heading for the bar. Maren excuses herself to the bathroom right as Shelby's phone rings. From the way her face lights up like a Christmas tree, it's got to be Cam. She holds up a finger and I wave her off with a grin.

"Hey, Lore," she whispers, peeking back around the doorway, her hand over the speaker, "it's actually Jazz with a cross-contamination question. If she wraps your cookies and has them displayed in a special box, can we still put them on the cake table? By the way, I can't wait for you to see them, they're darling!"

I'm already nodding. "Should be fine. Maybe put a little card next to them that says, 'Allergy friendly, gluten and dairy free' or whatever so no one accidentally grabs them instead of the cake?"

"Great idea!" Shelby's voice fades away as she's relaying what I'd said about the cards. I was diagnosed as celiac roughly six months ago, so I'm still getting used to advocating for myself and my strict diet. It's a tricky balance of not wanting to come across as a whiny pain in the ass but knowing if I don't speak up, I will literally have a whole lot of pain in my ass if I consume so much as a crumb of gluten or casein. And then I'll fall asleep faster than a dad on Thanksgiving. And I'll wake up with every single vertebra and foot and hand bone on fire. And then I'll be useless for an entire week with constant migraines.

This wedding is my first big test. I was tempted to pack gluten-free granola bars rather than make a fuss about the catering, but Shelby wouldn't hear of it. (I'm still packing the granola bars, FYI, and my enzyme pills, because I'm not about to interrupt my best friend on the most important day of her life to ask for my chicken to be sent back and baked in olive oil instead of butter.)

I sip the last bit of my watered-down gin, the ice having melted, and pull out my phone. I'd silenced it, but it appears Huck's been texting me a running commentary from the night. His sound engineer, Arlo, was holding a gender-reveal party at an ax-throwing place outside Nashville. A smile blooms across my face as I scroll.

> HUCK: These guys are too manly for me. This place is bleeding masculinity and not just because nearly everyone is a lumberjack homosexual. They all have beards. And giant forearms. Did you know there was a wrong way to throw an ax?

I snicker. Arlo is a pretty small dude, but his husband, Josh, is a burly pediatrician who comes from a large family of strapping men. They're having their first child via surrogate this fall and just had the ultrasound done this week. I'm dying to know what they're having.

> HUCK: Scratch that—the wrong way is throwing a sharp object in the first place.

HUCK: Update: they bought cigars. Know what's more ridiculous than a scrawny white dude whose preferred drink of choice is "your driest Cab"? A thirty-six-year-old trying to smoke a cigar for the first time. This is like when I was twelve and my friend Joe rolled literal swamp grass in a poison ivy leaf and tried to convince me it was pot.

HUCK: Seriously though, these guys are so nice. Arlo married up. I knew that, of course, but . . .

HUCK: Your song was just on the radio.

HUCK: And now my song is on the radio.

HUCK: They're song besties.

HUCK: I might be drunk. No one wants to share my wine. Not even Arlo. I need you.

HUCK: I mean.

HUCK: To help drink the wine.

HUCK: I don't NEED you. You should be having fun with your ladies.

HUCK: Ladies is a dumb word. Women? Girls?

HUCK: They just started a competition to see who can chop through a log in a single swing. Help!

HUCK: Spoiler: I didn't win.

I bite my lip to keep from giggling out loud. Man, he's fucking cute.

LORELAI: When is the reveal happening???

HUCK: . . .

HUCK: No way. You have to wait until you come back before I tell you.

LORELAI: What? That's not fair!

HUCK: Too bad. How's your hen party?

LORELAI: Is that what you landed on? Hens? Not ladies?

HUCK: Still workshopping it.

LORELAI: Fun! Shelby is glowing and the blackberry gin fizzes are out of this world.

HUCK: Are you getting nervous for tomorrow?

I'm singing tomorrow at the wedding, and I've been stressing about it all week.

LORELAI: Yeah. Still don't know why.

HUCK: Because you love them so much.

I bite my lip, warmed by how well he gets me.

LORELAI: That's exactly it. You're right. I should go. Maren's back.

HUCK: Tell everyone I said hi. I'll be around later tonight if you want to run through your performance.

I tuck my phone away and take another sip of my drink. Mindfuck indeed.

. . .

The following evening sparkles like the billions of stars in the crisp, clear northern night sky. Like the multi-facets of the glittering rock on my best friend's finger. Like the fucking beams of joy glowing straight out of Cameron's moony eyes when his bride literally danced down the aisle to his side.

It's all incredibly romantic and I find myself floating around most of the day in my lavender chiffon bridesmaid dress, feeling as though I'm an extra in a 1950s Rodgers and Hammerstein. But I'm a little sad, too.

I stopped imagining my wedding the minute things broke off with Drake, but before that, it's fair to say I was obsessed. As your typical small-town head cheerleader and prom queen, I used to sign up to model wedding dresses at bridal shows for extra cash on weekends during the season. After the runway shows, I'd walk around with my girlfriends, eating samples of sugary cakes and entering raffles for far-off Caribbean honeymoons. I had entire binders filled with clippings of my future wedding that I eventually replaced with multiple secret Pinterest boards.

And I know, now that I'm thirty-three and I've grown up and become someone who's a far cry from that giggling teenager, all of that is pretty materialistic. But I was so close, you know? To making even the wildest of my dreams come true. It was within my grasp, and even understanding how shallow it was doesn't seem to soothe the sting of not being wanted. Of not being worthy. I wasn't the right kind of person to win Drake's loyalty. He didn't think I deserved that dream wedding with him by my side.

I know. Fuck that. Fuck it all straight to hell, obviously. *Obviously.*

But just for a moment, in my yards of chiffon and half-drunk on champagne bubbles, I get to feel sad, okay? I get to mourn the *could have been* and maybe even get all the way drunk on champagne bubbles. I'll eat my lovely specially made gluten-free, vegan frosted cookies and watch the groom spin the bride around and around and remember that there was a time I hoped I could dazzle someone like that.

But I guess I couldn't.

Okay. Pity party over. I pull out my phone and snap a few pictures to post to social media, because at the end of the day, I still need to make sure I'm relevant or whatever.

I zoom in on Shelby and Cam, completely absorbed in each other as they sway back and forth to a Maren Morris song and click. Then I take a picture of my cookies, tagging the caterer and raving about how delicious and allergy free they are. Hopefully, they'll get a boost in their sales.

Finally I lean my head in one hand, tired, but still holding up nicely, and take an elegant selfie, tipping my champagne flute toward the camera in a toast, letting the twinkle lights soften my features and the alcohol widen my grin. I post the pictures, writing underneath:

Today was better than anything I could have dreamed up for my best friends. Only missing one scrawny thirty-six-year-old drinker of only the driest Cab.

Because I'm beginning to realize, whenever I've needed him, he's always been there.

4

CRAIG

STONE

My phone rings, jarring in the silence of an empty studio, and I knock over a mostly empty cardboard coffee cup. I can practically hear my engineer Arlo Bishop's lecture about the dangers of having liquids around his precious soundboard. In my (admittedly weak) defense, it's Saturday night and I'm alone. I paid for said precious soundboard and I can spill room-temperature Americano on it if I damn well please.

Nevertheless, I quickly swipe at the single drop of hours-old coffee precariously rolling between two levers and threatening to collapse four years of blissful partnership before reaching for my phone. Arlo might look like a small, pleasant Danny Kaye type, but he's a fucking barracuda on Jim Beam if you mess with his equipment.

I grin at the name that flashes on my screen. It's true I came here to be alone, but I'll never mind these kinds of phone calls.

"Hey, Uncle Craig, it's me, Dustin." Because all my nieces

and nephews announce themselves even though their names flash on the Caller ID. Dustin just got his first phone for his twelfth birthday and I'm one of the few contacts he's allowed. Ergo, I get a lot of calls from the little dude.

"Hey, D, how's it going?"

"Fine. Mom said I should call you and ask if you want to come for brunch tomorrow."

Just the thought of my older sister's homemade biscuits and gravy makes my stomach growl, and a glance at my wristwatch confirms it's long past dinner. "I'll be there. What's the occasion?" Not that I need a reason, but I don't want to show up empty-handed if it's someone's birthday or other. I stopped trying to keep track of the family calendar long ago. As the token (and much younger) bachelor brother, I'm basically exempt, anyway.

But I have a stack of used vinyl records that's historically worked in a pinch, especially for my older nieces and nephews, and they have the added bonus of spreading the gospel of lyrical brilliance.

I'm mentally flipping through my collection for one to part with when Dustin tells me, "Jenna got into 'Bama."

I groan with a laugh that echoes in the empty booth. "Oh, man, Uncle Scott owes me fifty bucks. I knew she'd Roll Tide in the end." While my siblings didn't inherit millions from Uncle Huckleberry, they haven't done half bad for themselves, either, to the extent that I'll happily collect my winnings.

"Yeah, he's not gonna be happy about that!"

Nope. But it's not my problem he ignored the near decade of intense loyalty pouring out of my niece's eyeballs every time someone brought up the Crimson Tide. I don't make a bet I don't already know I'm gonna win.

"My mom wants to talk to you, but me first. Can you bring your extra Xbox controller tomorrow?"

I bounce in my chair with an easy grin and adjust my ball cap. "Why, so I can beat the short pants off you in Fortnite?"

"As if, old man."

I snort at his razzing. He's getting pretty good at smack talk. I've taught him well.

"Yeah, sure. Put your mom on, kid. I'll see you tomorrow."

I'm the youngest by seven years, so I've always been sandwiched between my siblings and their kids. That means I'm the fun younger uncle but also that I have four additional parental types always on my case. My actual parents are long retired and settled in the Florida Keys these days. My siblings visit them often enough, towing their growing families along to enjoy the beach, but I don't get spring break or summers off. It's easy to see them only on Christmas.

Melissa, though. She lives right outside Nashville and always invites me around, making sure I eat vegetarian home-cooked meals and leave the studio often enough to absorb some vitamin D. No escaping that, not that I try real hard or at all. Like I said, my nieces and nephews are great, and Melissa's biscuits are mighty tempting for a guy who's rarely home early enough to cook a real meal for one.

After a few seconds of shuffling, my sister's familiar voice comes over the speaker. "Did D invite you to brunch?"

"He did. What time and what do I need to bring?"

"No earlier than eleven and why don't you bring Lorelai

with you? I've been dying to try out this gluten-free biscuits and gravy recipe I found, and I need to get her thoughts on this new chalkboard paint I picked up for that one wall in the kitchen."

"You do realize Lorelai doesn't work on *HomeMade,* and aside from being best friends with Shelby, has no special skills in home decor?"

I can practically feel my big sister's eye roll. She likes to pretend her kids get their sass from her ex, Randy, and we all like to pretend she's right. "I *do* know that, thank you very much. But she happens to have exceptional taste and I like having her around. She balances out all the testosterone. Ever since she's moved in, you're always hogging her to yourself."

This time *I'm* rolling my eyes when I notice a missed drop of coffee rapidly drying on the board. *Hell.* I dig around in the trash for an unused napkin. "Well, I'm sorry to say she's out of town at Shelby's wedding, so you're stuck with me and all my unchallenged testosterone. You can save your recipe for another time."

There's a beat of silence. "Oh, did you have to come back early?"

I pause my dabbing, mentally cussing out Arlo and his obsessive cleanliness. "From where?"

My sister huffs into the phone. "From the wedding? Tell me you didn't leave the wedding early to come back to Nashville to work? Oh, wait. Are you still there? I just assumed you were home."

"I'm home. Well, I'm in the studio, anyway. But I've been home. I didn't go to the wedding."

"Why not?"

I sigh at her incredulous tone. Big sisters. "Um, because, Mel, I wasn't invited."

"Oh."

I scrub my hand down my face, grimacing at the soggy napkin, forgotten in my hand, and toss it in the trash. "Yeah. *Oh.* Listen, I'm not sure what you think is going on, but Lorelai and I just work together. And she doesn't actually live with me, she rents the other half of my duplex." I don't mention it's at a premium and that I can hear when she sings in the shower, because that's not relevant information and my sister is on a strictly need-to-know basis. "We're friends. Nothing more."

Another loaded pause. "Huh. Well . . . so eleven tomorrow. Just bring yourself, then. And apparently your own Xbox controller."

"Any food or drink?" I offer for no other reason than I get the feeling I've let my sister down somehow and it's making me feel weirdly guilty.

"No. I've got it all under control." I bite back a groan at the obvious resignation in my sister's voice. She gets this way every other month or so. She thinks she's being casual about her over-interest in the way things are between me and Lorelai, but she's not. It's almost enough to make me long for the days on the road when it was clear to my family I wasn't gonna settle down.

I don't think the words *casual* and *big sister* go well together, even when you're a grown-ass man running your own successful business. Especially then.

"Okay," I say, trying to lighten the mood. "Sounds good.

I need to get going, Mel. I have an appointment with a new client soon."

"On a Saturday night?"

"The music biz never sleeps. I'll see you tomorrow." I end the call before she can ask me any more questions. Obviously, I would have gone to the wedding if Lorelai asked, but she didn't. And Lore isn't known for being shy, so if she didn't ask, she didn't want me there. The only saving grace to the whole thing is she didn't want Drake there, either. I smirk to myself, leaning back in my chair again, recalling the way his eyes bugged out when he saw me carrying off Lorelai's luggage.

No, she didn't invite me, either, but at least *he* doesn't know that.

And anyway, I don't even know if *disappointed* is the right word for how I feel. It never even occurred to me to be invited until I saw my former bandmate all packed up and ready to go on our porch. As far as I know, she's barely spoken to him since she returned to town. If he had the stones to expect an invite, maybe I should have?

But I didn't. That probably says a lot about the fundamental difference between Drake and me.

I think of Melissa's asking me to bring Lorelai tomorrow. As if it was some foregone conclusion we'd come together. Weddings and family brunch dates. Am I missing something? I mean, aside from my massively inappropriate and doomed-to-be-unrequited crush on my tenant-friend?

There's a tapping on the door and Arlo comes in. We don't make a habit of working Saturday evenings, but sometimes it can't be helped, and since I took yesterday off to drive Lorelai to the airport and help execute an ax-throwing baby-gender-reveal party, tonight is as good as any.

Arlo takes in my stretched-out form, my feet propped purposefully on the edge of the soundboard, along with the empty coffee cup and bag from my late lunch crumpled on the floor a foot short of the wastebasket, and a frown creases his pale freckled forehead.

"Been here a while? I thought Coolidge couldn't meet us until after eight?"

Jefferson Clay Coolidge is a former country wunderkind who burned bright and fast and burned out even faster. As a teen, he was picked up straight out of high school by the major labels and was fed all the best stuff, topping the charts and capturing a few Grammys his first year out. By the second year, he was slipping, however, and ended up shocking everyone by dropping off the face of the earth after a seemingly successful summer tour with a then-up-and-coming, now-unchallenged starlet, Annie Mathers. I don't know the entire epic story, but I know enough to make a guess based off his enduring sobriety and plans to reinvent himself.

The guy is still young. Maybe twenty-three? Twenty-four? But he has the chops. His songwriting is solid and classic, and he has this soulful voice that brings life to any lyric. Which means I'm super stoked for the opportunity to work with him. Does it help that Drake has always been jealous of the kid?

It doesn't hurt any, that's for sure.

"He's not," I tell Arlo. "I just had some things to do and wanted to take advantage of the quiet space."

"Right," he says, clearly dubious. Arlo agrees with Melissa

when it comes to how much time I spend in the studio. I sometimes wonder if either of them realize how much work it is to start a record company from ground zero. If I'm not here, work isn't getting done and money isn't being made and bills won't get paid.

Don't get me wrong. This is exactly what I've always wanted to do, and I know I'm good at it. But it's not like I can pass the buck to someone else when things go sideways. I'm the end of the line. It's awesome and scary as fuck for a guy who spent the first thirty-something years of his life coasting on the fringes of other people's career moves.

"There's nothing wrong with being professional and prepared for a new client. I've been listening to Coolidge's earlier work and making some notes. I've placed a few phone calls out for collabs so we're ready to run if things go well tonight."

I do have notes, that's not a lie. But Arlo knows me well enough to appreciate I could spout off thoughts on Coolidge's entire catalogue at a moment's notice, even before today. I know my stuff.

"Well, since you're here," he says, pretending to buy my bullshit, "I heard a story about a former partner of yours."

Arlo always hears stories. I don't know how, and I've stopped trying to figure it out. The man is more reliable than a gossip rag.

"Oh yeah?" I stretch back, casually interlocking my fingers behind my head.

"True or false, one Drake Colter turned up all remorseful smitten kitten on the very public doorstep of his luminescent ex-fiancé right as his former bandmate was *also* showing up and had a little shootout at the O.K. Corral moment in the front yard?"

I don't even know where to start. "What?"

Arlo's smirk is triumphant, and it makes me want to scuff his shiny overpriced designer boots. Rub dirt and grit all up in the nonexistent creases.

Instead, I drop my hands. "Colter showed up, yes. He thought to go with her to the wedding that he was definitely not invited to and she turned him down and then I dropped her off at the airport as planned. No O.K. Corral moment. Not even words. Just grabbed her luggage and took her to the airport. As friends do," I add plaintively.

Arlo sighs, heaving dramatically into the chair next to mine and spinning to face me with a frown. "That's not nearly as juicy as I hoped. Though I love the idea of him showing up only to have you sweep her off her feet."

I bite back a frustrated groan. "No sweeping. Just carried her luggage." This is starting to get obnoxious. "Did you talk to Melissa, by chance?"

He tilts his head to the side, his floppy red hair slipping over one green eye. "Your sister? No." He crosses one knee over the other. "But how is the hetero love of my existence?"

"She's fine," I mutter. "Invited me to brunch tomorrow." I straighten and pull myself to the soundboard, proper. "Listen, the last thing Lorelai needs is sweeping in any iteration from another guy in her life. She's already busy fending off Drake full-time." And let's face it, eventually he's gonna wear her down. It's the reason I didn't bother with a lease. I don't need the hassle of paperwork when she caves and moves in with him.

I'm not completely unfamiliar with self-preservation.

"She wouldn't need to fend him off if you were there."

I wave him away, switching on random levers that Arlo will fuss over later. "Something of which she is well aware. She didn't want a date this weekend."

He narrows his eyes shrewdly and I ignore him. He likely knows about my feelings for Lorelai. As I said, he knows everything. But up till now he's kept his thoughts to himself. After all, if he can see my feelings for Lore, he can also see her lack of feelings for me.

But before he can say anything more, I'm saved by Coolidge's arrival with his rusty-haired bandmate, Fitz Jacoby. We make introductions and I listen and watch the dynamic between the two musicians while Arlo runs through some logistics about our studio. It's clear Coolidge and Jacoby have known each other a long time. Fitz is well known for both his fiddle and guitar playing. He's married to Annie Mathers's cousin and bandmate, Kacey Rosewood. If memory serves, Jefferson was at least at one point very attached to Annie, creating quite a bit of overlap between the two bands. Jefferson and Annie oozed chemistry at the CMAs a few years back, setting off ripples of giddy speculation across the country music echelons. Even my front-row seat to Drake's hissy fit couldn't keep me from noticing.

I wonder idly how that's going for him and am relieved to see the camaraderie and respect between the two younger men tonight. Conflict is par for the course in the music industry, but I try to avoid it in my studio. It fucks with the vibes.

The two men play a few new originals for us that I really dig. A little Chris Stapleton–esque. If Chris had been twenty years younger and an unassuming underwear model type. Coolidge is genuine and poised. I was expecting youthful cockiness, but he seems to have grown out of it already, which is a huge point in his favor. Arlo offers refreshments, and while Fitz takes a beer, Jefferson sticks to water. He's refreshingly focused. I like him. A lot. Sometimes you just get gut feelings about people, and this is one of those instances. I'm happy to go with my instincts on this.

I lean forward in my chair with a soft squeak of leather. "So what exactly are you looking for from us?"

5

....

CRAIG

EVEN IF IT BREAKS YOUR HEART

Jefferson Coolidge settles back on the black leather sofa, crossing an ankle over his knee and draping an arm over the top of the cushion, looking every bit comfortable in his own skin.

"No offense," I continue mildly, "but I remember your being connected to Mathers. One tour with her and you'd be set. The labels have got to be knocking down your door."

Coolidge's face contorts in a boyish grimace. "They are, but I'm not interested in that route. Been there, done that, had my stomach pumped and vomited on the T-shirt."

My eyebrows shoot up at his frank response while a slow clap plays inside my head. "Ah."

"I know what lies that way," Coolidge continues. "It doesn't work for me. Annie's still touring stadiums and Suncoast is treating her like the royalty she is. I'm not interested in riding her coattails," he says with a smirk, trading knowing glances with his bandmate. "I've got new material I want to try out—experiment with, even. A little less refined than what the labels are looking for, but I think it could be something special under the right producer's magic."

"And you think I'm the right producer? I used to work with Colter, you realize?"

I don't like to remind people, but it's not like I can hide my former attachment. Especially in this case. Colter has long held a beef with Coolidge grown primarily out of jealousy. They faced off for Best New Artist and Coolidge swept. Then Drake faced off against Annie Mathers for Best Song the following year and lost again. It was mostly timing (not to mention, I was the one who wrote the song, so pardon if I didn't give a flying fuck about his feelings on the matter), but Drake's a dick. Look at the way he dropped Lorelai and she was his fiancé. And I haven't forgotten that he was relentless against Coolidge when the news started reporting his follies. It still riles me up to think about.

In my studio, however, Jefferson shrugs his shoulder, not shifting from his relaxed position. "*Used to* being the key. I heard you dropped Colter and picked up Jones."

I have to work so as to not react at her name. I put that aside for self-reflection at a later date, probably never. "No one picks up Jones. She's her own star."

He nods at me, a glimmer of respect in his eyes. "Then you get me. Did you know Annie and Lorelai sang together years ago?"

I shake my head, and he leans forward, elbows on knees. "Annie's looked up to Lorelai for years. Hated what happened to her and the way she was treated after the 'Ohio' incident. She was still in high school at the time. In Michigan, in fact," he says, and I don't miss the implication, as Lorelai taught school in Michigan. "Annie was the one to point me in your direction. Said if Lorelai Jones trusts you, I could, too."

I nod, feeling even more sure about the idea turning over in my head. I can feel everything clicking into place. "You can."

Jefferson holds out his hand. "Excellent."

We make plans for him to come back in toward the end of the week and workshop a few songs. He doesn't seem in a hurry and I'm okay with that. That's part of the reason why I wanted to go indie. It's not about the hustle. It's about quality and creativity.

Arlo ushers the guys out and I shove back in my chair, putting my feet back up and cracking my neck. It's late. I check my phone. Definitely after eleven. I've been here eight long hours on my day off. I'll definitely bum a ride off Arlo tonight. It's too late to be walking home. Scrolling through my phone, I open Instagram and check Lorelai's posts to see how the wedding went, thinking maybe I'll text her if it's over.

The first pic is a glamorous shot of Shelby and Cameron Riggs dancing together, completely lost in their own small world. Around them, the reception looks rustic and simple and fits perfectly with what I know of the pair.

The second is a beautifully decorated cookie with celiac as the hashtag. Lorelai's new to her diagnosis, but she's never been one to shy away from trying to use her name to do some good. Even if it's just normalizing that people with special diets want to eat good things, too. The third is a gorgeous selfie, with Lorelai in a fluttery-looking lavender dress, toasting the camera with a flute of champagne. My bleary

eyes skim over the caption, snagging on the familiar word-
ing, and read it through again, a smile growing on my face.

> *Today was better than anything I could have dreamed*
> *up for my best friends. Only missing one scrawny*
> *thirty-six-year-old drinker of only the driest Cab.*

I click the comment button to respond and write . . .
what? How do I respond to that without sounding pathetic?
Everything that comes to mind is . . . boring. Maybe she did
want me there, after all. At least to keep her company. Like
friends do. Unsure of what to say, I hit the like button and
close out, opening my other account. My anonymous poetry
account that was miraculously verified months ago because
of the sudden uptick in popularity.

I let the words, always there, simmering just under the
surface, spill over onto the keys

> *carefully uncork*
> *her all-consuming bouquet*
> *sipping*
> *holding*
> *soaking*
> *swallowing*
> > *savoring sweetly, so lush upon my tongue*
> *this insatiable thirst*
> *only ever quenched by her*

It's the closest I will ever come to a confession, my poetry. My filthiest pining on a very public stage, but with the

complete anonymity of the internet. It's mostly fine, except for the one time my sister reposted one of my less evocative lines to her stories and I realized she follows the account, and I couldn't tell her not to. So there's that.

Better than my mom, I suppose. I may be a grown-ass man in my mid-thirties, but there are lines you don't cross, and parents reading your erotic poetry account is one of them.

Arlo returns and I drop my feet to the floor, straightening up the space and making sure everything's turned off before locking up and walking out into the humid night air. It's late summer, so still warm enough that no one needs a jacket, even in the middle of the night.

He jingles his keys, aiming at his car parked behind our building and unlocking it with a beep. Even a few blocks off Broadway, downtown Nashville never really gets dark. Or quiet. For hours yet, the sound of a hundred open-air bars featuring the most talented musicians in the world vying for their chance at fame will float over pedaling bar carts filled with revelers celebrating everything from divorces to bachelorette parties. For the first few years, I used to pace these streets night after night. Sometimes with Drake, when we were young and dreaming of our shot, and still later by myself. Something about being surrounded by all this creative energy has always fed my soul. It's why when I moved back, I found a place not too far from the center of it all.

Arlo is quiet as he drives. It's late and he's had a long weekend and we're both worn through. I tell him to take his time coming in on Monday. Our first appointment isn't until after one. No reason to be there earlier.

Besides, with a new baby coming, I imagine the days he and Josh have left to sleep in are few and far between.

I studiously ignore Lorelai's lavender front door, extra pale in the moonlight, while unlocking the bright robin's-egg blue one that leads into my place and latching it closed behind me before climbing the creaky wood stairs up to my loft. When I get to the top, I flick on the dim kitchen light and toss my keys on the wood-block island next to my glasses, wallet, and phone. Pockets emptied, I circle the counter to my sparsely stocked fridge and pull out a container of take-out and a fork and eat in silence. Then I open a new bottle of Malbec and pour a generous glass, carrying it out through the sliding glass door of my balcony. Two stories up, I lean my forearms on the railing and sip the semidry red while taking in the glittering lights of the city.

On one hand, I love this. It's everything I've dreamed of. I have a job I can't believe I get to do every day. I live in the greatest city in the country, maybe even the world. I have supportive and talented friends and tons of nieces and neph-ews to spoil and even an asshole cat somewhere around here. If kid-me could see all of this, he'd fucking freak. He'd never believe it.

I can hardly believe it sometimes.

I'm so lucky. I'm also fucking lonely.

Only missing one fiery thirty-three-year-old drinker of the bub-bliest champagne.

6

LORELAI

IF I WAS A COWBOY

I knew I should have stopped. The literal minute the opening chords of "Ohio" lifted into the atmosphere, it was as though an enormous vacuum had sucked all the air out of the amphitheater, except for my lone voice. A hush swept over the crowd and sweat trickled into my eyes. This hadn't been in the show notes. Carissa and Lanie were offstage grabbing a drink and catching their breaths before the encore and I just . . . well. I don't really know what made me do it. It's not as though I set out to obliterate my career tonight.

Things started innocent enough. Okay, that's not true. "Ohio" by Crosby, Stills, Nash & Young is not exactly innocuous. It's pretty on the nose, in fact. There would be no mistaking my intent. But for fuck's sake, things were out of control in the headlines, and if I don't use my voice to make a point, what am I even here for?

I digress. "Ohio" was not exactly approved by my tour manager, Cassidy Faulkner, but it also wasn't not approved either. When I explained earlier in the day that I maybe wanted to do something possibly related to playing a cover of "Ohio," cool gray *eyes dipped in that unnerving way from the tip of my head to my toes and then to the side, as she dismissively took a drag from her cigarette.*

"Christ," she muttered, exhaling Marlboro Lights into the pink-hued Colorado sky. "Fine. Leave it at the song, though. For fuck's sake, Neil Young's Canadian."

"Canadian American, and also gun control is universal."

My manager glares, replacing her sunglasses. "Not in country music."

I let her go, not really fussed, since she's all bark and I never in a million years imagined things would turn out the way they would.

So there I was, in the middle of the stage, alone under the spotlight, holding my guitar for dear life. "Ohio" is about history, chronicling the moment in time during Vietnam when National Guard soldiers opened fire on a campus in Ohio, murdering four students during a peaceful protest. It's relevant, but not if you don't want it to be. Most of our songs are fun. And sassy. And rarely ruffle feathers. Here for a good time and all. We provide it.

But lately . . . well. Lately I've been feeling like I need to do more. Provide more than an escape. It probably stems from the years I spent just out of college, teaching elementary school. And the recent news of the latest school shooting in a middle school in a small town. Kids are being threatened and murdered in their schools and I want to do something about it.

At first the crowd was stunned, I think. Some of the younger fans likely weren't familiar with the song. But the older ones, they understood perfectly what I was trying to convey, and by the time I got to the chorus, the crowd went nuts. They were singing, chanting, screaming along with years of fear and rage and helplessness and more than a little drunkenness, and when I opened my eyes for the last verse, coming back to myself from the strange hazy plane of existence I escape to when I'm performing alone, a chill spirals up my spine and goose bumps flare on my bare arms and legs.

Fucking. Fuck. Fuck. What have I done?

. . .

The morning after the wedding, I wake up to one hell of a hangover, wicked rejection vibes, and someone licking my face.

"Ugh! Rogers! Gross!" I gather the slobbery wriggling mass of fur and puppy breath to my chest and sit up in the cozy guest bed I slept in. Then I tuck Maren's new wirehaired pointer pup under one arm and spin to the side, dropping my feet to the thick woven rug that covers the hardwood. Rogers continues his assault on the small vee of cleavage exposed in my sleep tank as I find my way to the kitchen, where I can smell coffee brewing.

Maren's eyes widen at my appearance and my cargo. "Rogers! Oh no! Did he wake you up? He was still curled up in my bed when I left."

"It's okay," I assure her. Putting down the squirming pup, I shuffle to the coffeepot and pour myself a generous mug full, black. "Honestly, it's the most tongue action I've had in years. I've woken up in worse situations."

Maren's eyes dance over her own cup. I notice she's already dressed for work in her khaki and olive-green park ranger uniform.

"I thought you had the day off?"

She sighs. "I did. But Paul's wife went into labor early yesterday morning and Shawn worked a double so I could go to the wedding. I offered to come in to relieve him so he can catch some sleep. Only until four. Then I'm all yours tonight before you fly out tomorrow. I thought we could go out to Potter's?" she says. "It's supposed to be another beautiful August day. We can sit on the pier and drink spicy margaritas."

I give Maren a warm smile. "Of course. That's perfect."

"You sure? I feel bad ditching you. We get so little time together in one place anymore. I was really hoping you'd sleep the day away and hardly notice."

"It's not a big deal. Besides, you're coming to Nashville in a month. That makes up for it."

I pull out a pan and quickly scramble some eggs and fry up some seasoned potatoes for Maren while she rushes around, getting Rogers settled for the day. I offer to take him for a short run, so she leaves his leash and halter where I can find them and then scarfs down her food, gracing me with one of her famous beauty queen smiles before flying off to save the tourists from bears or whatever else she does at her post as a park ranger for the US Forest Service.

I take my time, making myself a veggie omelet and having a second cup of coffee before dressing in my running clothes and collecting Rogers to head out. Maren's neighborhood is quiet and cute. A nice sidewalk and a bike trail wind along a small local lake. Rogers isn't the most coordinated of runners, but he makes up for it in enthusiasm. I end up slowing to a walk pretty quickly because of his tiny legs, but I don't mind. I started running years ago when I realized it was impossible to stay healthy on the road without some kind of exercise, and not every stop has a rocky ledge to climb (too bad, because there's no comparison to that kind of challenge). The habit's carried over and treated me well over the last decade. Running takes the edge off my anxiety.

But strolling with a really stupid-cute puppy is also fine.

I cue up some bluegrass, a band called the Infamous Stringdusters that Huck got me hooked on when I moved back to Nashville. He's forever on the lookout for good bluegrass. Neither of us really work in that genre but we were both raised on it: he, in a very rural area of the Smokies; me, on the shores of North Carolina. My mom sang in a small bluegrass band with her sisters when I was young and still lives there with her new husband, teaching guitar and mandolin. My dad lives closer to Nashville, but I don't see him much.

To be honest, I'm closer to Craig's, Shelby's, and Cam's families than I am my own. It's that whole "found family" thing at play in real time. Sometimes it just works out like that, I guess.

As I think about families, I pull out my phone.

LORELAI: It's been two days! Can you tell me the gender yet?

He responds almost immediately.

HUCK: Nice try, Jones. I told you. You have to come back first.
LORELAI: You're seriously holding this hostage? You know I could just text Arlo.
HUCK: You could try . . .

Which means he already swore his partner to secrecy. Damn.

HUCK: You busy right now? Melissa wants to ask your opinion on a wall or something.

LORELAI: She knows I'm not Shelby, right?

HUCK: I did explain that, yes. But she said something about your "exceptional taste."

LORELAI: Oh well, in THAT case . . .

HUCK: Picture incoming.

A moment later I zoom in on a photo of a wall in his sister's kitchen that is painted in what looks like two kinds of chalkboard paint. One somehow looks more rustic than the other, and from what I remember of her decor, it would match better.

I scroll to his name and hit call.

"Hello? Lorelai? Hold on. It's loud here. One sec. Don't hang up. I can't—hell, Meliss—" I can't help the smile pulling at my lips at the way he's stumbling over his words. It *is* unusually loud over there. He must be at some family get-together or other.

I hear a door close, and it's suddenly much quieter. "Lorelai?"

"I'm here."

"Sorry about that. My niece got into 'Bama. We're having a brunch celebration."

"Hey! That's fifty bucks to you, right?"

He chuckles low into the phone, and the sound warms me from the inside out.

"Yeah. So of course Scott's pouting into his beer."

"Too bad. Uncle Scottie should have paid better attention. Even I knew she was a 'Bama girl through and through."

"How was the wedding?" he asks, and I sigh, spotting a bench and sitting down. Rogers flops over in the shady grass, exhausted. I might have to carry him home. Oh *darn*.

"Beautiful. Gorgeous weather, gorgeous bride, awestruck groom, all the fixings for a disgustingly perfect day," I tease.

"How'd your song go?"

"Without a hitch. You were right. I shouldn't have worried. They loved it and Cam cried like a six-foot-two bearded baby."

I can hear the smile in his voice when he says, "I knew it."

It matches the grin in mine when I say softly, "You usually do." I fight the urge to clear my throat. I'm not usually soft. Only for Huck, I guess, which is concerning.

Silence fills the miles between us, and I rush to fill it. "So, the wall? The chalkboard paint? I say the more rustic one. It matches that whole farmhouse look Melissa has going on."

"That's what *I* said." He sounds aggrieved. "She was giving me all sorts of shit for not bringing you along this morning. I told her you were in Michigan, but apparently my family likes you more than they put up with me. What can I say?"

"Aw, that's not true. Your nephews adore you."

"Only the ones who haven't hit puberty yet. The older ones definitely choose you."

I laugh because he's probably right. "Fair enough."

"I should get back. I have to go kick D's ass in Fortnite."

I swallow back the disappointment. Which is stupid, because I'm sure I'll see him this week. In the next few days, even. Maybe I'll surprise him on our balcony tomorrow night when I'm back in town.

Oh god.

"Good luck!"

"Thanks for calling, Jones. I'll be sure to tell my sister I was right."

I laugh and we say goodbye and I end the call before slipping down to the ground to sit cross-legged on the grass next to Rogers. I smooth his little drooly jaw and stroke his speckled fur. I have no idea how long I sit there, but by the time I stand up and we return to the trail, I've made plans to invite myself upstairs to Huck's the minute I get back into town.

LORELAI

I TAKE MY CHANCES

After carrying one very tired puppy home and parking him on the bathroom rug while I shower off my almost-run and the wedding from the night before, I spend the afternoon catching up on work emails. Well, really just a handful of emails from the same person: my agent, Jennifer Blake. We go way back. Maybe too far back, if I'm honest. She was my agent before and up to when everything went haywire after the "Ohio" incident. When I was twenty-four, Jen found me in a tiny coffeehouse playing covers. Not long after that, she found my old bandmates, Carissa and Lanie, and we became the Belles. For several years, things were the stuff of dreams coming true. Sure, Carissa was a prima donna who always wanted to go solo and Lanie hated touring because it took her away from her model/actor boyfriend . . . so that was never ideal. Really, though, that only made things easier when they fell apart. No hard feelings. Or at least none outside of what I read in the comments section.

After "Ohio," Jennifer dropped me, but again, I couldn't really blame her. I mean, if my own fiancé . . . well, anyway. Maybe I should have tried harder to find new representation when I returned to Nashville, but after a few hard passes right out of the gate, and the widespread rumor that my name had been cancelled around town by several top executives, I was feeling lucky Jennifer didn't slam the door in my face. In fact, *she* came to *me*. Aside from Craig and Arlo, she was the only one. Besides, if *she* believed I had a chance to make it again . . . that's half the battle, right? Finding someone to believe in you?

Right. Or so I thought. The thing is, back in Michigan, I was all ready to say "fuck you!" to every single doubter and hater who gave up on me all those years ago. And then I got to Nashville, and everyone was kissing my ass and feeding me lines and offering me deals that sound suspiciously *exactly the same* as the ones they'd previously yanked away from me.

Including Jen. *Especially* Jen. Who very much wants me to smile pretty and say, "Oh gosh, thanks for giving me this second chance! I won't disappoint you again, mister!" She has this whole "apology tour" worked out. Wants me to sit in with country radio deejays and executives and recant my rebellious ways. Explain that I was young and rash and short-sighted, but *not anymore*. I've learned my lesson!

Which is a crock of shit, frankly. I've spent at least half a decade teaching in Michigan, and if anything, things are even more horrifying and I'm even more furious. I stand by what I did. I won't apologize for having a soul and the platform to use it.

But—and here's the real fucking crux of the problem—how can I effect change *without* the platform? If I don't kiss the asses of people in powerful positions, I won't have a career in music and I might as well go back to teaching third grade. Which, let's be real, is tempting.

I stare at Jen's email and click the respond button a dozen times before closing it out. Technically, I'm still in Michigan. This can wait one more day. Or two. I want to talk to Craig. If anyone understands my position and won't judge, it's him.

Maren's old grandfather clock chimes the hour and I figure I better get dressed to go out and maybe see if Rogers is ready for another short walk. Before I do, though, I open my Instagram. Force of habit, even though I was telling myself I wouldn't check social media while I'm out of town. I scroll through notifications, barely acknowledging them. There are too many to keep track of, and I learned long ago that if anyone important needed to get ahold of me, they wouldn't use social media. I pull up the feed. I don't follow very many accounts, but right on top is a photo dump from Shelby and Cam. She told me they made a deal with their network that they wouldn't allow any film crews or official photos at their wedding, honeymoon, or anything else, but instead would post their pics on social media in their own time and at their own pace. I loved that for them and for me.

I scroll through their photos, soaking in the happy smiles and relaxed poses. Their villa in Fiji is stunning and airy in that super tropical paradise way and I smirk, knowing they've probably had sex on every surface already. Good for Shelby. Lucky bitch.

I continue to scroll and my throat catches. Oh. He's posted. Hot damn. I'm already flushed and haven't even read the words yet.

So here's the thing. Craig publishes erotic poetry using an anonymous account. I found out by total accident a year or so back. In my defense, I already followed the account. Hell, *everyone* does. And by everyone, I mean it has multiple millions of (horny) followers. It's pure unadulterated sensual magic. Like, the number of times I've gotten off . . .

Ugh. I'm already sweating.

Anyway, like I said. I followed the account and I'm 99.99 percent sure he has no idea because he's never followed anyone back. He's exactly the kind of person who just throws his genius at the wall and doesn't bother checking if it sticks before logging out to do more genius things.

Super healthy and somehow even hotter.

For months, I didn't make the connection that it was Huck behind the account, until one day I picked up his phone to order us Grubhub at his request and his screen was full of notifications for his IG, under that very familiar screen name. I'll be honest. I about had an orgasm right there in the studio.

I know what you're thinking. Wow, Lore, that's objectification. He's your friend and you work together.

First of all, fuck you and the horse you rode in on, and second, I know. *I know,* okay?

But I would like to offer this as exhibit A:

carefully uncork
her all-consuming bouquet

sipping
holding
soaking
swallowing
      savoring sweetly, so lush upon my tongue
this insatiable thirst
only ever quenched by her

Holy . . . wait just one damn minute. Something clicks in my brain and I tap on the icon containing my own avatar, scrolling through my pictures. There it is: the wedding. Oh hell, I forgot I posted that champagne toast picture. I'm so obvious. But there's no response from him. Not there, anyway. I skip back to the poetry and look at the time stamp. Same night, hours apart. He's talking about champagne, right?

Well, no. He's absolutely talking about oral sex. But he's definitely using a champagne euphemism. How could that be a coincidence?

Blergh. I smack my forehead with my palm and cringe at my own embarrassing leaps. Huck isn't exactly shy. He's historically straightforward in his interactions with women, and here I am, basically that GIF with the guy and all the red string trying to connect the convoluted dots. He didn't even respond to my post. I (admittedly, drunkenly) made it so clear I wanted him, and he didn't comment or even text. And for all I know he schedules his poetry. For all I know, it's not even about champagne! I might write songs, but I barely passed college-level English. All that looking for symbolism made me want to scoop my own brains out with a spoon. I'm all about direct and to the point.

I imagine presenting my argument to Maren later tonight and the pitying look she'd give me. This is such a reach. I know it is. I'm seeing things where they aren't.

Just like I did with Drake. Years of imagining loyalty and love when it was all just a case of sexual attraction and career convenience. I need to stop this. I don't have time for any of it and I am nowhere near emotionally available right now. This is because of the wedding. Shelby's backyard was doused in lovesick happy sex pheromones all day yesterday and I'm still drunk off the what-ifs.

I'm thinking about this way too much for someone who isn't willing to act on it. He's my sort-of boss. And landlord. And one of my oldest, dearest friends.

Maren takes that moment to burst hurriedly through the front door. "Sorry, sorry, there was this family from Wisconsin that was trying to go 'off the grid' all weekend, which was so cute, but they insisted on using one of those fold-up paper maps and none of them knew how to read one. What a mess. Adorable. God, I hope they stay in a hotel tonight . . ." She trails off at the look on my face. "You okay?"

I quickly school my features. "Totally. Just an email from Jen. I'll explain over drinks. Why don't you shower and change, and I'll take Rogers for a short walk?"

Maren considers me for a long moment, and I can tell *she* can tell something's up, but Maren is also the most patient of the three of us. If Shelby had been here, I'd never hear the end of it, but Maren's good at waiting for the right time. And now isn't it.

Which has always been my problem.

. . .

In the late August sun on the shore of sparkling Lake Michigan, I explain my Jen-dilemma to Maren over margaritas, who hisses some uncharacteristically sharp words into the balmy freshwater breezes. Tequila brings out the fierceness in my best friend, and it's easy to imagine her beating off the less-than-kind side effects that come out of being born stunning. I settle back in my chair, letting her get angry on my behalf. It feels immeasurably validating to know it's not just me. Or even just me and Huck and Arlo. This is why I need to make sure I come back to Michigan more often. The perspective is so good for my pores.

"So what are you going to do? You're going to fire her ass, right?"

I make a face and brush salt off my fingertips with a napkin. "It's not that simple. I'm still a cussword behind closed doors. I doubt anyone else would touch me or my career with a ten-foot pole."

"Even after the success of 'What They Have'?"

"That was a song. Or okay, a *few* songs. It wasn't a career." She opens her mouth to protest and I raise my hand. "I'm not downplaying those songs. I promise. I'm saying those weren't enough to get me back in the good graces of country music. Might never be. Jen's plan is just that. One plan. It's not a bad one, exactly. She's not new to country music. She knows what it takes. I'm just not sure I'm willing to grovel. Maybe that's not what *I* want."

"Fair. So what do you want?"

I shrug a shoulder and sip my margarita before saying, "To write and perform music that changes the world."

Maren grins. "Is that all?"

"That's all," I say in a long-drawn-out Carolinian drawl, smirking to finalize the point.

"What does Craig think?"

I sigh. "I mean, I haven't talked to him about today's round of emails, so I can't say specifically . . ."

"But—"

"But he thinks I should say *fuck off* to country music. That they lost their shot at me, and I should go the way of Taylor Swift."

"Pop music?"

"Or something. Mainstream. L.A. That kind of thing."

Maren taps her lips, thinking. "And you don't agree?"

"I don't disagree," I say carefully. "I'm just not sure I have what it takes to make it in pop, and also I love my southern roots."

"Okay, what about Americana or indie folk? Indie anything, really. You don't have to walk away from your roots, but you don't have to be held back by them, either."

"Right. I could do that, too." Really love that idea, actually. "Huck seems to think I'm bigger than his record company and has been hesitant to produce me on a large scale up to this point."

She raises a brow and I sigh again. "I know. It's dumb. He's a genius."

"So are you. It seems like it's a match made in heaven."

"One would think."

Maren rolls her eyes, snorting into her drink. "Okay, can I just say something? You're fucking Lorelai Jones. The ballsiest woman I've ever known. This isn't a 'one or the other' kind of thing. You can have his genius brain and his heart and his cock. Just get after it."

See? Beauty queen on tequila.

I straighten to mirror her. "Who said I want anything to do with his heart. Or his cock?" I add, ducking my head and taking a long sip of my drink.

When I finally look up, Maren is watching me shrewdly. "Okay," she says after a beat. "If that's the way we're playing this, fine. Just his brain, then."

I ignore her dry tone. "This probably still won't work, though."

"Well, what do you want from me?" she asks, grinning. "I'm a park ranger, not a publicist."

. . .

Later that night, after I'm tucked into bed, my suitcase already packed and ready to fly back to Nashville, I pull up my phone and reread his poetry for too long.

Eventually, I close the app and pull up my messages.

LORELAI: Hey, can I see you tomorrow night after I get in?

His response is immediate.

HUCK: Of course. My place or your place?
LORELAI: Compromise on the balcony?

HUCK: I'll bring the gluten-free biscuits and gravy. Fly safe tomorrow.

I hesitate and then take a chance. A tiny one.

LORELAI: "Slow Burn"

I stare at the rippling gray dots, my heart inexplicably in my throat.

HUCK: "Fire Away"

A relieved breath escapes my throat.

LORELAI: Damn, that's a good one.
LORELAI: . . .
LORELAI: "If I Was a Cowboy"
HUCK: *groans* On today's episode of single lines of lyrics I wish I'd written . . . Point to Jones this round.
HUCK: See you tomorrow.

I click out and toss my phone on the nightstand, a tired smile on my lips.

8

. . . .

CRAIG

MERCY

I told Amos to take Monday morning off on account of coming in late on a Saturday night, but I couldn't help myself from unlocking the doors to our studio at seven A.M. We don't have anyone coming in until this afternoon, but I was crawling the walls of my too-quiet loft until the early morning hours and needed a change of scenery. I bought the duplex last year when the record company started to turn a steady profit and I needed a place closer to work. My plan was to eventually combine the two apartments into one open and renovated row house, but the rent income was hard to beat and I haven't exactly had free time to knock down walls.

My first renter moved out a few months ago after he got married and moved to Georgia, and I'd figured on leaving it empty long enough to make some headway on the renovation. But then Lorelai's former landlord raised the rent on her shitty studio, and I hated the idea of her essentially pouring her meager schoolteacher savings down the drain.

Am I playing with fire? Absolutely.

But it's not her fault I'm in love with her and entirely suck at boundaries.

Anyway, like I said, home was too quiet.

I flip on the studio lights, leaving the sound booth undisturbed since I'm not recording anything this morning. I cross the floor, carefully layered in thick woven rugs, over to the piano in the corner and settle on the bench with a creak. I place my thermos of coffee on the glossed black lid and remove my jacket, laying it over the back of a chair.

Sipping from my coffee, I idly lift and push back the heavy cover, revealing the black and white keys. Some studios prefer to keep keyboards in-house for public use. This Steinway is all mine, however. One of the first things I bought with the commissions from my songwriting, and since I spend more time here than at home, it just makes sense that it's here.

Besides, it sounds a thousand percent better on a recording.

I play with the keys, lingering on some and listening hard, concentrating all my earthly attention on the way the lower register haunts. Outside it's a sunny, nearly sweltering late summer morning in Nashville. In here, it's cool. Lonely. Achingly sad. In other words, the perfect climate for a hit single.

Ever since I met with Coolidge, I haven't been able to shake this melody, and in my gut, I know it's a duet. I initially felt it could be for him and Mathers. But I was wrong. This song needs Lorelai. It's not romantic on the surface, although I know it could be taken that way. For Lorelai and Coolidge, this could be a song about leaving behind an old identity and finding a home in something new. Duets can be a lot of things: a tool to capitalize on chemistry, or a mutually beneficial career boost, or even a publicity stunt.

But a well-done duet can also be a signal of something more to come. Firing a flare into the deep, dark sky. A statement made by the united front of two powerhouse vocalists with through-hell-and-back stories using only their own force of will and industry-blinding talent.

They just need the foundation, which happens to be my specialty.

I spend the next five hours workshopping a song I haven't even confirmed will see the light of day. But that's how writing is. It's yours and only yours until maybe one day it's not. Nothing is guaranteed, but the chills I have zipping up and down my spine confirm *something* is happening, and those chills are rarely wrong.

Before long, Arlo arrives, his usual Lucky Work Fedora in place and a new set of shined-up loafers on his feet, with his jeans cuffed higher than I would know what to do with. This morning, he reminds me of Jason Mraz, minus the penchant for environmental activism and hipster jams. His arrival is followed by a folk band named Baker's Dozen, who've spent the better part of the last two decades touring small music festivals and coexisting in a refurbished school bus with their commune of children. These guys are low maintenance to the nth degree, despite my every effort to instill even the smallest amount of professionalism in them. But really, they're not in it for the money. Which is a good thing, because I doubt they manage to break even, selling their CDs quite literally out the back of their bus. They like my studio, though, because of the "vibes," and they're polite, which to be honest is rare and appreciated around these parts.

All of this is to say, I let Arlo take the reins on recording Baker's Dozen and instead send a text to Coolidge, confirming where he's playing tonight. He mentioned he likes to lay low and hit small bars off Broadway to stay fresh, and I thought I caught one of his stage aliases on the listing at the legendary Lulu Mays. He texts back quickly to confirm, and almost immediately after, I have a text from Lorelai, letting me know she caught her flight and would meet me on our balcony at seven.

I bite back a sigh, trying not think so hard about why this feels significant. Or why I *want* it to feel significant. Or why I need to just get the fuck out of my head because this is the same Lorelai I dropped off at the airport three days ago.

Christ. I run my hand through my hair and scratch against the scruff covering my face and grimace. I could use a haircut. Melissa mentioned it a time or seven yesterday, and while I don't love admitting she's right, or giving her fuel to think she can convince me, a grown-ass man, to do anything I don't already want to do . . .

She might have a point.

I tap my phone: 5:01 P.M. Two hours before I'm meeting Lorelai. I decide to make myself an appointment at my barber for thirty minutes from now and duck out early. Arlo promises to clean up and practically shoos me out when I tell him I'm going to get a trim, which is all the confirmation I need that I'm looking rough. I spend the couple of blocks' walk to the barber convincing myself I would be getting a haircut regardless of my night's plans. It's overdue and I look like a seventh-year college student who has run down his scholarships and is shacking up in the depressing attic at the frat house. I might not be your typical buttoned-up record executive, but I am the boss. I should look it.

At least that's what Arlo and Melissa are always telling me. I'm not entirely convinced it matters, but I guess it doesn't hurt.

Burl Matteson has been cutting my hair since 2015 and hasn't once asked my opinion. I can't tell if that's because he knows exactly what looks best on me or if he just gives the same haircut to everyone. His shop is so small, he doesn't accommodate lines. It's like the barber equivalent of Fight Club. No one talks about it. Every now and again, I'll see someone with a vaguely familiar hairstyle and wonder if they know Burl, but I won't ask. It would feel like a betrayal.

All of this to say, I don't change it up this afternoon, but I do ask for a shave. I've been halfway growing scruff for the better part of the last few years, but I wouldn't call it a beard. It would be an insult to real bearded men everywhere. At best, it's a near goatee, at worst it's mossy laziness. Burl gives me a smooth finish and surprisingly does something a little different with my unruly hair. My hair's never been what I would consider stylish so much as . . . convenient.

"You got a lady friend in your life, Mr. Boseman?"

I start to shake my head and he holds it still, scissors held precariously close to my earlobe. He meets my gaze in the mirror and raises a pair of well-groomed brows. I exhale.

"No, sir."

"Man friend?" He checks in a notably judgment-free tone.

"None of those, either, though I'm less inclined in that direction."

"Are you one of them perpetual bachelor types?"

This is more talk than I've gotten from Burl in the entire eight years I've been going to him. If you pressed a gun to my head this morning and asked me to identify his voice in a lineup, I wouldn't have made it to this afternoon. Because of this, I really consider my response. "I'm only thirty-six, Burl, so I don't think that qualifies me as a perpetual anything. But I guess I wouldn't hate to have someone to talk to at the end of the day."

He continues to nail me in the chair with that discerning look until I squirm. "Why'd you ask?"

He doesn't say anything, just nods to himself and moves to block my view, tugging on the ends of my hair and pursing his lips under his massive mustache.

When he finally turns me around, I'm shocked to see the difference a few well-placed snips and a close shave can make. I run my fingers through my short lengths and turn my head side to side.

"Damn, Burl, what kind of magic you got in those scissors? You mean I coulda looked like this all along?"

Burl only grunts, brushing off my neck and removing the collared cape.

Guess we're done talking.

Still flummoxed over the entire encounter, but incapable of finding fault with the results, I pay Burl, including a generous tip, and head home to shower off the loose hairs scratching through my shirt. It's after six and I'm feeling the press of time.

Lorelai. Lorelai. Lorelai.

She's here by now, in Nashville, and it's almost like I can feel her. Like the air feels different—more charged—when she's here. As if the entire city is waiting to see what she's gonna come up with next.

9

CRAIG

HURRICANE

I get home and shower and change into a fresh pair of jeans and a clean V-neck T-shirt before fiddling with my hair the way Burl did, using a tiny bit of pomade that Arlo gave me last year for Christmas. I'm still early, so I decide to hit the liquor store around the corner from our place and pick up some wine. Next to the register is a display of Prosecco and champagne, and for an insane minute, I contemplate buying her a bottle before offering to act out my most poetic fantasies.

But I don't, because a good haircut a personality change does not make. I learned long ago her type was everything I'm not. Smarmy, classically good-looking lead singers like Drake, not snarky, scruffy, soft guys with bad eyesight and poetry accounts.

When I make it back to the duplex, I see a light on downstairs, confirming she's made it home, and once I've climbed the stairs and closed the door to my loft behind me, I hear the groan of old pipes letting me know she's in the shower.

I pause too long, my feet frozen in place, listening hard and allowing myself the split-second assault that familiar groan stirs behind my eyelids . . . steaming hot droplets of water mixing with peekaboo suds and chasing one another across and down the smooth bare surface of her skin, the pulse of the showerhead massaging her toned muscles, tight from travel, as she lets out a tiny moan of relief or maybe even bliss before . . . *before* I'm rapidly shaking my head to rid myself of the fantasy and grab a couple of wineglasses as I head out on the balcony to wait.

Maybe noise-canceling headphones would be a good investment. Or one of those white noise machines. *Alexa, play something annoying whenever my neighbor turns on the shower and let's reverse-Pavlov this shit in the bud.*

And then it's seven and I can hear her steps on the metal fire escape as she makes her way up toward me. A moment later, her tantalizing fresh-from-the-shower scent reaches my nose a split second before the rest follows. Her shiny blue-black hair pulled off her forehead in a clip but left long around her shoulders. When she first came to Nashville months ago, Lorelai's hair was a deep chestnut shade, but since then, she's back to embracing her natural black-as-night waves. I'm glad. The contrast suits her. Now, her dark brown eyes crinkle with happiness. Her small, athletic frame is stunningly on display in a pair of well-worn jeans and a plain white tee. I put down the glasses and wine just as she's throwing her arms around my neck in greeting.

Hell.

I shouldn't be caught off guard because this is classic Lorelai. She's always been generous with her affection when it comes to her friends. I manage to hold tight, wrapping my arms around her and squeezing. Truthfully, I give good hugs. I learned from Melissa, who, despite our more conservative parents, hugged me long and often. "Squeeze the toxic masculinity right out of you," she'd say.

For what it's worth, I do not lose myself in this particular hug, closing my eyes or swaying in place like a masochist. Much, anyway.

Lorelai pulls back and tugs me toward the small wrought-iron table for two, pressing me to sit before doing a double take at my appearance, her full bottom lip finding its way between her teeth and making me sweat in long-ago memories.

"You got a haircut!"

The thing about the scruff—it wasn't much more than Astroturf on a mini golf course, but it knew its job and it covered the rising pink. *Now* I remember. I, Craig Huckleberry Boseman, blush more than a debutante with wardrobe malfunction.

Fuckin' a.

I try to play it off. "Yeah, well apparently Burl *does* have one other trick up his sleeve."

The corner of her pretty mouth lifts as she takes the bottle from my hands and gestures with her head to my kitchen before saying in an easy-breezy way, "I like it. You look hot, Huckleberry."

I choke out a "Thanks" before mentally punching myself to get my shit back together, shifting my focus to the way

Lorelai's jeans hug her curves and her simple white tee rides up ever so slightly, revealing a strip of smooth pale toned waistline. A waistline that was wet only minutes ago.

Which is the direct opposite of helpful . . .

She pours the glasses, thank fuck, and I hustle to the kitchen, realizing I left Melissa's biscuits and gravy on the kitchen island. I grab the Tupperware and a couple of forks and join her back on the balcony, holding out the leftovers.

"Melissa's been hell-bent on figuring out a decent gluten- and dairy-free biscuits and gravy recipe for when you visit . . . This one doesn't suck, though I swear it tastes better cold for some reason?"

We settle in on the iron chairs and sip from our glasses as she pries open the cold leftovers and digs her fork in. She takes a bite, her eyes immediately rolling to the sky and a heady groan coming from the back of her throat. The sound shoots tingles through my veins straight for my groin and I quickly prop my ankle over my knee to hide any evidence. Blushing and getting sprung like a seventh grader at his first coed pool party. Two for two, Boseman.

Lorelai offers me a bite and I wave her off. That's just what I need, to share her fork and imagine her taste on the tines.

She finishes, licking her lips clean and wiping with a napkin before taking another long sip from her wineglass.

"I love your sister."

I laugh. "Pretty sure that's mutual."

"So . . . I got an email from Jen," she starts, changing the subject. "While I was in Michigan."

I don't bother to hide my judgmental eye roll. Lorelai knows how I feel about her so-called agent. "And?"

"And she's prepared this sort of 'apology tour,' hitting up all the key country radio stations and executives. She wants me to go in there ready to grovel and promise to never, ever think for myself ever again."

"Did she phrase it like that?" I ask, amused despite my annoyance at the nerve of Jennifer Blake.

Lorelai sighs, pulling one knee to her chest and resting her heel on the chair. Her toes are painted a deep dusty pink, and while I'm not usually a foot guy, I could easily compose a song about Lorelai's cute toes. I won't, obviously. But I could.

"Just about," she concedes wryly. "She seems intent on this course. Doesn't see much chance of a career in country music without it."

I don't offer my opinion. This isn't my choice and it's not my career. It's Lorelai's, and I know how much country music means to her. She's not ready to walk away and I respect that. "Is that the route you want to take?"

She shakes her head. "I thought about it. Talked with Mare. I haven't responded to Jen yet, but no. It's not really what I want. I don't regret what I did. In fact, I'd do it again in a heartbeat, so how the hell am I supposed to grovel? The problem is, I don't see another way."

I nod, silently relieved. "I might have some thoughts. Maybe not an answer to the apology tour, but rather an alternative?" I offer. "If you aren't afraid of being creative."

She turns to me, tilting her head against her knee. "I'm listening."

"How well do you know Clay Coolidge?"

"Enough to know that's not his name anymore."

I raise my glass in acknowledgment. "He's my newest

client. Met with him over the weekend. He's looking to re-invent himself."

"I thought he was already doing that with Annie Mathers?"

I shake my head. "He was . . . but he said he's not in-terested in riding her star to make it happen. He wants to change things up a bit and do something different. Country, but more retrofit. Classic, minus the historically problematic penchant for sexism, classism, racism . . . And he wants to do it his own way, without the interference of the record labels. Whatever he's cooking up, I definitely want in. I've already started writing with him in mind and I can't wait to collabo-rate, but . . ."

I trail off, and take another sip, knowing I need to proceed with caution. I don't want Lorelai to think I don't believe in her. Or to think I'm trying to swoop in and save her. It's not like that.

"But?" she leads, her hand doing a little elegant twirl in the balmy summer evening air.

"Well, okay." I turn to her, placing both feet on the ground and my empty glass on the table between us. "Not so much a *but* . . . More like a possibility based around a caveat."

"Caveat first, then. Lay it on me, Huckleberry."

I can't help my grin at how she always manages to say that name with a straight face. "The caveat is you know I think you're fucking out of this world talented on your own."

She presses her lips together and crosses her dark eyes comically. "Okay. Noted."

"So I've started writing a duet for you and Coolidge. No pressure. But if there's anyone who knows about reinvention, it's him, and I just got the feeling . . . you know . . . the tingles." I point to my arms. "Like this could be magic."

"He's with Mathers."

"Nothing romantic," I clarify in a rush. "And nothing manufactured for the sake of attention. I'm thinking more along the lines of a statement. What's better and more influential than one beloved star jilted by the industry powers that be?"

"Two," she whispers as a smile spreads across her lips.

"Two," I agree.

"In theory, it's a great idea," she says. "But I haven't talked to Coolidge in years. Not since Drake threw his tantrum over Best New Artist. I imagine I'm the last person, next to Drake, he wants to work with."

"Not at all. He knows that wasn't anything to do with you, and he even told me he sought *me* out because I produced your most recent songs. You impress him. I think he'd be down."

"But you haven't brought it up yet?"

I'm already shaking my head. "No way. Not without asking you first. That's not how this works," I say, gesturing between us.

Now her smile is full-blown. "You realize you're a rarity around these parts, Huck?"

"That ain't hard to be," I grunt easily. "I said I didn't ask him yet, and I didn't, but I happen to know he's playing at Lulu Mays"—I glance at my watch—"in thirty minutes. If you want to go check him out and see what he sounds like these days."

Lorelai's face smooths out, and while she didn't look

particularly stressed before, I can see a marked difference now and I want to slump with relief because it's clear she really *doesn't* hate the idea.

"I think that sounds awesome. I haven't been to Lulu Mays in forever."

. . .

Lulu Mays is one of those institutions in Nashville that locals are born knowing about and tourists wait in line to experience. It's history, pure and simple. All the legends have played in this tiny bar and café at one point or another. The dingy walls are soaked in decades of grease, black coffee fumes, and the sweetest melodies to ever come out of this town. I will sometimes come just to sit outside on the curb and listen, letting the music roll over me and feed my soul. The proximity is enough. When I was a kid and my sister first moved to Nashville for school, she would let me stay with her some weekends and take me out. We went to the Country Music Hall of Fame and Museum and the Johnny Cash Museum and the Bluebird Cafe and all up and down Broadway. I knew from the very first moment this was exactly where I needed to be and what I wanted to do with my life. Eventually Melissa got married and moved out to the suburbs, but I've never left. Not really.

This is home.

The warm night means there are no doors or windows to be seen. Already, music pours out of Lulu Mays into the street, and it's excellent.

Lorelai leads us to a small table right in the front that

FRIENDS DON'T FALL IN LOVE

a couple had fortunately vacated as we were walking in. Coolidge looks up from his mic, recognition flitting in his eyes underneath the brim of his hat, and without breaking the song, he sends a nod in our direction. I turn to Lorelai, who's nodding back, a reassuring smile in place. We order a couple of inexpensive glasses of house White Zin (Lulu Mays isn't the kind of place to serve red) and settle in our chairs to listen.

Jefferson's accompanied by his usual rusty-haired fiddler, Fitz Jacoby, and a dark-haired drummer who looks vaguely familiar, but I can't automatically place him. After a minute, Lorelai leans over and says in my ear, "Is that Mathers's drummer? Diaz?"

Instantly, I know she's right. I'll have to confirm if he'll be the one recording for Coolidge or if he's just in town for tonight. The three play seamlessly for over an hour. That Jefferson has someone as talented as Jacoby on the fiddle opens a lot of doors. I wonder if he plays the mandolin or banjo? I don't think he's mentioned it. I let Coolidge's whiskey tenor roll over me and allow my mind to wander, mentally skimming my catalogue for songs that might work for him. More than anything, though, I imagine his vocals layered with Lorelai's against the backdrop of the lyrics I wrote this morning.

Soon it's break time and they make a beeline straight for our table.

"Craig, you made it." He shakes my hand. "You remember Fitz, and this is Jason Diaz," Coolidge says before motioning to a server, who quickly brings him a tall glass of ice water and Fitz and Jason a couple of beers. Then he turns to Lorelai. "I'll admit, Ms. Jones, to being a bit starstruck that you're here. I'm honored you came."

Lorelai holds out her hand. "Fuck's sake, please call me Lorelai. Y'all make me nervous calling me Ms. Jones. The honor is mine. You play beautifully, and that tone of yours is a goddamn dream."

Everyone settles around our table and compliments pass back and forth for a little while. Lorelai asks after Annie Mathers, telling Jefferson she remembers her from when she was a child. He tells us she's in L.A. doing promo for a song she has featured on a blockbuster movie soundtrack. Because of that, Jason Diaz is on loan for the next few months and has committed to laying down tracks for Coolidge, which answers that question. Honestly, this keeps getting better and better.

"My girl's in town for a few months," Diaz tells me with an easy lopsided grin, his foot tapping a backbeat on the sticky linoleum. "So I'm happy to overlap here in Nashville and help out."

I tell them that works for me. After hearing how cohesively they play together, I'm thrilled to put Diaz on the record. Someone from Lulu Mays gives them a discreet five-minute warning.

"I have a proposition for you," I say. "No pressure and I don't even want to know tonight, which is why I'm only bringing it up now. I was working on a little something original this morning. I've sent it to your email, as well as yours," I say to Lorelai. "A duet, meant for two talented vocalists looking to reinvent themselves in this industry. Like I said, no pressure, but the timing is pretty perfect for you both."

Coolidge looks surprised but intrigued. "Okay, I'll definitely listen."

Lorelai looks a little relieved, maybe that Jefferson seems interested in sharing a song with her and her reputation. She doesn't have anything to worry about on that front, though. My gut tells me this is a good thing.

"Me too," she says with a grin.

I nod my head, indicating that's settled. "Awesome. That's all I ask, and then we can revisit next week sometime if it turns out you're interested."

The men return to the stage, but it's late and Lorelai traveled from Michigan this afternoon, so we decide to give up our table. Outside, it's even more dark and humid, and when combined with the half bottle of red from earlier and the more recent two glasses, I'm feeling plenty loose-limbed and drowsy. We decide to forgo a ride and instead walk back to the duplex, allowing us some time to sober up and stretch our legs.

The sidewalks still hum with music and laughter and the clinking of bottles, but they're less bustling than they are on the weekends, so we stroll side by side. Our hands dangle between us, occasionally tangling but never quite catching, and I ignore the way my skin practically vibrates from the closeness.

"Do you think he'll want to do the duet?"

"Do *you* want to do the duet?" I toss back.

She looks over at me, her dark eyes penetrating. "Well, yeah. You had me at 'I'm writing a song for you . . .'"

"Okay," I concede, fighting the urge to smile, "but I would write you a song either way." Every day until the day I die if she wanted.

She slows to a stop under a glowing neon sign flashing a pair of dancing cowboy boots. "Have I thanked you lately?"

I pause alongside her, the corner of my mouth lifting. "For what?"

She raises her hands and gestures around. "For everything, really, but mostly for being such a good friend."

My mouth goes dry because that's me. *A good friend.* "Oh. Well." I shrug a shoulder, looking forward at nothing and grateful for the flashes of blue and green neon when I feel my cheeks flame. Might as well let the moss grow back and retain the tiny shreds of dignity I have left. "You really don't have to thank me for that."

She's quiet and eventually I turn to look at her. Her brows are pulled together and her lips are tight. I wait for her to say something, but she doesn't. She steps into my space and gingerly lifts her hand toward my face. Eventually her cool palm finds my burning jawline. She stumbles the tiniest bit forward and I reach up my hand to steady hers on my skin. This close, the scent of White Zinfandel mixes with her breath and covers me in soft puffs of sweet air.

"I've been—um." She pauses. Starts again. "Your face. It's so smooth. I wanted—" She swallows, her eyes searching my own. She has to be able to feel the way my blood is rushing beneath my skin. The way I can't help but sway toward her, magnetized. "I was curious if it was as smooth as it looked." Her thumb brushes along my cheekbone, back and forth, and I'm pulled closer still.

"Is it?" I ask her, dumbly.

She blinks, her lashes fluttering, and I sway even closer. Her inhales are bringing her chest within inches of mine. I don't dare look down to confirm, but I swear to Christ her breasts brush against me. Her lips are open ever so slightly. I can practically taste her. If I just bent the slightest bit . . .

"Look out!" Suddenly I'm swept to the side and knocked off-balance as someone zips past on a rented scooter, reeling out of control and shrieking over their shoulder, "Sorry, man!"

Lorelai untangles herself and straightens first, eyes bright and brimming with amusement. I shake my head, getting to my feet. "Are you okay?" she asks, holding out a hand. I take it, but she releases it almost as quick, biting her lip. The moment, whatever the fuck it was, has passed.

"Yeah." I laugh once, rubbing at my bruised ass. "Yeah, I'm . . . fine. Good. I mean, I think I broke my tailbone, but it's nothing an inflatable doughnut seat can't fix."

My bruised pride, however? That's gonna need something stronger.

LORELAI

SOMETHING TO TALK ABOUT

Is my breath wasted if it's only exhaled between your lips
If my fingers print the sway of your hips,
If my eyes crave to trace your freckles unseen,
If my tongue licks and lingers just in between,
If I tease out your cries,
If I spread apart your thighs,
will you save your sated sighs
only for me?

I say a quick good night to Craig on our porch, and by the time I hear his feet ascending the staircase and his apartment door shut, I'm already wearing my hardwood floors smooth with my pacing. Thankfully I'm on the first floor, so he won't know by the creaking of floorboards that I'm emotionally and physically spiraling. What just happened between us on that street corner? He definitely leaned. Full frontal leaning. Slow-motion nipple brush. There was contact. I felt it zing-ing straight to my damp panties and circling wildly through my bloodstream. If that guy on the scooter . . . if we hadn't been interrupted . . . was he about to . . . was I about to???

I flop on my navy faux-velvet sofa with a loud sigh and slip out of my boots, letting them thud softly against the inexpensive blue-and-white area rug I picked up at Target when I realized the duplex was outfitted in hardwoods. I still haven't bothered with lights. There's a full moon shining through the slats of my blinds, painting everything an ethereal blue, pale enough to see my way around. My phone buzzes, and thinking it might be a text from upstairs, I check it, turning the screen light way, way down. But it's only an email. Instead of closing out, I listlessly scroll through Instagram, not really taking in the images posted by people I wouldn't recognize if I encountered them on the street.

Another zing of awareness breaks through the inattentive fog. He's posted. Not on his account, but on his *other* account. The poetry one. I wish I knew if it was scheduled or if he wrote this after leaving me . . . I settle against a cushion to read.

And read again. And again.

I probably have every one of his poems imprinted in my memory. What makes his account so popular, and likewise his lyrics, is the uniquely sexy accessibility of his words.

Blah blah blah, now I'm horny and he's literally just upstairs. What fresh hell. I try to shift mental gears, but all I can come up with is the accidental nipple brush from an hour before. Which makes me even hornier.

My eyes slide shut and my head is full of traitorous thoughts, images conjured within and filling the spaces between his written words. I imagine them precisely chosen to trigger a reaction in me. Which, honestly, is so unfair, and the next time I'm drunk, I might tell him, because, right now, inside the hidden walls of my mind, I see only him, his dark brows drawn together, his newly shaven cheeks flushing, his breath panting between us.

I think of the way his air traded places with mine on that street corner, twining and covering us in things unspoken. In my imagination, we're not interrupted. Deep inside the secretive hollows in my mind, his long fingers reach for my waist and tug me close. Close enough that our hips meet and sparks fly. And it's with intention. There's nothing accidental about it. His blue eyes dip, just long enough to be followed by his hands.

And like that, I lose control.

My imagination takes over, or maybe my memories. Behind my closed eyelids, I watch as he unbuttons my shirt (because of course I'm wearing a button-down—way sexier than a tee), popping each individual button through its hole and placing a cool, open-mouthed kiss on the feverish skin left bare by the effort. On my couch, in my apartment, only one floor away from him, I clench my knees together, but his words echo inside of me and spur me on . . . *if I spread apart your thighs,* and I let them fall open. My skin is aflame in nerve endings and sensation and I quickly unzip my jeans, my fingers ghosting inside my panties to find the exact spot where I'm soaked and aching. I imagine his hands, his mouth, his breath all over me. I imagine him hard and thick inside the cradle of my legs and I press and tease and expertly dip the way I wish *he* would. My free hand finds my breast and I cup and pluck and roll until I cry out into the silence, shattering against wave after wave after wave of real release.

But when I finally open my eyes, wrung-out and half dreamy . . . the room is dark and still. My body is left unfurled on my navy couch, the moonlight slanting through the windows and my phone discarded on the floor.

I'm completely alone and he was only words.

. . .

The following morning I wake up in my bed, grumpy and a little dehydrated. For the dehydration, I guzzle a tall glass of tap water before popping a pod of caffeine in the Keurig. For the grumpiness, I text my best friends on my walk to my favorite rock-climbing gym.

LORELAI: How do I make someone want to have sex with me?

MAREN: Is this rhetorical?

SHELBY: No, I bet this is Craig Boseman.

LORELAI: I'm positive he almost kissed me on a street corner last night. There was definitely leaning. Maybe even nipple brushing.

SHELBY: *eyeballs emoji*

MAREN: NOT NIPPLE BRUSHING!

LORELAI: Ha-ha, laugh it up, Beauty Queen.

SHELBY: So lean . . . more. Seal the deal, Jones.

MAREN: He wrote another poem last night.

LORELAI: OH I KNOW

MAREN: *smirk* I'll just bet you do.

SHELBY: Does he know you know he writes those? (whew that's convoluted)

LORELAI: NO. And I don't know if I can tell him.

LORELAI: It might make him feel weird that I know.

MAREN: Weirder than you knowing makes YOU feel?

LORELAI: Doesn't make me feel weird. Unless weird is a euphemism for "excessively turned on."

SHELBY: I'm with Mare. He posts on Instagram. It's not like he's writing it in a locked diary or something.

SHELBY: Are you sure you're not reading into things because you're actually looking for a repeat of history?

SHELBY: Because it sounds like you might be.

MAREN: No judgment, obviously.

SHELBY: Absolutely not.

LORELAI: Ugh.

LORELAI: See, it worked last time because it scratched multiple itches (ie: Fuck off Drake and also that whole "wonder what it'd be like to have sex with Huck?" thing)

LORELAI: with the benefit of getting on a plane the next morning and never having to face him again . . .

MAREN: No strings attached.

LORELAI: Exactly. The cleanest of breaks.

SHELBY: But now you work together and see each other all the time and also you're very single, so rebound sex isn't a thing.

LORELAI: Right. So this would be a fuckbuddies sitch and I saw that movie.

LORELAI: Twice.

LORELAI: It's super messy. And I don't want things between Huck and me to ever be messy.

SHELBY: Well, you could, you know, date him. Like for real.

MAREN: Ope!

LORELAI: *hyperventilates* Not happening.

MAREN: The way I see it, you have two options: Find another fuck buddy to call after Craig's poetry gets you all hot and bothered or invest in more batteries for your vibrator.

LORELAI: Are those my only choices? Surely we're forgetting something.

SHELBY: Yeah, you're forgetting that you could just DATE HIM. You get the orgasms, you get the friend, you get the feelings. It's win, win, win.

LORELAI: I also get the insecurity, the jealousy, the battling careers, the abandonment issues, the commitment phobia . . .

LORELAI: Y'all, I can't go there.

MAREN: RIP your nipples, I guess.

SHELBY: *sigh* "Hey, Alexa, add 'send rechargeable batteries to Lorelai' to my to-do list."

. . .

Full disclosure: I'm not a stranger to sexting. Back in Michigan, before my last album and before returning to Nashville and before . . . whatever this is, Drake used to sext me on occasion. And if those occasions lined up with a night I was feeling especially horny or lonely or maybe just empowered because I knew if he was texting me, he wasn't hooking up with someone else . . . well, I'd respond. I knew damn well nothing was ever going to come of it. It's true I thought I really loved him once upon a time, but it turns out I was young and influenced and I don't know. What I thought was love just faded? Turns out, being left at the metaphorical altar really just squeezed out all the love I had inside of me.

Besides, Drake's an opportunist. He's too self-absorbed to put actual effort into loving someone, but if the right situation presents itself, he'll be the first to jump on it and ride the easy wave.

Which is exactly why the minute, and I mean the *very* minute, he tried to play the "Baby, I still love you, what are you wearing right now?" card, I quit that shit cold turkey. I might be an idiot who stayed with the guy way longer than I should have, but I needed to learn my lesson only once.

Anyway, I don't want that with Craig, not the long-distance sexting and not the epically terrible one-sided relationship. As hot as his poetry gets me, there's a reason the account is anonymous. It's the same reason he played bass in the shadows instead of up front and center, despite his enormous talent. And the same reason I like him so damn much. I can't just send him a text saying, "Fingered myself to your poem last night. Want to meet up?"

(Also, meet up where? On our balcony? In our driveway? Want to meet me downstairs in my apartment that you own?)

Just. Ugh.

By the time I've run all my favorite routes up my favorite wall a half a dozen times, I'm feeling an intense burn in my shoulders that's gonna follow me into tomorrow and I've come up with a plan. It's not quite so elaborate as "anonymous erotic poetry account," but it's close.

I shower, change into jeans and an old Hootie & the Blowfish tee (because I liked Darius Rucker before he was country music cool), and make myself two toasted sandwiches on tiny gluten-free slices of bread. Then I pick up my guitar and get to work. I'm not as exceptional a songwriter as Craig, but I'm good in my own right. And occasionally, I'm even brilliant.

A few hours later, I've got a decent start on a new song. Only this one will never see the inside of a booth. This is just for him, and it's not finished yet, but as it is, it should get his blood pumping. Praying that I'm not making a huge mistake, I hit record on my laptop, strum the opening chords, and sing.

The words you said
echo softly 'round my head
Whisper sparks along my skin and
I can't help
Tracing patterns from the lines
Fingertips drawing where your eyes
Set me on fire

You breathed me in
Stealing air and sense away
And planted longing deep inside
I can't stop
Imagining your lips
Kissing every inch of me
Burning for you

It records in one take, and I don't even bother listening back. I'm not aiming for perfection. Frankly, I'm aiming for his cock.

I save the file and send myself a copy so that I can access it on my phone. I don't want to send this through our emails like a business transaction.

I open my text app and tap on his name.

LORELAI: I worked on a little something today. It's not finished
yet, but I wanted you to hear it first. <<< File.ForYou.zip>>>

He doesn't respond right away. In fact, he doesn't respond all day. To the point that I end up turning my phone
off and on again to make sure it's working. But I get texts
from Shelby asking for an update while I'm eating a comfort
dinner of boxed gluten-free vegan mac and cheese, so I know
everything is operational.

I'm halfway through a draft of a text where I tell him it
was an accident, and I wasn't ready to send that song and to
please disregard, when I see the gray dots of his reply pop
up. I sit back on my heels, my heart in my throat. Oh god.
What if he was grossed out? Okay, probably not grossed out.
We're adults. And he was definitely into it that one time. But
he *could* be trying to figure out how to let me down easy? To
be professional. Holy fuck he owns his own recording studio.
What was I thinking?

I panic, flipping the phone facedown on the table and
jumping to my feet. For a second, I stand in indecision. I
have to go somewhere. Do something. Out of the corner
of my eye, I see the small stack of dishes from dinner and
so I methodically make my way through them, hand wash-
ing and drying and putting them away. Then I move on to
laundry . . . I need to keep on top of my sweaty running
clothes, after all. When I've exhausted the too-short list of
housekeeping chores, I turn to my phone, my lips pressed
together. It's only a text, Lorelai. Fuck's sake.

I reach for my phone and on the count of three, I flip it,
revealing the empty lock screen.

FRIENDS DON'T FALL IN LOVE

No notifications.

He didn't respond. He saw the text and started to respond . . . I saw it. I know I didn't imagine it.

But then *he just didn't respond*. He's never not responded to me before.

Oh my god. What have I done?

11
. . . .

LORELAI
MAYDAY

It's been five hours since I made it back from Denver—my tour officially canceled, my future officially fucked—and my fiancé still hasn't called me back. Someone else in my position might worry he's giving me the cold shoulder, but I know better than to panic. Well, panic about that, anyway. This is standard Drake. He's notorious for holing up in the studio and turning off his phone, shutting out the world so he can become one with his process or whatever. Case in point: his grandmother had a terrible stroke last fall and it took me flying in from D.C. and literally pounding down the studio door to notify him she was gone. Even then, I got to him only because Huck answered the door.

So his silence isn't that unusual. But hell if it's not aggravating as heck and a tiny bit hurtful. On the surface, I'm pretty independent, and we've never had one of those clingy relationships (the man is deathly allergic to PDA), but for just once in our lives, I could use a hug and some fucking reassurance from the man I'm marrying. If ever there was a time to be needy . . .

I try his cell again. And again, nothing. By the time he checks, he's gonna have seventy missed calls and probably freak out.

Which, well. Considering I just crashed and burned my entire career with one four-and-a-half-minute protest performance, maybe it would help. I would love to not be the only one freaking out.

I nearly smile to myself. Yeah, right. Famous Drake Colter lose control of his careful facade? Not a chance. One of the things that first drew me to him was his calming presence. Nothing rattles him. I could use a voice of reason. Encouragement. Logic.

I call again. "Pick up, pick up, pick up . . . Hello? Dra—"

"Shit. No, I'm sorry, Lore, it's Huck."

I pull the phone away from my ear and double-check the name on the screen and bring it back to my ear in time to catch Huck still speaking.

"I should have used my phone, but I have just a minute and I saw your name flash on the screen and—"

"Where are you guys?"

I can hear Huck's exhale. "New Orleans."

"Oh. Well, that explains it. Have you been in the studio all day? I've been trying—"

"Yeah, we have," *he cuts in, in a rush.* "But listen to me, Lore. Drake already knows. What happened at your show and with your tour . . . He's being a dick, okay? He heard the news right away. Powers called first thing this morning." *Huck's tone is pained as he mentions his and Drake's slimy manager.*

"Oh," *I repeat, icy realization cooling the blood in my veins, freezing me in place.* "I see."

It's quiet a beat before Huck speaks. "I'm sorry, Lore. I've been trying to get him to take your calls, but Powers told him not to talk to you until he figured things out or some shit. I'm not supposed to

be talking to you, either, technically, but that's such bullshit. I'm—
this is just all so fucked up. You didn't do anything wrong, Lorelai."

"He won't talk to me because Powers told him not to?" I ask,
snagging on the detail.

"Yeeeah." Huck exhales loudly over the speaker. "Yes."

I swallow back the sudden rush of emotion, feeling the hot sting
of tears for the very first time since this whole thing began, and
clear my throat before saying, "Just to clarify, the man I am supposed to marry, tie my life to—who is supposed to love me in sick-
ness or health, for richer or poorer—he won't talk to me because his
manager told him not to."

"I know. It looks bad. It is bad. One hundred percent. I'm sorry.
I feel shitty even telling you, but I couldn't handle him ignoring
your calls. You needed to know."

"I understand. Thank you. Bye, Huck."

"Lore—shit. Okay. Right. Bye, Lorelai. I'll call you later, okay?
To check in."

I hang up the phone, feeling numb, and slump back on my bed
with a shaky sigh, rubbing my hands over my eyes until eventually
they, too, fall against the rumpled quilt.

My high-rise studio has been half unpacked for over a year. Its
honestly more of an overpriced storage facility at this point. I was
supposed to move in with Drake, but he's home even less than I am.
I guess it's good I never did.

It hasn't always been this way. At the start, before we had
things like careers and commitments and tour buses, we spent all
our time cuddled up on a secondhand couch we found on a street
corner for free. We'd drink cheap beer and smoke questionable weed
and dream about our futures as mega super famous country stars
and then make love on his piece of shit mattress laid right in the

middle of the floor on the wood. It was humble, and maybe even a little trashy, but we were happy. We were on the cusp of something big and filled with all the hope starry-eyed twenty-somethings in Nashville can hold.

And then our dreams came true. Labels signed us. First me, but he wasn't far behind. And albums were recorded and tours were planned and we could afford things like box springs and couches that didn't have mysterious stains on the cushions.

And with every granted wish, we pulled further apart. On our three-year anniversary, he took me to St. Croix and asked me to marry him. I said yes, obviously, and I thought maybe that was the missing piece. That if he could make that kind of effort—go to all the trouble to coordinate our schedules and plan this whole beautiful trip and pick out this perfect ring—maybe our relationship wasn't ill-fated. Deep down he knew me more than anyone and he understood.

Of course I found out later my agent Jen did most of the planning, but that's not unusual. Our schedules were super busy. It's hard to plan a surprise trip with someone who reports to an entire management team.

My apathetic musings are interrupted when my phone buzzes. I grope near where I dropped it, grabbing it and blinking against the brightness to read the Google alert.

COUNTRY STAR DRAKE COLTER BREAKS SILENCE WITH SOCIAL MEDIA POST AFTER FIANCÉE LORELAI JONES MAKES POLITICAL GAFFE AT SHOW

I sit up, clicking on the link, my heart in my throat. I don't even read the article, just follow the blue-lined text to Drake's

Instagram. "Don't you dare let me down, Drake Colter," I mutter, swiping at my eyes and sniffing as the video loads.

There's no sound. It's just one of those screen scrolls. It's his phone calendar and he scrolls to the month of May. The month we're getting married. Then the date. There it is on the screen.

Marrying the most beautiful girl in the world.

He deletes it. Letter. By. Letter.

And the video goes black before cycling through again.

I blink, confused. What does that even mean?

Wait. Holy fucking shit, did he just break up with me via a fifteen-second clip on social media?

I watch as the video repeats over and over. Marrying the most beautiful girl in the world.

Marrying the most beautiful

Marrying the most

Marrying the

Marrying

I can't stop the bark of laughter that creeps past my throat and ends on a loud sob.

Oh my god. I've ruined everything.

I've ruined everything.

I need a drink.

. . .

The following morning, I'm just pressing the start button on my coffee maker when I hear a knocking at my front door. My head slumps forward on my shoulders and I groan, forcefully smacking the button three more times for good measure to speed things up. I've overslept, which is absolutely because I spent half the night tossing and turning before actively googling "Is it possible to unsend texts?" and "Can you delete a file after sending it?" sometime around two A.M.

The knocking continues its assault until it's topped off by the doorbell, which is one of those annoying old-fashioned buzzer types. "Ugh, I'm coming." It's not until I'm halfway down the hall that it occurs to me it might be Craig. That maybe he's here after getting my song and made himself wait until this morning so he could come over in person and press me up against my wall and kiss all the way down my body and . . .

I dash into the powder room and dig for a sample bottle of mouthwash courtesy of my last dental appointment, swishing it around my sleep-fuzzy teeth while simultaneously splashing ice-cold water on my face.

I spit in the sink and blot my face dry, combing my fingers through my tangled hair in the mirror, tousling it in a way I hope looks artful and not frizzy. I can see the vague outline of my nipples through my white sleep tank, but maybe that's a good thing. A little visual reminder of what *could be.*

Not once, not *once,* do I question why Craig would be knocking *and* ringing the doorbell when he lives upstairs and can just, you know, text back and I could unlock my door and—

The doorbell buzzes again. "This is it," I tell my reflection.

A moment later, I pull open my front door and immediately realize it's definitely *not* Craig.

I lean against the doorjamb, immediately crossing my arms over my nipples. "Speak of the never-lovin' devil."

Drake beams a confident, too-sexy grin. "So you were speaking of me?"

"Fuck no, I wasn't. But the point stands."

His face twitches. A too-familiar indication of his annoyance, but he recovers quickly and holds out a small package. "For you."

Holding one arm across my breasts, I reach out for the box and shake it a little.

"From the farmers' market. Vetner's strawberry shortcakes. Those are your favorite, right?"

I'm busy sniffing the box but slowly lower it at his words. I narrow my eyes at him, bemused. "They are. I'm shocked you remember, though I guess you're bound to be correct every once in a while. I'm pretty sure you used to have Craig or Levi pick them up for me whenever you were in town."

He affects a wounded expression, his hand clutching his chest. "Ouch. I did ask you to marry me, Lorelai. I wanted you to be my wife."

I tilt my head to the side. "Until you didn't, Drake. Thanks for the shortcakes. You're right. They *used* to be my favorite. Before my diagnosis. Now one bite would put me in bed for a week, which you should know, given the way you stalk my Instagram, but that's neither here nor there."

I start to duck into my foyer, swinging the door shut behind me, when his arm reaches out. "Jen's been in touch. Asked about the potential for a reunion tour this winter." He shrugs. "You could have just asked me in person, Lore."

My mouth drops open and it feels as though the ground shifts under me. "She did what?"

"Makes sense. I should have done it a long time ago. You were right. I messed up. But better late than never, right?"

"I didn't—I don't want—" I swallow, trying to regain my

composure. "She never should have—she went behind my back. I never would have asked you that."

His brows draw together. "Why not? You don't have to act too proud with me. Look, I'm sorry about the shortcake. I forgot, okay? I can't keep track of all your diets. But you have to admit, the tour is a brilliant idea. You could celebrate your reemergence on the country music scene aaand . . ." He trails off meaningfully, stuffing his hands in his designer jeans pockets in a way I know he thinks is down-to-earth and charming. Spoiler: It's neither.

"And what?" I ask. My patience is way past running thin and I'm not the least bit interested in putting words in his mouth.

"And . . . I don't know. Let whatever happens between us, happen. C'mon, Lore, you know our chemistry is off the charts. It's inevitable."

I could slam the door in his face. I should after all he's put me through. But all the insecurities from the last six months—hell, six *years*—prevent me from completely shutting down this opportunity. I don't want Drake. I don't even think I want the tour or the inevitable career boost. But I backed myself into a fucking corner and I've spent years trying to muscle my way out.

"Nothing is inevitable, Drake. Least of all, a reunion between us." I pretend to perk up at something over my shoulder. "I think my phone is ringing. I should go." I wave the box in my hand before pressing it firmly to his chest. "It's not a diet, by the way. It's a chronic autoimmune and digestive disorder, you *ass*."

I shut the door with a soft click and lock it before leaning against it and sliding down to the floor, dragging my knees to my chest and exhaling, dropping my head back against the door with a thud.

What was I even thinking coming back here? It's like those years in Michigan made me forget how jaded and impossible this industry is. Did I really think I could just waltz in with a new sound and everyone would magically forget what I was about the last time around? Did I forget how rare it is to get one shot in Nashville, let alone two? What makes me so special that I deserve to keep making music?

No, I don't want to join forces with my ex, but I don't want to do an apology tour, either. The fact is, I might have to swallow my pride and do both if I want a second chance, and I'm in no position to refuse help, no matter how much said help makes my stomach churn.

I know what Craig would say. He'd tell me to trust in the duet. But that seems even less likely a scenario than the tours. I'm not saying I won't do it, and I know if Craig writes it, it *will* be a hit. No question. I'm all in, I just don't see how one song is going to fix the mess I've made.

And really, it's easy for Craig to say. He's not the one bumming a living off his friend's generosity. He's not the one shutting the door in his ex's face and he's not the one watching his meager teaching savings slip away month after month.

I don't begrudge my friend's success. He's worked his ass off and he deserves every bit of happiness. But at the end of the day, I don't have an eccentric wealthy uncle who died and left me the ability to take career risks.

And of course, that's not all that's bothering me. Right this moment, when I'm feeling all tender and decidedly not my usual bad bitch self, I'm worried that I've misread things with my best friend/professional partner by sending him (half) a dirty song.

And if I'm being honest, that feels worse than the rest of it put together.

Emotions are weird motherfuckers.

In no time, hot tears are pricking in the corners of my eyes. What a fucking disaster. It takes me a minute to realize my phone actually *is* ringing from my bedroom. With a loud sniff, I scrub at my mostly dry face and scramble to my feet. By the time I make it to my phone, I've missed a call from Jen. I imagine she wants to fill me in on her "huge move" in scooping a Drake Colter tour. Thanks for nothing on that one.

It really would be so much easier if I could wipe the slate clean with Drake and fall into his convenient (cold and largely calculating) arms. Even if it wasn't real, I was happy enough while it lasted. And I would have my patched-up career to keep me warm at night when he'd inevitably be off changing his name to the Artist Formerly Known as Drake Colter or pretending to write his own songs or working out. Whatever the fuck Drake does when he's busy avoiding meaningful relationships.

Except even the perceived happiness I found with Drake— the touring and screaming fans and gold records and award shows—stopped being enough the first time I sat on Craig's balcony with a bottle of wine and a couple of guitars between us.

I sigh, picking up my phone and putting it to my ear, halfway listening to Jen's voice mail and confirming her glee at having "the offer of a lifetime." I go to delete when I notice another notification—a series of texts—and I quickly tap the icon and HUCK is lit up with messages.

> HUCK: Sorry I didn't get back to you last night. I was in the studio late.

I chew my lip. I suppose he might not have listened until this morning. That's reasonable. He *is* working, after all.

> HUCK: I listened right away but was dog-tired and needed to let it marinate. It's different from what I've heard from you before, but I think you know that.

Hell, is he critiquing this? Is he really that dense? I huff, swallowing a frustrated growl, and continue reading.

> HUCK: Come to my place tonight? After eight?

I freeze, my phone clutched in my hand. Okay. That's . . . good. He's not so disgusted that he's avoiding me. He's not asking to see me in a neutral location like the studio. Holy fuck, the overthinking is going to murder me.

> LORELAI: You provide the wine; I'll bring the takeout.

12

CRAIG

SHOOT ME STRAIGHT

It's not even lunch and I'm ready to call it. I slept for shit last night, getting tangled up in my sheets for hours before caving finally and throwing myself on the couch and cracking open a YA novel about teenage country music stars that my niece, Jenna, lent me, reading until the sun came up. I crawled into the studio before seven, guzzling so much caffeine, it feels like I've swallowed a pair of Lorelai's running shoes and they're completing a 5K in my gut.

Baker's Dozen were back again bright and early (for them, anyway) to re-record a track they felt wasn't *vibing* well with the rest of the album. Thankfully, they didn't require my expertise as much as my equipment and Arlo was able to get it laid down, because I've been consumed with fielding legal calls from fucking Colter all fucking day.

Note to self: If some jackhole narcissist invites you to be his writing partner and tour with his self-named band, *run in the opposite direction* to avoid *years* of aggravation.

This could all be solved if Drake had (a) not used the songs I wrote years ago on his latest album or (b) just credited me as coauthor and paid me my due.

It's a hundred percent my own fault I'm still in this mess years after the fact. I didn't fight him on "Jonesin'" like I should have. I wanted a clean break and a clear conscience after hooking up with his ex on the down-low, then quitting his band on such short notice and starting my own indie label. So when I heard "Jonesin'" on the radio a year after I'd walked, I didn't push for credit. Not hard, anyway. I figured, I'd give him one album and that would be that. My business had been taking off and I didn't need to be greedy, and honestly, I didn't want the hassle.

Though I wish it hadn't been that song. That one was personal. But how was I supposed to call him up and be like, "Hey, man, I wrote that song about your ex, whom I slept with that one time after you broke up and might've fallen a little bit more in love with her that night, and so it would be awesome if you'd fucking stop using it already."

Regardless, that was two albums ago, and Colter is still using my lyrics, uncredited. And this time there's been talk about one of them being a contender for Song of the Year.

Song of the Year would be a hell of a résumé boost to a guy seeking validation with his own indie record label in a town chock-full of record labels and songwriters.

DRAKE: Just sign the goddamn release, man. It's not like it matters to you. You're solid with your other songs.
DRAKE: This could be a game changer for me. After you left, it's the least you can do.

There it is. The guilt treatment. As if my leaving was crushing for him and his career.

DRAKE: Is this about "Jonesin'"?
DRAKE: We wrote that together. It's legit.

That's debatable, but still.

CRAIG: And yet only one of us got paid for it.
CRAIG: I'm getting real tired of hearing my songs on the radio and not getting paid for them, Drake. All you have to do is credit me and we're good.

But we both know he won't do that. I doubt it's about the money. He just knows if he changes the songwriting credit now, it could mess with his chances for Song of the Year, and if he doesn't change it, I have every right to contest it.

Would I? I honestly don't know. I should, though.

I *should*.

He's taking advantage and I'm letting him, based off one morally iffy night with his ex years ago. How long am I gonna let this go on? Until he gets his CMA? His Grammy? His fucking Lifetime Achievement Award? When exactly does the punishment fit the proverbial non-crime?

Drake doesn't respond the rest of the day, not that I expect any different. He prefers to let his lawyers do the talking. Two emails' and three voice mails' worth. The thing is, we wouldn't even be having this conversation had we worked on these songs in the studio or under contract. He would have had the might of the record label behind him if that had been the case. But these songs were written and workshopped on our own time, in my apartment. I have entire notebooks of them. Drake's a pretty average lyricist, if I'm being honest. He's great at a generic summertime banger, and his overall look and vocals lend themselves to a superstar, but he's meant to be *written for.* That's what made us a great team. I wrote the songs and he made it look good. Then I left, and he kept using my work instead of finding himself a new lyricist. It's hard to say no to Drake and he knows it. He banks on it. Always has. First with Lorelai and then with me.

Which is why when I wake up this morning and see his douchey thirst trap of a shirtless selfie with the caption *Netflix and "Jonesin'"* on my Instagram feed, I don't immediately assume he's talking about Lorelai.

Or at least he's not talking *with* Lorelai. He's absolutely talking about her. But there's nothing going on between them. I would know if there was.

Pretty sure.

Colter likes to pass out mindfucks like he's tossing candy from a parade float and I'm about over it.

I groan, exhaustion heavy and pressing me into my chair. I drop my phone to my desk, remove my glasses, and rub the heels of my palms into my eyes until colorful fireworks burst behind my lids and the tension ache in my neck weakens to a dull throb.

This is the exact shit I didn't ask for when I opened my own record label. I just want to make music.

My phone buzzes with yet another text, and for a minute, I ignore it, still forcing pressure into my eye sockets to keep the threatening migraine at bay. Some days are just like this.

The constant assault of contact followed by an entire week when I don't even open my office door.

Not today, though. I've barely left my desk all morning. Curiosity wins out eventually, and I pick up my phone, holding it a little closer to my face to read the small print.

LORELAI: You provide the wine; I'll bring the takeout.

I release a slow whistle under my breath. Lorelai. I invited her to my place tonight. For the hundredth time, so it's nothing new, except that song.

Holy fuck, that song.

And now we come to the reason for my tossing and turning all night for the second straight night in a row. If I'm honest, my friendship with Lorelai Jones has been the cause of an increasing number of sleepless nights over the last decade. It's also the impetus for my poetry account.

I needed an outlet for the feelings she's stirred up inside of me. After that song, however . . . there aren't enough poems in the world.

Arlo knocks and pokes his head around the corner of the doorjamb. Today he's wearing a striped vintage bowler shirt and pointed leather shoes that complement his burnt orange fedora perfectly. I crack my neck and replace my glasses to see him better. "Baker's are all wrapped. Josh offered to pick up some lunch and bring it in. Want anything from Shelia's?"

At the barest suggestion, my stomach rumbles loudly, echoing in the silence of my office.

Arlo grins and pulls out his phone. "Toasted artichoke sandwich with tots it is."

I make a face, Colter's douchey shirtless selfie in the forefront of my mind. "I should probably eat a salad or something green instead of the tots."

My friend blinks. "You are literally eating a veggie sandwich."

What am I even doing? It's not like I've ever been fit or muscular in my entire life. Not gonna change today if I skip out on the tater tots. Besides, they're fried in truffle oil. It would be a sin to turn that down. "You're right. Close enough. Give Josh my thanks."

"You can tell him yourself. He'll be here in fifteen. So." Arlo folds his arms across his chest after pocketing his phone. "You're looking like someone scratched your collector's copy of *At Folsom Prison* and set it on fire."

"Shows what you know. I have *two* copies, and one is locked in a fireproof safe along with an original *American Recordings*."

Arlo remains unfazed. I sigh. "Colter wants me to sign over my rights, uncontested."

"The fuck he does."

My face twists in a grimace. "Yeah. That. His new tactic appears to be 'wear him down,' and it's nearly working because I don't want to fucking think about him and his thirst traps anymore." I consider a second. "But this is what kept me up all night."

I turn to my phone and tap around for the link Lorelai sent me. While I work, Arlo moves in, and forgoing the chairs, he circles around and perches against my desk, facing me. I turn up the Bluetooth speakers next to my monitor in time to hear the opening chords of Lorelai's song.

Just like the first, second, third, *and* fourth times, I have an immediate and visceral reaction to her voice. There's a breathless quality to it I know I haven't ever heard from her before. At least not in years and definitely not stone-cold sober. It's sexy and sensual and teeming with . . . something *I won't actually say out loud.*

Something that brings to mind shifting silhouettes and soft, pliable skin. Moonlight crisscrossing and bleeding through drawn blinds. Swallowed whispers. Feverish wanting.

I come back to myself, double-checking my lap is securely hidden under my desk and clearing my throat. All of that might be in my head. The power of suggestion, maybe. Likely that, even. Which is why I want Arlo to hear. I need to know if I'm projecting before I see her.

Arlo's expression is hard to read. "Where's the rest?"

"That's all there is."

"She sent a half-finished song?"

"Yeah. And she texted it, rather than emailing like usual."

Arlo taps to play the song again, possibly because he likes to torture me.

I try not to listen so close this time—to shore up my defenses against the siren's call of her voice—but it's inevitable.

So you want me to cannonball into the icy depths of the Pacific and swim until my internal organs flatten and my eyeballs explode? Sure. Just let me take off my shoes first. Can you send them to my nephew along with my spare Xbox controller?

This time, when the last of the clip finishes, Arlo appears different. Smug, even.

"Tell me."

ERIN HAHN

He shakes his head, playing at being demure. "I mean, I'm no expert in women."

"You're the closest I have."

Arlo smirks, fedora snugly in place on top of his curls. "Which is to your detriment *for sure*. Nevertheless," he says. "I would venture to say she's making a move."

"A move?"

"Yes, Craig," he drawls slow as honey from the comb. "A move. She's trying to get your attention."

"For what?" My friend stares at me. "Not for *that*," I insist, even as my heartbeat kicks into a trot. "This is Lorelai we're talking about. She was engaged to my bandmate." I've never told him about the one night years ago. It's never seemed worth mentioning. Ancient history and basically a fluke.

He blows a raspberry right as there's a knock at the door. It's Dr. Josh with our lunches. Arlo jumps up from my desk, skipping over to his husband and kissing him on the cheek. "Come on in. We're gonna eat with Craig. He needs our homosexual input on his hetero life choices."

To his credit, Josh doesn't so much as bat an eye. He settles down in one of my office chairs, scoots close to the desk to use it to eat off of, and unwraps his sandwich.

"Play the song for him."

I peel open my sandwich and frown at it. "*Pfft*, I've heard it enough today. Besides, it feels like an invasion of privacy." I shrug at Josh. "Sorry."

Arlo hums in the back of his throat. "Interesting that you think it would be an invasion of privacy. It's a song. You're a songwriter and she's a renowned country artist. This is the business we're in, isn't it?"

I swallow my bite before speaking. "I guess, but it's half-finished."

Arlo's sandwich remains untouched in front of him. He leans forward, elbows on his knees. "Exactly. That she sent through text, rather than email, like usual."

"Right. We said this all already."

"Recapping for Dr. Handsome over here."

"Oh. Right."

"Basically," he explains to Josh while finally tearing open his sandwich, "Lorelai sent our Craig a sexy nibble of a song via text, unprompted. And he doesn't know what to make of it."

"How sexy?"

I feel my face burn beneath the barely day-old stubble and Arlo's eyes glitter with triumph. Josh nods sagely. "Well, if the guy moonlighting as a famous erotic poet on Instagram is blushing . . ."

So Arlo and Josh know about my poetry account. Don't ask. Just know it involved the one time I tried to record a spoken word version in the studio after-hours and a horny Arlo thought to sneak Josh in for a little late-night lovin'.

"It's not like that. Exactly. But yes, it's pretty sensual. Of course"—I massage the back of my neck, the tension ache returning in full force—"I think everything Lorelai does is sensual. Clear bias in this vicinity." I wave a hand up and down myself. "Which is why I asked Arlo to listen."

"Naturally. So what did you say to Lorelai when you got the . . ."—Josh casts an amused glance at Arlo—"sexy nibble of a song?" His husband winks over his grilled chicken Caesar wrap.

"Nothing. At first," I rush to clarify. "I was super busy in the studio yesterday. I listened for the first time between clients and couldn't actually believe what I was hearing, so I waited until things quieted down and . . ."—I sigh, beyond humiliation at this point—"listened a thousand more times before bed."

"Where you shot your man-custard all over your duvet like a fifteen-year-old, presumably."

My face is the surface of the sun. "Jesus, Arlo," I mumble. "I texted her back this morning, apologizing for taking so long to respond. I explained how busy I'd been and asked her to come over tonight."

"She's coming over?"

"Yeah." I gesture at my phone, resting on the desk between all of us. "She just confirmed."

Arlo falls back in his chair and lifts his wrap to the heavens. "Praise the Lord."

"Arlo, Lorelai comes over all the time. She literally lives at the same address. We share a balcony."

"Yes, but not *after sexting*. This is definitive progress."

"It wasn't a sext!"

Arlo looks to Josh. "Survey says?"

Josh gives me an apologetic look, nudging his frames up the bridge of his nose. "It's a sexy text, so calling it a sext isn't that far off the mark. I'd say for two people who are so into the written word, as you two clearly are, this is legitimate."

I take in his reasoning and roll it around my brain as we finish our lunches. It's not that I don't think they know what they're talking about, but the risk is high. Higher than I'm certain I want to pay. If we're reading this wrong and Lorelai *isn't* making a move, I could blow years of friendship. She doesn't need another guy she trusts sniffing around her, hoping for sex. Not that that's what I'm about. Not totally, anyway, but the fact remains, she's a beautiful, fiery, out-of-this-world talented woman and I'm . . . the guy who's been hiding his hard-on behind his sound booth for the last twelve months.

The conversation changes to more mundane things, and eventually Josh packs up his things to return to work. Arlo collects the trash and walks his husband out while I tidy up my desk and check my calendar for the afternoon. I have one more client today, and they're going to require my full attention. It's time to do what I do best and put the rest out of my brain.

13

CRAIG

COME OVER

I get held up with a late phone call with a guitarist I'm hoping
to arrange for Lorelai's record (and who's currently residing
three time zones away), so I'm hustling up the sidewalk just
as she's parking her car on the street in front of our place.

Lorelai closes the car door with her hip, balancing a takeout bag in each hand. I rush to offer my assistance but stop
short when she circles the car and heads up the walk toward
me. She looks like—

Well, she looks like—

Like—

Fuck. My brain short-circuits as I hold open the front
door and she ascends the stairs to my place ahead of me.
Lorelai's wearing a dress. Or a long shirt. Honestly, the best
I can come up with is a shirtdress. With rolled sleeves and a
belted waist and a skirt that reveals her miles of suntanned
legs. *Miles* of them. Her skirt isn't short and I'm not *trying*
to look up it, but the way it flips off the back of her legs

keeps flashing little glimpses of heaven at my eye level and my mouth waters and . . . *stop*.

I have to stop.

I slow my climb, letting her get far enough ahead of me to where I'm no longer within kissing distance of the backs of her toned thighs. Distance gives me the chance to take in the rest of her. She's in leather sandals and her dark hair is pulled up off her neck in a high knot, and the overall effect makes her look stretched out and elegant and sophisticated and—

I can't stop
Imagining your lips
Kissing every inch of me

—the keys?

"Did you forget your keys?" she asks me. She's standing on the landing, hip cocked, and I can't tell for sure, but her grin might be *knowing*. As if she can read the scrambled thoughts straight from my brain and knows the exact effect the words she sang, coupled with her miles of legs and that flippy skirt, are having on me.

Right. I need to unlock the door.

"Uh. No. Sorry. Long day." I reach into my pocket to retrieve my key ring and quickly unlock the front door before taking the bags from her hands and gesturing for her to enter first. Lorelai flips on the light and my cat, Waylon, rounds the corner and dashes between her legs, nuzzling her ankles, that bastard. I drop the food on the counter as Lorelai is kicking off her sandals and scooping Waylon into her arms.

My cat hates everyone, including me, but for some reason loves Lorelai. Lore says it's because "a catty bitch knows another catty bitch," but I think it's because they're both secretly softies.

Or maybe *I'm* the softy.

Never mind, I'm definitely the softy.

With the exception of my cock, that is.

Moving on.

After an appropriate amount of baby talk and cuddling, Lorelai lets Waylon go to do whatever it is asshole cats do when no one's looking and hops up on a stool at the island, sipping from the glass of Pinot I've poured her.

She swirls it a little and I can feel her eyes on me as I divide dinner between two plates to take on the balcony.

"Go ahead and ask," I say mildly, taking too much care to scrape the bottom of an already empty container of brown rice.

"You listened to my song?"

I roll my eyes lightly, not reminding her that we already established I listened last night and again this morning. "Of course I did."

She's quiet a beat and I put down the Chinese takeout container to give her my full attention. Lorelai's dark eyes are bright in her pale face, and she's worrying her bottom lip between her teeth. This is the Lorelai no one sees. The one I've had the privilege to know almost from the start.

The one I've loved nearly as long, but we don't need to rehash that shit again.

I lean forward, moving before I've even made the choice

to do so, and with my thumb, gently tug her chin, freeing her lip. "I have a question but I'm not sure how to ask it."

She nods, reaching for her glass, but only playing with the stem, her eyes intent on mine.

"This is seriously the most humiliating thing I've ever asked, and depending on your answer, we might have to crack open a bottle of absinthe so we can erase it from our memories." Old Huck, the one from all those years ago, had a lot more swagger when it came to women. He could wash down awkward conversations with a beer and laugh off rejection with an overabundance of youthful, fame-adjacent bravado.

Craig of today pre-games with ibuprofen and wakes up every morning feeling the press of time in his bones. He couldn't spell *swag* with a dictionary. And he really needs not to ruin things with his friend. She's too important.

The corner of Lorelai's mouth quirks ever so slightly, as if she can read my hesitation, and somehow that familiar movement strengthens my resolve.

Because I know I'm important to her, too.

"Was that a real song or . . ."

"Or . . . ?" she prompts, her eyes dancing over the rim as she takes a healthy sip of Pinot.

Christ.

This one time when I was in junior high, my sister took me to a water park in Georgia and forgot sunscreen. I had second-degree burns all over my body. I peeled like a fucking rattlesnake for weeks after.

But that was nothing compared to my face right now. I swallow and take a deep breath. "Or was it just for me?"

Lorelai's cheeks puff as she exhales before licking the wine off her lips. "Maren and Shelby told me to pretend to accidentally sext you, but of course that's asinine, so I decided to write a song that was the equivalent of a sext."

My air rushes out of my lungs and I slump against the top of the counter, trying to stave off the tunnel vision. "Oh god, Arlo was right. He's never gonna let me live this down."

"You told Arlo?"

I speak in the direction of the oiled wood block underneath my sweaty palms. "I thought it might be a real song."

"Bullshit!" she cries out, slapping the island and laughing, startling me into looking at her. "You know me better than that."

And suddenly I know I do. I've always understood Lorelai Jones. I get her quirks and love her instincts. Even if I didn't have secret deep-seated feelings for her, she's still the one person I like the most.

And right now, I feel like I am knowing things—potentially scary things—about Lorelai that maybe she doesn't even know about herself, and what the ever-living *shit* am I supposed to do about that?

Just roll with it, I guess? That's what Old Huck would do. Find an equilibrium. Or at least a baseline we can both live with.

"Which is *why*," I say even louder, cracking a smile, "I assumed it was a song. Because you couldn't possibly mean to send me something like that. Not now, anyway. Years ago, maybe . . ."

She grabs up her wine and snorts into the glass before swallowing another gulp, and I'm mesmerized watching her long throat work. "Yeah," she hedges softly. "Well. Not all of us have"—she makes air quotes with her guitar-callused fingers—"*anonymous poetry accounts*. Some of us have to get creative when expressing our . . . desires."

At the last word, my heart seizes in my chest and I can feel the blood leaching from underneath my skin, every last drop on a raging course south. My voice comes out hoarse when I say, "Jesus fuck."

She raises a fine brow and puts down her glass. Having pity on me, she nudges mine toward me. "Take a big sip. The Pinot is delicious and especially fortifying tonight."

I reach for it. "I think I'd rather have the absinthe."

"Get ahold of yourself, Huck. This isn't the time for being shy. You regularly write about oral sex on a public forum."

I choke on my sip and Lorelai flushes prettily, her lips pursed. "Are you gonna deny it?"

I chug the entire glass, which in turn burns my entire esophagus, but desperate times and all. "How long have you known?"

"That you have an anonymous erotic poetry account on Instagram or that you're writing about me?"

I clear my throat and retrieve the bottle, refilling both our glasses. "Both," I rasp.

"I've known about the account for months. I've followed it for longer, but I didn't know it was you until I accidentally saw your phone notifications that one time we were ordering from Sweet Tomato. As far as knowing you were writing about me . . . I didn't. Until now, anyway. I guessed. Or hoped rather, after the sunflower poem."

I wrote the night after she made me pull over at a field of

sunflowers and we wandered in between the rows. She was tipsy and I was feeling especially poetic.

So she knows. She . . . *knows*.

"And then the champagne poems from the other night . . . after I posted from the wedding."

I spread my hands on the countertop, dropping my head and taking a deep breath.

"Still need the absinthe?" she asks quietly, and I recognize the offer for what it is. A chance to pretend this conversation never happened.

I shake my head, still reeling, but not a complete idiot. I know what she's asking for. I can recognize the come-on for what it is. Of course she wants Old Huck. The good-time guy. The no-strings-attached fuck.

That's what sexts are for, after all. Even ones set to music and sung in the loveliest voice. Not once did she mention love or feelings or taking our relationship to the next level. Which, okay, neither have I. My poetry has been purely physical. About her, but not. About us, but not.

Because the one thing Old Huck and New Craig have in common is an ironclad sense of self-preservation.

Find an acceptable baseline, Boseman.

I decide to be honest. This is new territory for me. "I don't know where to go from here, though."

Lorelai drops down from her chair and pads on bare feet around the island to stand in front of me. Just as close as she was the other night on the corner when we nearly . . .

She raises her eyes to mine and her mouth follows. Her lips a millimeter away from my own, her wine-soaked breath making my mouth water. She trails her fingers along the back of my hand, still on the countertop, grounding me; up my tense forearm, over my shoulder, and around my neck.

"You could start by kissing me."

Without conscious thought, I'm reaching for her hips, my fingers eager, dragging her close. I swallow hard. "Okay." My voice comes out sounding like it's been dragged across sandpaper.

"Thank god."

The words have barely passed her lips before I let it all go, diving down to capture her mouth, my fingers carding in her hair, and tilting her face so I can consume her. Her lips fall open with a surprised gasp and I finally get my first taste of her.

Hell. She's better than I remembered.

I taste over and over, my greedy tongue tangling with hers, hers curling against mine. A hungry moan escapes the back of her throat and I swallow it, with a quiet growl. I drop one hand to the small of her back, pressing her against me, and she hooks one of those mile-long legs around my hip, bucking slowly, tantalizingly, and I don't think I've ever been so hard in my life. I have handfuls of her shirt, dress, *whatever*, in my fists, and her soft panting in my ears. She pulls back to place hot wet open-mouthed kisses from my ear to my collarbone, and I can already tell it's been too long for me and I don't have an ice cube's chance in hell of lasting tonight.

After waiting for this woman for so long, I refuse to let that happen. I quickly spin us around and press her back

against the island, tugging her mouth to mine and stroking a long, teasing finger back and forth against her center
before taking a step back with a smirk, my dick fighting a
losing battle against my zipper. Lorelai whimpers softly in
protest at the loss of contact, her dark eyes flashing open
before I drop to my knees and slip a hand up her dress.

14
....

LORELAI

ACTING UP

He drops to his knees in front of me and I nearly pass out.

It's happening. Thank fuck, it's finally, *finally* happening.

I thought I was ready, but then he brushes ever so softly against my center with the knuckle of his thumb, gripping my trembling thigh between his palms and bowing his head like he's giving a benediction.

I thought I was ready, but then he slips my damp underwear down my legs, inch by inch, covering the blazing trail left behind with his cool, wine-rich mouth.

I thought I was ready, but then he glances up at me, his blue eyes dark with lust, and in a low rumble tells me to keep my hands on the counter.

I thought I was ready, but then he lifts my leg, nibbling playfully at the inside of my knee before draping it over his shoulder, offering me up before him.

I thought I was ready, but then he spreads me apart with his talented fingers before deliberately pressing his hot tongue against me, tender and coaxing, savoring me into near incoherence.

I thought I was ready, but then his tongue curls and circles, relentless and almost rude in its insistence to make me come. He's devouring me, his talented fingers playing all the right chords until I drop over the edge, wildly bucking against his mouth. Until I cry out his name, clenching again and again, and sing my own incoherent benediction to the rafters. Until I find my feet, stunned, sated, and irrevocably changed.

Until I let go of the counter and run my fingers through his hair, collapsing to my own knees there on the kitchen floor in front of him, still trembling with the aftershocks of what I've just experienced.

What he's done to me.

I wrap myself around him and he holds me close as a second skin. We share breaths. We share heartbeats.

I come back to my senses when I realize I can feel him hard as steel beneath me and pull away, reaching for his belt buckle, eager to return the favor, but he stops me, his hand covering mine.

"You don't have to . . ."

"But I want to."

He's completely still. So quiet that I can literally feel him withdrawing and the space between us grows suffocatingly thick with something unrecognizable. Craig gets to his feet and offers his hands to help me to mine. He's careful and attentive and something is very, very wrong because I'm still tingling from my orgasm and his face is a mask of politeness.

"Why don't you . . ."

He shakes his head. "We've done enough tonight."

My face burns white hot. "But I don't understand. Is something wrong? Did I do something wr—"

"No!" he assures me, but his expression is still weird. Like him, but also not at all. "No," he repeats, quieter. "Nothing is wrong. I just . . . you know. That was a lot. For one night. And all those things we talked about before . . . and just." He swallows, his Adam's apple bobbing and his bare cheeks flushed. "Nothing is wrong. I loved doing that for you. I . . ." He smiles, finally, and it looks more real this time. "I've wanted to do that forever. It's late . . ."—he gestures to the food left scattered and cold on the counter—"and we didn't even eat dinner."

I swallow. Unsure of what is happening still. The words coming out of his mouth don't seem to match up with the way this is feeling.

He starts to pour the food back into the containers. "I have some work to do tonight. I forgot, but Arlo was going to email me some tracks from today that I need to work on before a client early tomorrow." He doesn't meet my eyes. Just offers me the bag of food.

"Okay," I agree weakly, accepting the bag.

He walks to the door ahead of me and opens it while I stop to slip on my sandals. When I reach him, he's got his hands stuffed in his pockets and he looks . . . I don't even know. I reach for him, pressing a soft kiss to his cheek. He still smells like me and I almost wince from the memory so recent. So different from this stilted awkwardness.

"We're okay?" I check because I can't help myself.

He reaches for my face, but at the last second, tucks a

wild strand of my hair behind my ear and lets his hand fall to his side. "We're okay," he insists. "Text me when you get home," he teases and it's so familiar I nearly sob. "So I know you made it safe."

I don't respond. I can't, or he'll know I'm on the verge of crying. Instead, I walk out his door and down the stairs, wondering what the fuck just happened.

. . .

(SIX YEARS AGO)

Before I even open my eyes, I know I'm not in my own bed. My cold, empty bed in my barely furnished apartment that still smells like fresh paint and lemony furniture polish from my weekly cleaning service. No. This is different. This is better.

Because this is Huck's bed in Huck's apartment. It's neat as a pin and warmly decorated because his big sister lives close enough to care. It smells like clean laundry and brewing coffee and maybe also like the things we did last night.

I should be freaking out. I'm aware enough to know that, though I haven't bothered to open my eyes. I'm no longer engaged to be married. My tour was canceled. And I had sex with my best friend. Drake's partner. Huck.

Twice.

Without conscious thought, my body stretches languidly all the way down to my toes, and I feel tender in places I haven't felt tender in a while. The good kind of tender. A tiny smile curls in the corner of my lips before a soft groan next to me startles sense into me.

Right. Freaking out. My heart skips in my chest with a delayed pang. Of course this was a terrible fucking idea. What was I think-ing leading him back here? I was engaged to be married less than twenty-four hours ago. He was in New Orleans less than twenty-four hours ago.

My thoughts snag. He was in New Orleans with Drake yester-day. I don't know what time it was when he found me at Georgie's last night, but he had to have hopped a flight.

Huck left Drake and flew to me.

Eyes still closed, I swallow hard against the wave of emotion squeezing my chest.

"Whoa, hey. Lorelai? Oh god. Hold on. Let me . . ."

I open my eyes and see Huck hopping on one foot, trying to shove his leg into a pair of discarded jeans. "No, don't look!" he says, alarmed, and I close my eyes again, confused. "Don't freak out. It's okay. Fuck, I knew this was a bad idea. I'll get some clothes on and run out and you can just, um. Fuck." I hear the sound of his zipper and some more muffled cussing, presumably as he pulls on a shirt. I sneak a look, and his expression is pained.

"I'm gonna go."

"Huck." I start to get up, the sheet pooling around my bare waist, and this time he crushes his eyes closed, slapping a hand over them for good measure. I bite back an exasperated laugh. "Okay, you don't have to cover your eyes. You literally had your tongue inside—"

He holds one hand out, halting me from saying anything else, his other still covering his eyes.

"Don't. Don't say anything else. That was last night. In the dark. After a few beers and sexy dancing and my hips—fuck. I rolled my hips at you, didn't I?"

"Well, sure, but I didn't mind."

He drops his other hand, but he's still looking at the ceiling. "Of course you didn't mind. They're irresistible. It's my sexy superpower. Which is why I swore to never use them on you. It's, like, a rule."

"A rule?" This time I don't stop the smile, even if he can't see it.

"A code," he insists. "That says you don't use any sexy super-powers on your bandmate's fiancée."

"Ex-fiancée."

He huffs. "That fucker. He's so stupid."

"Look at me, Huck."

He shakes his head. "I can't. I need to go. You can stick around as long as you want. Move in if you want. Just let me know and I'll find another place to go."

I finish pulling on a random shirt I've dug out of the covers and realize it's his from the night before. "Huck," I repeat, scrambling across the bed and parking myself in front of him. I tug gently on his chin, so he's forced to look at me. "I'll go. This is your place. I need to figure some things out anyway."

"I'm not trying to kick you out," he says in a quiet tone. "This isn't like that."

"I know. I don't think that. I think you're the guy who dropped everything, hopped on a flight, and tracked me down to get drunk at a dive bar. You're also the guy who gave me the first orgasms"—I emphasize the s and his eyes flare with heat—"I've had in a re-ally, really long time. Well, ones I didn't give myself, anyway. So thank you."

"Be that as it may," he says in a slow drawl, "I don't think we should have done that. It crossed a line that can't be put back up."

I lift a shoulder, too exhausted and feeling the weight of all the things I've been through in the last few days. "Consider it a goodbye gift, then. From me to you and you to me."

His hands curl around the tops of my arms and his thumbs trace back and forth. "You're really leaving?"

"I have to. I'm not welcome in this town right now, and sticking around isn't doing anyone any favors. I don't have the first clue what I'm gonna do, but that's okay. I'll miss you, though."

He grimaces and I press my lips together. The look on his face is so self-deprecating and familiar.

"I still think it was a mistake. For the record. Sex always complicates things, and—"

I press my finger to his lips, cutting him off. "No one ever has to know outside of me and you, and anyway, we may never see each other again. So no harm, no foul. I'm glad I got to experience your superpower at least one time."

I drop my finger and he exhales long and slow.

"Fine. There's coffee downstairs. I'm gonna run out and grab something for breakfast. Want a doughnut?"

"Sure," I say lightly, but we both know I won't be here when he gets back. This is another gift he's giving me. A chance to escape. I fucking hate goodbyes.

"Great." He leans forward impulsively and presses a warm kiss to my forehead for a single beat and then turns around, grabbing his keys and wallet and shoving them in his pockets. "The place on the corner is closed, so I'll be a bit. Take your time."

"See you," I say, drinking in his tall, comforting form one last time. He raises a hand in farewell, not bothering to look back, and then he's gone and the door closes behind him.

I don't waste much time slipping on my pants and shirt from

last night, refolding Huck's T-shirt and placing it on the bed. I consider keeping it, but I don't. I don't want any reminders. Not that I could possibly forget, but I'm making a clean break. From everyone and everything.

And when he comes back, I'm long gone.

15

LORELAI

BABE

The following day, I'm sitting perched on a rocky shelf in one of my favorite high places outside of Nashville, letting the September sun warm my skin and clear my head. This is as good a place as any to wander amidst the thriving field of my many, many tactical missteps. Steamy excerpts from the night before intersperse with the painful memories of a night all those years ago. A clear pattern emerges, and I don't love what it's saying.

Because it appears my gut is unreliable.

Time and again, it nudges me into action, and time and again that action results in a fucking mess.

Like when I loftily decided I was going to make concert-goers stop and think. Reset their minds. Engage with some empathy. Instead, I flushed not only my career but the careers of my bandmates and my manager down the proverbial drain. I thought it would be a flash in the pan. Maybe a headline or two, but certainly everyone would forget about it and move on to the next bit of news . . .

Except no one forgot. Not country music radio, who refused to play any of our recordings, including the old, politically mundane ones. Not Nashville, where the glass entrance to my condo building was spray-painted with the words *Yankee Bitch* and restaurants refused to seat me. Not my bandmates, who had to completely fall off the radar and restart their careers from scratch. Not Jen, who was hired out by the label to someone just getting started.

Not my fiancé, who took three days to call me back (*after* publicly canceling our wedding) just to tell me he thought it was time for a break. "Not because of the Neil Young thing," he insisted. "But because we've been drifting apart, and I need to focus on my art right now."

Everything, gone. One song to ruin it all. Fucking Neil Young.

Ugh. I don't mean that. I love Neil Young. And I sang what I sang, and to this day, I stand by it. I just wish taking a stand hadn't cost me everything I had. Utter cancellation.

And last night? I mean. What the actual fuck happened last night? I squirm on the giant boulder I've claimed, darting glances around to double-check that I'm still alone up here, and release a humiliated groan even as my thighs clench against the tiny and persistent residual zings of a phantom orgasm.

How dare he be just as miraculous at oral sex as I'd remembered.

How dare he . . . what? Give me one hell of an orgasm and refuse to allow me to pay back the favor? The audacity of the man to package up leftovers?

Like, on paper, it was a good night. He didn't technically "wham, bam, thank you, ma'am" me and shove me out the door to call my own Uber. So why does it *seem* like that's what happened?

Why do I have this sick feeling in the pit of my stomach like it was all wrong? I confessed feelings, he confessed feelings, and then we made out, which led to kitchen-counter cunnilingus. The stuff of literal fantasies.

But my fantasies never ended with me falling asleep alone, in a disgusting puddle of snot and tears. As hot as that was, and it really, *really* was, I would trade it back a hundred-fold if I could just have a little platonic cuddling followed by the security of knowing my friend was still my friend and nothing had changed.

I know. I hardly expected it myself.

Eventually I force myself off the boulder and hike back down the short trail to the parking lot just as the first cars filled with morning sightseers are pulling in. I go home, make coffee, and eat a breakfast of soy-sauce-free Chinese leftovers, cold and straight from the container.

By the time my phone rings with a FaceTime notification from Maren and Shelby, I'm wrung out and ready for bed. It's all of 11:30 A.M.

"Hey," I answer.

"Oh shit, you saw already?" Maren says. She's clearly in her office, from the amount of planed timber and the "Poisonous Plants of Northern Michigan" graphic over her shoulder.

"Hold on!" There's the generic racket of construction happening over Shelby's speakers, and I watch her gingerly step out onto the green porch of some project or another, slamming the door shut behind her.

"What did I see already?" I ask dully.

"Oh shit, she *didn't* see." Shelby's eyes grow wide.

Maren's normally sunny face slips into an apologetic wince. "Drake's post on Instagram this morning about you two going on tour together. You're *not* going on tour together, right? You would have told us. I mean . . . not that there would be anything wrong with that." She immediately changes course and I cut her off.

"No, I'm not. At least I haven't decided yet but probably not."

"Just probably?" Shelby asks, squinting in the sun and jabbing on a pair of what look to be Cameron's sunglasses.

I release a breath and settle in against the back of my couch. "Almost definitely. It's just . . ." and all of a sudden, I can feel the tears sizzling in the back of my throat. Fucking a. I wave a hand in front of my face, trying to stave them off.

"Lorelai!" Maren gasps, alarmed, as if she's never seen me cry. Which, to be fair, she hasn't. Aside from the snot fest last night, I haven't full-out cried since my parents told me they were getting a divorce when I was a kid. Not even Drake dumping me after "Ohio"-gate made me this emotional, but these last few weeks have got me weeping like Shelby.

Which, ugh. Probably means something extra shitty.

"What happened?"

I take a deep breath. "Huck went down on me and it was perfect and then he got all weird and sent me home with leftovers." The last part is half whine, half sob, and all embarrassing.

There's a long, awkward silence before Shelby asks, "Did you say you hooked up with Craig?"

I nod.

Maren. "Is *leftovers* a euphemism?"

I shake my head.

Maren's expression is baffled. I hear you, sister. "But why are you crying? Was it bad?"

"It w-was . . ."—I hiccup—"so hot. I've never come so hard in my liiiiiiiife," I sob.

Through swollen eyes, I see Maren and Shelby exchange looks before Maren guesses, "So . . . you're crying because it was good?"

I take another cleansing breath, trying to pull myself together. Then take two more for good measure. Yoga breaths. I fucking hate yoga, but the breathing thing is objectively useful. "I'm crying because afterwards he got all weird about it and sent me home with the rest of dinner. Alone."

My best friends look pained, which is answer enough.

"I don't know what went wrong," I say. "We talked about our feelings . . ."

"You did? You told him how you feel?"

I think back. "Well, I sent him a sext . . . or a sexy song, anyway, like you said, and then I confronted him about the poetry account and we started making out and he just dropped to his knees right there in the kitchen."

Shelby whistles low. "I mean. We all knew he had it in him, but *damn*, girl."

Maren fans her face. "I'm not trying to visualize, but I'm not *not* trying, either. Sorry," she confesses wickedly. "It's been a while."

I wave her off. "Fair." I exhale with a huff. "So that's that. I don't know what happened and I need to talk to Huck, *clearly*. What's this about a tour with Drake? I told him no when he showed up, uninvited, again, yesterday morning."

"So you did see him yesterday morning?"

I deflate. "Not on purpose, why?"

"Well, you should probably sign on to your Instagram and get caught up. We'll wait."

I prop my phone on a cushion, leaving it lopsided and likely showing them an excellent view of my ceiling, and pull my laptop close. Instagram is still open in a tab, so it takes me no time to find what they are talking about.

"Ugh, Drake, *seriously?*"

On my screen is my ex, as per usual, shirtless and so obviously aware of his appeal it makes me roll my eyes. Twice. The caption reads something about Netflix and "Jonesin'." "Real original, you dick," I mutter as I scroll up to see that last night he posted another photo, this one pretending to be a candid shot of his songwriting, and the caption says, *Six years later, and it's still hard to keep from writing all my songs about you.* With the hashtag #togetheragain #summertour.

"Fuck's sake!" I shout, slamming my laptop shut with an unsatisfyingly soft click and grabbing for my phone. "What is he talking about? He didn't even write 'Jonesin''! Last I knew, he didn't write any of his songs, let alone about me! He's so full of shit. And the hashtags! What the ever-living fuck is he on about? 'together again'?!" I mock in a douchey voice. "Please."

"Well, that clears up that," Shelby says, amused.

"So . . . if we saw these, what are the odds that Craig saw these?"

My chest pulls tight and the blood drains from my face. "Oh god, you don't think he still follows him?"

"I wouldn't if I was him," says Shelby. "But Craig is still in the industry, and I bet for business reasons, it behooves him to be in the know or whatever."

"So wait, Drake didn't write 'Jonesin'?" Maren asks, frowning.

I shake my head, distracted. "Craig was the songwriter. Drake was the face. They shared credit, but it was pretty clear, even back then."

"But that song released after they parted ways."

"Yeah, I know." I shrug. "I don't really know why Craig didn't fight for credit, but I would guess he was trying to be nice and let Drake take that one. Which apparently Drake is going to run into the fucking ground. I'm *this close* to changing my last name from Jones to Springfield."

"Or Boseman," Maren offers slyly.

Despite the chasm that's burst between me and Craig in the last twelve hours, a tiny irrational grin tugs at my lips.

"Well," I say, getting back to business. "It looks like I've put off returning my agent's call for too long, so I better let you two go."

. . .

Predictably, Jennifer is reluctant to outright turn down Drake's offer and was definitely not going to follow through with my suggestion of "tell him to go to hell."

The best compromise we could come up with was to give her so-called apology tour a chance.

"I've got it all arranged. A couple of willing local radio stations, an interview on Square TV, and . . ."—there's a pause and some aggressive typing on her end of the line—"I'm sending you the contact information for a publicist who's known for being able to perform damage control. I can't reveal her client list," she whispers into the phone, "but trust me. She's worth every penny."

I try to keep my voice even, but my agent loves to play tone-deaf on the whole "Lorelai needs to make money to spend money" side of her job. "How many pennies are we talking, Jen?"

"Okay, I can reveal a little," she says in a rush, ignoring my question as expected. "Remember that cute little chickadee from that one children's show that had the sex tape?"

"No."

"Exactly. She won an Oscar last year and no one suspects a thing."

"Huh?"

"Call the publicist, Lorelai. I'll put off Colter's team for now, but this offer isn't without an expiration date. I'll make the arrangements for your first few radio interviews and see if we can't get the ball rolling on the apology tour."

My head is spinning a little by the time I hang up, but that's nothing new. It's not like I didn't know I'd have to eat some crow in the process of getting back on track. Might as well start now.

I open my text messages, rereading from last night.

LORELAI: Made it home safe.
HUCK: Good. 'Night, Lorelai.
LORELAI: 'Night.

With a sigh, I toss my phone down. Maybe I need to add Craig to my apology tour, but for the life of me, I can't figure out why?

16

CRAIG

DOIN' THIS

These days, when I'm struggling with something, I go to the studio. I pull out my guitar or sit at my piano and I write until I've nailed down exactly what it is that's holding me down.

Unfortunately, right now I know whatever is bothering me won't be fixed in a studio, and home is the last place I want to be when every creak, groan, and door slam reminds me how close I am to Lorelai.

Instead, I cleared my meetings for the next forty-eight hours, told Arlo to take a long weekend, and walked my Harley out of the garage behind the duplex like a fucking chicken-shit teenager sneaking out past curfew. I pack an overnight bag and some well-used camping gear and hit the open road for my favorite spot up in the Smokies. It's a tiny one-room cabin my uncle Huck built several decades ago to hide away from the world and focus on his art, which, honestly, ain't a bad idea. The journey's a four- or five-hour trek, depending on traffic, but I don't mind, and for once, I don't bother with music. I need a break from melodies, instead choosing to let the rumble of my bike and the relentless battery of wind fill my brain. It's not a perfect solution, but for a short while, with all my attention focused on the road, I stop seeing *her* laid out before me. The heady scent of hot asphalt and pine trees erases the taste of her, and over the roar of my engine, I'm unable to hear the echo of her moans.

Most of all, I don't see the memory of her stricken expression as I packed up leftovers like some fucking douche, opening the front door and telling her to text me when she made it back downstairs to her place, safe and sound.

Years. Fucking *years* I've spent dreaming of kissing her—of bringing her to the brink—and it was even better than I remembered. So of course I panic and fuck it all up with my overthinking.

I thought I could do casual. I'd convinced myself that whatever Lorelai could give me would be enough and I would be okay with that. People do it all the time. Hell, I've done it for years with other women.

Turns out, shocker, I can't do it with Lorelai Jones. Not this time. It's too much, too close to what I've always wanted, and now I've gone and hurt her.

Icarus, meet the fucking sun. She's sure pretty, ain't she?

By midmorning, it's already scorching. The pavement ripples, potent and pungent under a cloudless Tennessean sky. I turn my bike down the unmarked but familiar dirt road that leads to the cabin. Within minutes, I'm dropping the kickstand, hopping off on slightly unsteady feet, and removing my helmet, letting a gentle breeze off the lake lift and tug at the damp ends of my hair. I remove my leather road jacket, slinging it over the seat, while I unbelt my pack and the small cooler of food I brought.

The front door isn't locked. As far as I know, it's never been locked. My great-uncle used to leave the cabin stocked with canned goods and firewood over the winter months for strangers who found themselves without shelter, and I've kept up the tradition. It's rustic up here. No electricity, water via a well pump. Outhouse dug downwind from the back porch. It's not the kind of place someone with nefarious intent would bother taking advantage of, but it's just enough for someone in need.

Today and tomorrow, that someone is me.

I ignore the only locked building on the property, the pottery shed. Not even the promise of mindlessly creating with my hands, allowing my muscles to take over and shape something unseen, can tempt me. Maybe another time. This visit is about avoidance and feeling.

It shouldn't make sense, but it does. I'm here to write.

I shove open the heavy hand-hewn door with an almighty creak and leave it propped with a brick that's been used as a doorstop since before I was born. Light streams in, revealing an uncluttered dusty space. I make my way through the cabin, which doesn't take long, as it's only one great big room. I open windows and wipe off surfaces before sweeping it all out. Once everything is habitable once more, I pull out the bedding I brought from home and make the bed.

And that's it. Luxury, it is not.

My stomach grumbles and I eat a banana but know that's not gonna hold me over for long. I pull my phone out of my pocket and confirm there's no signal out here. Since there's no point in keeping it on, I power it off and tuck it away in my back pocket. Arlo knows where I am in case I don't return, but there's not much else I can do to be accessible.

Which is kind of the point. Being unreachable is the best part of this place. No phone calls from lawyers, no texts with sexy siren songs, and no fucking thirst trap social media posts using my fucking songs to further someone else's career.

Just me and the fish. I grab the old cane pole leaning up against the log wall in the corner of the room, along with a tiny rusty tackle box, and head out back toward the dock.

My older brother and I fixed up this dock a few years back, but it could already use another coat of finish and some basic maintenance. I roll some rocks back along the shoreline and find a few juicy night crawlers, jabbing them through with my hook and tossing it out into the water. After a while, I perch on a boulder we creatively named "the fishing rock" as kids and cast. In general, I don't eat meat, but lake perch fresh-caught from the fishing rock is my one exception. It takes most of the afternoon to catch my dinner, but that's all right. I end up cleaning and cooking my catch over an open fire out back, tossing the guts and bones out into the woods to make it real easy for the bears, before sitting by the fire until long after sun fades from the sky, sipping straight from a bottle and thinking.

About her.

I write some lines down. A few stanzas. Some are even good. Maybe the best I've ever written.

Stark honesty usually is.

And then I rip the pages out of my notebook and throw

them on the flames so I can watch them curl and turn to ash before floating on embers up to the sky.

Eventually I throw dirt on the fire and make my way to the dark cool of the empty cabin.

Grabbing the battery-powered lantern hanging by the door, I switch it on and light a fire in the small iron stove. It's cooler in the mountains, but mostly I just want the friendly firelight and soothing crackle to keep me company until I fall asleep.

But as I lie on top of the quilt, in the near perfect dark, the quiet feels deafening. Repressive. Smothering. I usually love this part—being left alone with only my thoughts to keep me company. I've always been an introverted extrovert and have long felt comfortable with my own company. I didn't think it would be possible for me to ever feel lonely.

So when I woke up this morning with the itch to escape the loudness and color of Nashville, I thought this would be the perfect reprieve.

Turns out I was wrong. I do have the capacity to feel lonely. Just without her.

The uncomfortable truth makes me squirm in the dark, scratching at my own skin and rustling against the bedding. I exhale loudly into the silence just to hear something.

I miss my friend. I need to find a way to make this work.

· · ·

Decision made, I drift off uneasily sometime in the middle of the night and wake blearily with the sunrise. I boil some water over the stove and make myself some coffee in an ancient French press I've tucked away in the single cabinet before eating an unsatisfying breakfast of a protein bar and another banana. I finish cleaning up after myself, double-check the stove is cooling, and close the door behind me.

I stop on the porch, sucking in the crisp clean air and absorbing what remaining refuge I can from the silence. Eventually, though, it's time, and I tug on my helmet and kick-start the engine to my bike, putting the Smokies behind me. I don't stop, except for gas, until I'm pulling down my street. Our street. I'm unshowered, smell like a firepit, and have barely slept, but I know in my gut this won't wait another minute.

She's sitting on our balcony, pretty feet perched on the railing and guitar in her lap, when I pull up, my bike revving. I pull off my helmet just as she stands, guitar forgotten, gawking at me.

"I thought you got rid of your bike!"

I shake my head, grimacing at the sweat matting down my hair. "What gave you that idea?"

She lifts a shoulder. "Guess I don't know. You always walk and I haven't seen it all year."

She's not wrong. I do prefer walking everywhere around town. Especially since my apartment and my work are only blocks apart.

But I'll never get rid of my Harley.

"Wanna go for a ride?"

She takes a moment to consider, and my chest constricts because I need to fix this thing between us. She doesn't need to go for a ride with me, obviously, but it'd help. At least that's what I've convinced myself in the last five hours coming down from the mountains. If she's not into it, I probably should head up to my apartment and shower before banging on her door to plead my case. Either way, I have to talk to her.

"You sure?" she checks, already collecting her things, which definitely include the shredded pieces of my pride.

I move closer so that I'm right under the balcony. "Wouldn't have asked if I wasn't. I think I have a spare helmet in the garage."

She grins, and the next words out of her sweet mouth knock my heart clear out of my chest. "No need. I still have mine." She turns for her house, closing the sliding glass behind her, and I wait, trying to breathe, practicing what I'll say.

A minute later, she's closing her front door and locking it before practically skipping over to me. She pulls on her old hot pink helmet, strapping it under her chin, and slips behind me.

"Where're we going?"

"Does it matter?" Because I have no idea.

"Fuck no. Take me away, Huckleberry."

17

CRAIG

YOU WRECK ME

We don't go far. I weave us through downtown, past the tourists, bachelorette parties, and circus of lights and music pouring from every doorway. I drive us over bridges, through neighborhoods, and finally out into the open road. We don't talk, but at some point, she wraps her arms more snugly around me and I press my arm over hers, lacing our fingers together.

I write words for a living. Words that people all over the world use to access their feelings. But right now, with her, I'm speechless. My feelings have been too much for too long. I choke on them whenever I try to explain myself. So instead, we ride, twined together like this, until my stomach growls and I make the impulsive decision to pull off at a roadside ice cream stand.

"Dinner?" I ask, grinning.

Her matching smile looks genuinely happy, and I'm flooded with relief. "You read my mind."

We get a couple of enormous tin roof sundaes (cashew vanilla ice cream for hers) and perch on the top wooden rail of a fence, letting the breeze cool our skin.

We're gazing out into a large expanse of rolling green hillsides when I finally speak up. "I'm sorry for the other night."

"You're okay?" she checks. Not "What the hell is wrong with you?," I notice, which is what I fully deserve.

I nod. "I got in my head. Just real good at overthinking."

"That's new. You didn't used to do that, if memory serves."

I don't say anything, because the truth is I started overthinking the day she and Drake broke things off, and she doesn't need to hear that. Bad enough I have to know it.

"You don't, um . . ."—she captures a loose strand of dark hair and tucks it behind her ear, blushing—"you're not regretting what happened, are you?"

"Not in the slightest."

"But you probably don't want to do it again . . ."

"Do you?" I ask, disbelieving. "After I got all awkward and practically shoved you out the door?"

She smirks. "Well, that wasn't great, true. But prior to that, things were going all right."

This time I'm the one who's blushing. "I can do better."

She pulls her hair back again, revealing a raised eyebrow. "I find that hard to believe, Huck."

Yep. I'm definitely red, but I've managed this much. "I want to prove it to you, but . . ." I blow out a breath. "The thing is, I don't have a lot of practice being fuckbuddies . . ."—I wince at the crass term—"with an actual, uh, buddy. I can do it, though," I rush to assure her. I'm determined to. If that's all I can have, I'll take it and be happy about it. It's the conclusion I came to on my long ride down the mountain this morning. "I think I just panicked because we work together, and I don't want to make things uncomfortable. Plus, Drake—"

Lorelai, who has been listening intently, her eyes focused on her sundae, snap up, her gaze meeting mine. "What about him?"

Great. I don't need her to think I'm a jealous idiot. Because I'm mostly not.

"Nothing. I don't know why I said anything about Drake. He's got his lawyers breathing down my neck about song rights and his name just came out . . ."

"Wait, what?" She holds up her hand, halting my rambling. "Hold on. What do you mean, he's got lawyers breathing down your neck. Why?"

"He's up for Song of the Year for 'Best Worst Case,' and he wants me to sign off on something that says he's the lyricist."

She hisses like a bobcat, and I can't help but grin at the sound.

"So it's your song. Obviously," she says. "Like 'Jonesin'.'"

I feel my cheeks flame, but I nod. "And pretty much all of his top hits in the last four years."

At this, she outright shrieks and smacks my shoulder. "Craig Huckleberry Boseman! What the actual fuck?"

"I know," I say, grimacing. "Believe me. It's my own fault. I let it go uncontested for the first album, including 'Jonesin','
since I felt bad for leaving him hanging before the tour."

"So basically the equivalent of a pity fuck, but in songs."

I give an internal shudder at the image. "I guess. Sure. But it's getting old, clearly, and not only is he not paying me for my work, he's not crediting me for it, either. Eventually, he'll run out of my material, but asking me to sign off on 'Best Worst Case' when it's up for Song of the Year is out of the question."

"Jesus, Huck, Song of the Year," she whispers.

"Yeah, I know it seems petty, but the validation would be huge for On the Floor Records."

"No, you misunderstand. I wasn't calling you petty. You're a fucking genius, is what you are. You amaze me. Every day."

I side-eye her, feeling pleased, and dig my spoon into the rapidly melting ice cream. "Yeah. Well, it's mutual, Jones."

"So what are you gonna do?"

I shrug. "Not sure yet. I'm running out of time."

"He invited me on tour this winter."

"I wondered if that was what he was talking about on Instagram."

She makes a face. "Ew, you saw that?"

I don't respond and she sighs, using her spoon to chase down a maraschino cherry at the bottom of her dish.

"I told him no. I told Jennifer *hell no*. She wants me to try this apology tour first . . . I don't know." She shakes her head. "I don't want to think about it right now. We were talking about sex," she reminds me, exasperated. I choke on a chocolate peanut, and she laughs. "How'd you let me get so far off track?"

"Sorry?"

She gives an affected sigh. "Guess you'll just have to make it up to me. After you let me make it up to you."

Her words shoot right to my cock and her triumphant smirk tells me she knows it. Hell, she's sexy.

"Dinner first?" I offer.

She presses her lips together, but I see the smile she's hiding. "Can we take the bike?"

"So you like the bike?"

"I fucking *love* the bike."

"This weekend, then? I have late nights the rest of the week to make up for leaving town."

"Where'd you go?"

"My cabin. Maybe I'll show you sometime. It's pretty rustic, though," I warn her.

"Bed?"

"Yes."

"Shower?"

"Lake?" I answer her question with another question.

Her eyes spark with interest. "A Harley and a cabin in the woods. Any other secrets you hiding in there?"

"I mean, you already know the dirt on my poetry account."

"Oh, I know alllll the dirt." She fans herself. "Okay, I need to get home. I have an interview with a radio station in the morning and a public apology to issue."

. . .

It's the middle of the night. I can't sleep and I'm in my studio. Not my studio studio, but my office studio, in my loft.

The one no one knows about. Turns out I've been keeping a lot of things to myself. I don't know why I haven't told people about the cabin or my bike or even this small one-room office recording booth.

Why so secretive?

Maybe I was just waiting to share myself with the right person. Or maybe I'm a coward.

I've been thinking about what Drake is asking and how Lorelai reacted. The way she said, "It's your song, obviously. Like 'Jonesin'.'"

It's not just that Colter released my words and made money off them. Or that he continues to use it again and again to publicly court Lorelai. That's all obnoxious, of course, but the worst thing is, it's not even the real fucking song.

Drake never had the entire song. How could he? He didn't write it, and after he released what he had, I didn't want to correct him because the bridge was personal and there was a reason I didn't share it. It was my confession. I was in love with my partner's ex. My best friend. My soulmate. And I couldn't tell her.

But she has a way of seeing all the things I don't say and knowing all the things I don't know, and maybe it's time I claim "Jonesin'." It's too late to actually get credit. The song released years ago.

But I'd know. And she'd know. And Drake would know.

And maybe he'd see the threat for what it is and stop stealing credit for my other songs. Because if I wrote "Jonesin'," there's a good chance people will want to know what else I wrote for Drake.

I don't need words or even the music. When I write a song, it glues itself inside of my brain forever. A creative muscle memory, of sorts. I'm not an awesome guitar player, but this song was meant to be acoustic. You're supposed to hear every slide of the strings and feel the space between every resting sigh.

I hit record, close my eyes, and sing for her, the way it was always meant to be done, and when I get to where he stopped, I keep going.

So I'm here, my door unlocked
My bed unmade, my heart unblocked
I'm right here, begging you to come back
To reach across, to be my one
And only then, will I find peace
My soul can rest, I'll breathe with ease
Until that day, here I'll remain,
Craving her, I'm jonesin'

And it's time for me to show her I mean it.

18

LORELAI

9 TO 5

Jen has another client meeting in Memphis this morning that conflicts with the kickoff of my apology tour, so instead I'm stuck listening to her on the phone as she preps me from the back seat of her Uber on the way to the airport. She keeps giving the driver directions in between instructing me.

I cross my legs, one foot bouncing, careful not to meet the eye of anyone listening to my half of the conversation in this shiny lobby.

"If Drake or the summer tour comes up, I want you to play it off like it's all still under wraps. Okay, Lorelai? I know you're a bit rusty at the PR, but . . ."

"I told you I'm not interested in the tour."

"Right, but—"

"And before that, I made it clear to *Drake*." I say his name in a whisper, my hand dancing in front of my mouth, blocking it from sight, like I'm a defensive coordinator in the Orange Bowl. "That's why I'm here, playing nice."

"I know that," Jen responds tersely. "No, not this exit. The next one. I'm not paying you one hot cent more for your delays. Take the next exit and get me out of this car. Sorry, sugar." Jen's tone artificially sweetens as she switches her attention back to me. "I know that," she repeats. "But all that hinges on how well you play your part. Until then, let's avoid burning bridges. Drake's ready and willing. Let's not look a gift horse and all that."

"These people are like vultures," I insist. "Give them an inch to speculate over and they'll have us reengaged and pursuing shotgun nuptials faster than you can say JLo."

Jen gives a pleased hum in the back of her throat and I scowl at the fresh-faced receptionist, clearly eavesdropping. "That's all I'm asking for, Lore. An inch. Do not confirm or deny. Just apologize, and dammit, be sincere about it. You're too fucking smart for your own good. The industry doesn't favor smart women. It favors respectful women who know their place, and I'm not saying I agree with it, but for the love of Pete, leave the intelligence and forward thinking for your songs."

I snort, but she remains quiet. "Wait. You're serious."

"Perfectly serious," she says, her tone growing harsh and censuring. "None of your usual shit, Lorelai. That's what got you into trouble in the first place. I opened the door for you. I told them you were contrite and the last few years have humbled and matured you. Get in there and prove it." The call disconnects and I can't tell if she hung up or lost the signal, but it doesn't matter. The receptionist calls my name and I tuck my phone away in my purse. I get to my feet, pressing my sweaty palms against my denim skirt and brushing my long dark waves behind my shoulders before following Bo, a young intern, toward the studio.

I've dressed as instructed. "Front pew on Sunday morning with a dash of the sex kitten we all know and love." Yeah, I'm not exactly sure what that's supposed to be, either, but I decided on a simple white cotton cap-sleeved blouse and a classic jean skirt that hits closer to my knees than my butt cheek but still shows plenty of tasteful leg.

I haven't been out of the industry that long. Despite what my agent apparently thinks, I'm not a complete idiot when it comes to what sells.

There are a bajillion women just like me out there with talent. Some sing better than me, some are prettier, some are more gifted writers, some play guitar like the dickens . . . But I also know I possess a package that sells. A chemistry, if you will, that draws people in.

I have *it*. Even now, years after they forced me out on my ass, I still have it. It's why when Shelby and Cameron were *this close* to losing their show and falling right into the pit that Shelby's ex, that fucker Lyle Jessup, dug for them, I was able to fall back on my social media following to pass them a shovel. Country music might've turned its back on me, but my fans haven't. Not yet. I just need to find a way to reach them again.

Bo makes me wait for the on-air light to click off before opening the door into the booth. He presses a hand to the small of my back, escorting me in. I'm sure he thinks he's being reassuring, but inwardly I bristle at the touch, at the insinuation, slight as it might be, that I need help.

I'm Lorelai fucking Jones, and it's about time I remember that.

And that right there is the moment where everything starts to go south.

I'm introduced to Carl and Reggie, the morning show on-air personalities, as well Marissa, their producer. Marissa looks to be about my age, though she dresses older, and it's clear after only a few minutes that she's honestly sick of Carl and Reggie's bullshit. Which, who can blame her?

Carl is flat-faced and soft-bellied, with a shock of orange-red hair that pokes out of his head in tufts over his headphones. He reminds me of a blustery horse, the way he punctuates everything with a raspberry or a noisy, hawking yeehaw.

If such is possible, Reggie is worse. Even sitting down, I can tell he's tall the way he curls over his mic. His eyes are beady behind thick frames, and he leers at anything with a vulva. Marissa's conservative clothing choices are making more sense by the second. This guy looks like someone Taylor Swift would sue, and I mean that exactly how it sounds.

Jen wants me to apologize to these two? Not fucking likely.

But I have to try, because the alternative is touring with my ex-fiancé for an entire winter while people watch my belly to play the game "Is it deep-dish pizza or baby Drake Jr.?"

The commercial break ends, and Reggie takes the lead in my interview, introducing me on the air with a crass summary of my past discretions, which he's ever so creatively dubbed the *Neil Young Debacle*.

(I want to correct him and let him know that Crosby, Stills, and Nash were also present the day they produced "Ohio," but I figure that's not the point and also I remember just in time I'm not supposed to be smart.)

"Lorelai Jones, forced retirement suits you. Where've you been these last few years?"

"Oh gosh, here and there. I spent the majority of my time in Michigan teaching third grade, if you can believe. Hi, class," I say into the mic, waving at my invisible students as if they're listening. "Make sure you're doing your homework."

Carl raises a brow. "You mean to tell me you had students?"

"Thirty every year."

"Now that's something I wouldn't mind seeing," Reggie says. "Gives a new meaning to the words *hot for teacher*. I bet those boys had a hell of a time paying attention with you strutting around."

Carl gives a honking laugh and in a breathless falsetto says, "Now, class, today we're going to learn about sex ed . . ."

I don't cooperate. "Yes, well. Again, third graders, so not exactly."

"So the dads, then," Reggie says to Carl. "Plenty of parent/teacher conferences happening after hours, I bet."

I press my lips together, controlling my breathing. "Not really, but I've recently moved back to Nashville and am hard at work on a new album."

"Right, right." Reggie clears his throat. "Well, I'll be honest with you folks; Lorelai looks as incredible as ever. That northern air did a body good. But has it improved your attitude, young lady?" he asks in a fatherly tone, and my throat fills with acid.

"Well, if you mean, have I stopped playing protest rock, sure. I've been focusing on my own music."

"Something lighter and little happier, I hope? None of that fuddy-duddy depressing social awareness crap?"

I hedge my answer. "Certainly more mature, yes. I've grown into my vocals and have had the priceless opportunity to step out of the spotlight and into real life for a bit. In some ways, I'm more socially aware than ever. Hard not to be after the state of things over the last few years."

Carl blows a fat raspberry and Reggie cackles. "Blah-blah, that sounds boring. People want to escape their lives, Lorelai. They want a pretty voice to listen to and a pretty face to look at while they're listening."

I press my lips together to keep from spewing any words I can't take back and grin. "Well," I drawl, "I can certainly provide the people with what they want."

"Can you sing a little something for us now? Something new you've been working on?"

Jen hadn't mentioned this, but I'm perpetually ready to sing, and have been since I was born, so I agree. "I don't have my guitar, so I feel a little naked," I say coyly, knowing exactly how I sound and hating myself for it.

Reggie winks and I suppress a shudder. "That's all right by me, darlin'. You all right with that, Carl?" Carl makes one of those cartoon *ayy-ooga* noises and I deserve a million bucks for not vomiting.

I press forward in my seat, closing my eyes against the

room and the pigheaded men in front of me, shutting out their leers as I sing a few verses of "What They Have," the song I wrote about Shelby and Cameron, picturing my friends and ignoring the pang of homesickness.

When I'm finished, I settle back, opening my eyes, and to their credit, Reggie and Carl look almost gobsmacked. I honestly don't feel cocky at their expressions. After all, like I said, I have *it*.

But I can't help but feel the steady sinking in my gut, because I know this wasn't enough to soothe anyone's opinions of me.

19

LORELAI

MY GIVE A DAMN'S BUSTED

The rest of the week is much the same, and it's pretty clear by Friday afternoon that the overall result was underwhelming and ineffective.

Even Jen's early return from L.A. on Wednesday morning could do nothing to curb the intense dislike reflected on the faces of the gatekeepers of country music radio. In the beginning, I really did make an effort at earning their good favors. Not everyone was as despicable as Reggie, but the disapproval was clear. No matter how demure I pretend to be, no matter how self-deprecating, no matter how fucking charming (and I'm charming as hell when I want to be), it's not enough. The best I can figure is because what I stand for, what I'm about deep down in my center, still remains, and they have to sense that.

They aren't ready for that version of Lorelai Jones.

"They feel duped," Huck tells me over the phone after a particularly shitastic interview with a popular conservative deejay on iHeartRadio. "You made them fall in love with you and shower you with praise. You were everyone's pliable darling until you showed your claws. You pulled the wool over their eyes and made them look stupid. Not only that, you made the rest of the country stand up and take notice of the more backward traditions in this industry, and they're slow to forgive that."

"I'm not the only one, though. Look at Kacey Musgraves and Annie Mathers. Miranda Lambert. The Highway Women. Mickey Guyton."

"Would it make you feel better if I told you that I think what happened to you opened doors for others? Jefferson said Annie sent him to me *because* of you. Because she admired you and never thought what happened to you was right. I've heard she has a clause in her contract that says she can speak about whatever she wants, and her label can't legally drop her for it?"

After that, the apology tour was pretty much a joke. I went through the motions twice on Thursday and three times this morning, but I shouldn't have bothered. At the last, disastrous meeting, the deejay, wearing a T-shirt that read GET YOUR HANDS OFF MY SECOND AMENDMENT, had cued up a bootleg recording of my performance of "Ohio" before my ass even touched the seat across from him.

"How do you feel about the Second Amendment now?"

I can feel my agent's eyes boring holes into my skull as if to give me the proper response, telepathically. *Don't mess this up, Lorelai. Be vague. Polite. Play stupid. Anything but the truth.*

Fuck it.

"I think assault rifles hadn't been invented when it was

written. I think the right to bear arms and a well-regulated militia have no place in school buildings or college campuses or hospitals or cemeteries or grocery stores or churches or any of the hundreds of other mundane locations where people, completely innocent and nonthreatening human beings, are going about their right to life, liberty, and the pursuit of happiness. *That's* what I think."

Jen has her head in her hands, but I can't make myself care. If this is the only way back to music, I guess I don't want it. I'll return to my classroom and sing to my third graders every day for the rest of my life before I offer one more lie to appease these people.

I shake my head, feeling the weight of the headphones over my ears, and lean toward the mic one more time, feeling more myself than I have in months. "I sang a song. That song, the one you just played, to a stadium full of people years ago. My heart was broken, and like a thousand times before, I sang that broken heart into a crowd where other people could share it. That's what music is supposed to be about. A shared experience. A transfer of emotions and understanding. Empathy.

"I sang that song because I couldn't let one more minute pass without saying it. And I was told to shut up. The proverbial mic was stolen from my hands and the lights were shut off. Because of me. One tiny woman singing a song that wasn't even mine. I don't know why that scared y'all so much, but I'm done apologizing for it. I'm taking my *sorry*s back. I'm not sorry. I'd do it again in a second. Just watch me."

And with that, I remove my headset, my hands steady and my breathing calm. I scoot back in my chair, whisper my thanks to the production team, and walk out into the waiting area.

Jennifer is pale and shaky. She looks like I kicked her puppy, and that won't do. Clearly I've outgrown her.

"I just got off the phone with the Square network. They canceled your interview for tonight."

"Already?" I quip. "That was fast. Well, I think we can officially call this apology tour an epic failure."

Jen straightens, running her trembling fingers down her pencil skirt. It's fascinating to watch. She reminds me of a cartoon Transformer, reconfiguring herself back together.

"I'll get on the horn with the Colter team."

"No," I say, my voice soft but strong.

"What do you mean, no?"

"Jen, I'm releasing you. Be free of my bullet-train-off-the-rails of a career."

"It's not as bad as all that. I'll have to sweet-talk Marty, but he's always had a soft spot for you. You know what? Even better." She's nodding to herself and brushing her manicured fingers down her fitted jacket. "Let's head on over there together. He won't be able to turn you down to your face. You won't have to even say a word . . ."

I blow out an exasperated breath and hitch my purse higher on my shoulder. "Fuck's sake, Jen. I'm firing you. I don't want Drake's tour; I don't want an apology tour, and I don't want whatever plan you've cooked up next."

Jen gives a pitying sigh. "You'll never sing in this town again, Lorelai."

My smile is sad, I know, but it's also genuine. "Maybe not. But that's no longer your concern."

Which brings me to now. Sitting on the balcony, under heavy cloud cover, my bare feet propped on the railing and a half-empty bottle of Two Buck Chuck sitting on the side table next to me, Taylor Swift's *Midnights* soothing my prickly feelings and filling me with female righteousness.

In my lap is a well-loved spiral notebook filled with pages of thoughts and lyrics. I'm not writing for me right now, but there's comfort in the familiar process. I've been collecting words since I was a lonely teen in my bedroom while my parents worked through their bitter divorce. The unlikely but all-too-real contrast to my head cheerleader and weekend bridal model persona. Lines from poems, stanzas from songs, pages out of books, copy from glittering magazine ads. Thoughts borrowed from strangers that feel like connections. A stunning web of like minds, all carefully collected and copied down in blue ballpoint pen.

Whenever I've felt my craziest, I've gathered my courage from these pages.

You're not alone, they'd whisper to me over and over. *You're one of us.*

As of tonight, I have no recording contract, no credibility in country music, no tour with Drake Colter, and no agent. I've nearly run out of my savings, and I have no source of income to speak of. I have notebooks of songs, but they're all pure country, so that's a bust.

I could return to Michigan—to Shelby and Cameron, Maren and my students. There's a pang in my gut, however, at the mere thought of leaving Nashville, and I'm not sure if it's only about the music or if it's something more. Some*one* more.

A light drizzle starts to fall and with it, the smell of an impending storm. I slap my notebook shut and collect my bottle and pen just as the drops start to fall heavier and closer together and jog down the metal stairs and into my apartment, sliding the glass door shut behind me.

I turn on the light from the kitchen, putting away the rest of the wine and pulling out a jar of kalamata olives from the fridge. I grab a fork and then flop on my couch, pulling my tablet onto my lap, figuring to find a good serial killer doc to distract me from my current state. I've been avoiding email and social media since I left the radio station earlier, but I'm just tipsy enough to face them, so I make a detour from Netflix and click on my Instagram. I bypass all the DMs, since I already know that way lies madness. My notifications are so chaotic, I can't even keep up, but from skimming the tagged posts, sound bites, and clickbaits, I have to say, it feels fifty-fifty on the hate scale. Which, honestly, isn't terrible. There's a clear separation between national coverage and conservative coverage, but at least no one is telling me to shut up and sing this time. I'm trending on Twitter, but it's just my name, so I'll take it.

My eyes snag on another trending name. WhoIsCraig-Boseman and "Jonesin'."

Huh. What?

I revert back to Instagram, and there on the home page is a face dear and familiar to me. He's posted a video. He never posts videos. I click on the link and turn up the volume. Huck rarely sings. His voice isn't really anything extraordinary, but I have to admit, the low, kind of growly tone of it sends little spasms of attraction through me, anyway.

He's strumming a guitar, and if I didn't know him, I wouldn't be able to tell it's not his instrument of choice. Not even the top three, but he plays smoothly.

But that's not what everyone is talking about. It's the song he's playing. *His* song. I've heard it a million times. Everyone has. Drake made it famous, but this is different. It's as though Craig is playing it the way it was meant to be played—the way it was meant to sound. Drake's version is polished and precise. Manufactured in an expensive studio with the best, highest-quality equipment available.

Craig is playing it in a tiny, dark space. The sound quality is more than fine, but it feels intimate. Uncut and raw, somehow. Like he's playing it from his bedroom the morning *after*. Like I just left.

And then he surprises me—surprises us all—with an entire bridge never heard before.

> So I'm here, my door unlocked
> My bed unmade, my heart unblocked
> I'm right here, begging you to come back
> To reach across, to be my one
> And only then, will I find peace
> My soul can rest, I'll breathe with ease
> Until that day, here I'll remain,
> Craving her, I'm jonesin'

I press my fingers to my lips, my eyes filling with proud tears. "You brilliant man," I whisper to the ceiling between us.

He's done it. He's found a way to claim his song.

CRAIG

ASK ME HOW I KNOW

Craigboseman ***Presented Without Comment***

1.2 million views

Liked by Annie Mathers and 200,514 others

View all 8,104 comments

AnnieMathers Always loved this song, but that bridge? *chef kiss*

JeffersonCoolidge About damn time.

Sparklegrrl I like this more than the original!

IversMusic Wait. I thought this was about Lorelai Jones

Faltercation Colter always claimed it was . . .

Iversmusic Is Lorelai Jones the new Layla??????

Momof3weeee *fans self*

Eddvark85 Drake sang it better, but I'm digging the unplugged feel

BakersDozenTheBand We knew you could write, but singing and playing? A man of many talents!

Musky.Maren I knew you had it in you, Huckleberry.

ShelbySpringfieldRiggs Get 'em, Tiger.

JaketheSnake I heard Boseman wrote all of Colter's songs

Faltercation Worst-kept Nashville secret

CameronRiggs Looks like someone needs a music video . . . I might know a guy.

CMT *eyeballs*

Arlo.in.the.fedora Glad to see our luncheon helped!

LorelaiJones Huck, could not be prouder of you, darlin'.

. . .

Arlo picks up my phone, powering it down and tossing it onto my desk with a thud. "If you aren't gonna answer, and believe me, I understand why you aren't, then let's just conserve the battery, and by default your sound engineer's sanity, hm?"

"Sorry," I apologize distractedly. "It's just Drake. Or his lawyers. Or Drake *and* his lawyers."

"Or, you know, CMT calling our offices. Pretty eventful stuff. Incidentally, boss, I wasn't aware we had a landline listed. Anyone who knows better just reaches out to you or me directly."

I'm clicking around on my laptop, putting together a couple of demo tracks I lined up for Coolidge, aside from the duet, to play for him today. "We don't have one listed. I haven't bothered because then I would have to hire someone to answer said landline."

"We should set up a voice mail at the very least."

"Someone would have to check it and respond. You want to be that person?"

Arlo scoffs, adjusting his hat. "I'm a sound engineer."

"And I can't be answering it, because I'm the fucking CEO, so what we're gonna do is let it ring, without a voice mail, and if they really need to get ahold of either of us, they'll call our cells."

"I'm sensing tension."

I continue clicking around, unseeing. "I'm not tense, I'm tired and I'm busy and I'm preparing for our next client who is supposed to arrive any minute and I can't concentrate with my phone ringing and vibrating every forty fucking seconds with notifications from Colter because he's anxious about his precious Grammy nod. I just need a moment of fucking peace and quiet to hear myself think."

"Riiight. Got you," Arlo stage-whispers before turning for the door. When he reaches it, he glances over his shoulder with what I am positive he thinks is a jaunty smirk. "And so we're clear, you *don't* want to know when there's a power-house brunette pacing outside our front doors?"

I raise a single eyebrow, but my gut tells me I already know the one he's talking about, and therefore I'm rolling back in my chair to the lone window, peering through the slats in the wood blinds. "What is she doing outside?"

"No idea, but I'm betting she's not here for me."

I watch Lorelai pace a small circle in high-heeled boots before jumping to my feet and marching out of our offices and down the stairs and shoving through the heavy metal door.

"You're not on the schedule, are you?"

Lorelai shrieks and jumps three inches in the air. "Jesus Christ, Huck, are you trying to kill me?"

I lean against the doorjamb and cross my ankles. "More like trying to figure out why you're out here and not in there?"

"Well, I don't have an appointment, as you said."

I scoff good-naturedly. "You know I was being flippant. You don't need an appointment here, and besides, it's never stopped you before."

"I know, but I figured you'd be all super busy and famous and I wasn't sure after . . . well." Her arms drop with a giant sigh. I look at her, taking in the dark circles under her eyes, just barely hidden under her large sunglasses, before my gaze wanders to the defeated droop of her shoulders. She searches around, as if looking for a crowd carrying pitchforks. "I didn't know if you heard the interview and what that might mean for . . . our partnersh—us. What it means for us."

Hell, is that what this is about? I shake my head and swing the door open behind me, standing there, waiting for her to pass. She freezes in place, her eyes wide for a long beat before her expression melts ever so slightly and she quickly ducks past me. I tug her to a stop and lean in so I can see past the shaded lenses of her glasses.

"I fucking *loved* the interview. Arlo thought I was being attacked in my office because I hollered so loud. I'd guess it would be the equivalent to competitive guys watching the Super Bowl, the way I carried on. Not that Arlo or I would really know. That deejay baited you and you handed him his ass *live* on the radio. You didn't back down for one moment, even though literally everything that mattered to you was on the line. Do you realize how incredible you are? I'm in awe of you. I'm not ashamed to be seen with you, I'm fucking *honored* to share your air. You can have your own office space if you want. I'll change the name to Lorelai Jones Recording Studio. I'll have merch made with your gorgeous face on it."

Lorelai huffs softly, "Huck—"

"No. You need to hear this. This isn't the same as last time, and I'm not Drake Colter, so *whatever* this is . . ."—I gesture between us—"it's not dependent on you hiding yourself away and staying the quiet and perfectly submissive starlet. I have no interest in that version of Lorelai Jones. I want the one that cusses out the patriarchy and plays Neil Young and writes whole-ass songs when they could just send a text. I *like* the schoolteacher activist."

"I might never sing in this town again," she says.

"I'd love to see them try and keep you out." I wrap my arm around her, leading her upstairs with me. "Now, I have Coolidge on his way and he's putting up with me and Arlo only because he thinks you're part of the package deal, so maybe I really will get merch made. Some T-shirts or those trucker hats that were super popular a few years ago. We'll bring sexy back."

Once we hit the top of the stairs, I stop her one more time before we enter the studio. "You good?"

Lorelai takes a deep breath and pulls off her sunglasses, tucking them away. "Yeah."

My expression is skeptical, and she smirks. Something inside of my chest loosens at the sight. "I'm good. Fuck them and the horse they rode in on and all that. I'm over it."

And you know what? I know she isn't really over it, but I believe she's on her way.

21

. . . .

CRAIG

DIE A HAPPY MAN

Not only did Coolidge bring fiddler Fitz Jacoby and drummer Jason Diaz, he also brought Annie Mathers, reigning queen of country. Mathers immediately made a beeline for Lorelai and the two beauties huddled together, giving the men shit and presumably draining the planet of its talent just by their mere existence.

Before today, I obviously knew there was a dynamic between Coolidge and Mathers, everyone did, but it's something else to experience it up close. The way they challenge each other with just a word or a look. It's a language all their own, equal parts friends *and* lovers, and it rings familiar in a way I'd better not overthink.

Right now, Coolidge and his bandmates are sitting in the dim studio while Arlo and I man the board. Annie's over Arlo's shoulder and Lorelai's sitting behind me, her eyes closed, listening to his rich vocals.

He's singing an original right now. He's a more-than-decent lyricist, singing lines that speak to experiences he shouldn't have but believably does. The honesty in his tone is kind of unsettling, but I'm into it. I let his vocals wash over me and allow them to soak deep into my bones, not interrupting him. Just letting him do his thing and get comfortable behind the mic. Already my brain is picking up on a kind of funky vibe that I want to eventually explore with him. Almost R&B. There's an edge to him that has a cross appeal. A little bit of a Babyface or an old-school Usher vibe.

It's a direction country artists cycle through every few years, but it's tough to manage without outright appropriation. Coolidge is a farm boy from Indiana, but he's also danced with the devil. No parents and an older brother who died while serving in the military overseas. His reputation for getting into trouble as a kid is well known, and I think that innate recognition of survival comes across.

It's no wonder he and Annie found each other. Mathers is practically country music royalty. Her parents were Cora Rosewood and Robbie Mathers. Think Tim and Faith if they hadn't overcome the odds and turned vegan. Literally everything crashed and burned for Annie's parents in the most horrific way. She was sent to live in Michigan to grow up with her grandparents away from the lights and toxicity of Nashville and returned a young woman with a good head on her shoulders and talent shining out of her pores. Fate brought Coolidge and Mathers together for a summer tour, and as far as I can tell, they've been intertwined ever since. Even when Coolidge stepped out of the limelight and walked away from his career, they've remained intact.

Jefferson moves into a new song, pressing his lips to the

mic and meeting our eyes. "This one's untried. I wrote it a while back and kind of threw it to the wayside, but I'm suddenly feeling it." He looks over his shoulders to his bandmates. "I'll go solo on it unless you wanna jump in."

Then he meets Mathers's eyes and starts to strum.

Within a few chords, I know this has to be on the album. I can also tell it's exceptionally personal and probably biographical. A glance at Mathers and she's pressing her lips together, pushing her big bold curls out of her face and revealing glittering eyes. The song is about a sinner in love with a saint and is told from the perspective of *after*. Not as if whatever they had was over, but instead it's because she's no longer a saint. He's corrupted her with their shared sensuality.

By the time he's done, both Annie and Lorelai, who's come alongside me, are fanning their pink faces. Arlo removes his hat, swiping at his forehead, and everyone laughs.

I press the speaker and lean forward. "Okay, so that's going on the album."

"Gotta check with Annie first."

"Oh, sure," Annie pipes over the speaker, chuckling despite the flush in her cheeks, "ask me *after* you've played it for everyone."

"Easier to ask for forgiveness than permission, darlin'. Learned that one from you, little Miss 'Coattails.' And 'You'd Be Mine.' And 'That Man's Gonna.' And—"

"Okay, okay. We get the picture. I'm just kidding, anyway. How dare you sing that when there's glass between us and witnesses, including one I'm practically related to."

Coolidge winks and drags his callused fingers over the

strings, and I clear my throat. "Right. We'll come back to that one and the one before it because as far as I can tell all the songs you have stockpiled there deserve to be laid down as tracks. I have some thoughts on some engineering stuff with regards to overall vibe and maybe some crossover potential if you're amenable, but first, while I have Lorelai here, what are your thoughts on the duet?"

Annie presses forward again on the button, but she's talking to Lorelai behind me. "A thousand times yes."

Coolidge laughs into his mic. "Yeah, what she said. Let's do it."

Within moments, we're settled on chairs, sofas, stools, and even a pair of cushions that Arlo dug out of his office, all cozily crowded around the sound booth. Waters, beers, and for Lorelai, a cup of honey lemon tea are distributed as we workshop the duet. Annie is an impeccable resource on timing and delivery, taking my lyrics and parsing them in a way that feels fresh. After barely thirty minutes, they're ready to lay it down and head back into the studio, picking up their headphones and stepping up to the mics.

I'm not sure I've ever had a recording go so smoothly. I'd sure as hell never experienced anything like it from the other end when I was working under Drake. Everything has come together so seamlessly, it almost makes me second-guess myself, but I can't second-guess Lorelai and Jefferson. Truth is, sometimes that's the way it works. Things just click and personalities jibe and vocals marry, and anyway, I called it from the start. I knew these two would be perfect for this song.

After the duet, we decide to call it a night. It's not that

late, but I don't need anyone straining their vocals and this is a good stopping point. Plus, and maybe more important, I'm dying to get Lorelai alone to talk. We've barely scratched the surface on the conversation from earlier and I've been itching all fucking day thinking she might still be questioning whether she should be here with me. With us. The duet should have proved it a hundred times over, but I need to be sure.

I more than anyone know firsthand how fucked up Lorelai was after Drake's rejection, followed by the rejection of the entire industry. It's been years, but the writing's on the wall. It's all coming back in full force, and I can't let that happen.

Last time, I let her leave and have her space. I won't be making that mistake again.

"Come back to my place?" I ask, before realizing how it sounds and feeling my face burn.

Lorelai's face lights up with *something* and I bite my tongue to keep myself from walking back the offer. After all, I chose this. I made the commitment that whatever she needs, I can do that.

Am I seriously questioning the chance to pleasure this woman? What the fuck is wrong with me, acting as if I haven't been fighting off hard-ons all day just breathing in her scent?

"Should I stop for some pad thai on the way?" Lorelai asks, completely unaware of my inner turmoil.

Resolved, I shake my head and lean closer, my voice barely a rasp. "I'm hungry for something else tonight."

That mysterious something is back, lighting up her features again as her full lips spread in a sexy smile.

. . .

We barely make it up the walk before I've pressed her up against the front door, the callused pads of my fingers smoothing unspoken thoughts into her petal-soft skin, my split-second decision made that tonight is about Lorelai. After all, it's what a *good friend* would do.

I dip my head, capturing her mouth in a searing kiss, and gently suck her bottom lip between mine before using my teeth. Lorelai responds immediately, bucking her hips against me in a torturously slow roll, and my grip on her tightens, my body molding against hers. She twists her tongue with mine and I swallow the little gasps that escape when I drag my thumb across her sensitive nipple hidden under the layers of her tee and bra, once, twice, three times circling in time with my hips.

Her hand reaches between us for my buckle and snaps me back to attention. I pull back, as if drugged, my senses reluctantly allowing in the world around us, and I remember it's barely dusk and we live on a busy street. Thankfully, we seem to be alone, but it's Nashville, so I hold a fingertip to her kiss-swollen mouth and turn to unlock and open my front door.

I don't resume kissing her right away, instead reaching for her hand and leading her in behind me up the stairs and once in my apartment, planting her firmly on the love seat. "Close your eyes and give me a few minutes."

A teasing smirk dances around her lips. "You're gonna clean, aren't you?"

"Hush, woman. Rest up. I have big plans for you."

Shocking us both, she relents, shutting her eyes and leaning back against the armrest, slipping out of her boots and crossing her socked feet on the cushion.

"You have five minutes, Huck, before I start stripping."

All the blood rushes from my head, and my cock gives a painful throb against my constricting jeans. Lorelai, eyes still shut, grins triumphantly at my groan, and I hustle before I change my mind and decide to just do it her way.

First, I open a bottle of wine and let it rest on the island while placing two stemless glasses next to it. Second, I pull out my phone, turning off all notifications before scrolling to some music. Willie's "Blue Eyes Crying in the Rain" cues up and I increase the volume. It's not the sexiest song, but it does a good job of setting the atmosphere and I instantly feel more relaxed.

And believe me, I need to calm the fuck down or this is gonna be embarrassing. One day, maybe, Lorelai and I will have enough sex that I can convince my dick to be patient.

Today is not that day. Tomorrow isn't looking great, either.

Then I rush to the living room, where there's a small brick fireplace in front of the couch where Lorelai is pretending to rest. I grab the bundle next to the hearth and have a cozy fire going in under a minute, crackling softly and painting everything in a warm glow.

For a final touch, I spread a large quilt on the floor, tossing a few throw pillows around and laying a couple of extra blankets over the opposite arm of the love seat just in case. I'm about to change the song to something sexier when a soft snore stops me in my tracks.

Hell.

She's asleep.

In an instant, I'm shifting gears. A blanket covers her exhausted form, the music is turned down, and I collect a few more logs off the back patio to stock up for when the flames get too low. When I return, she's snoring louder and I'm staring at her like a sappy lovesick idiot. Before I overthink it too much, I grab a book off my shelf, this time a collection of Mary Oliver poetry my parents bought me for my high school graduation, and gently lift her feet before sitting and replacing them over my lap. I slip on my glasses and settle in. Maybe reading will keep me from dwelling too much on how this feels exactly right and how if I got nothing else for the rest of my life, this would still be enough.

22

LORELAI

BREATHE

I wake up and it feels achingly familiar. An echo from a long-ago memory. Before I even open my eyes, I can feel him—his steadfast presence, solid and comfortable wrapped all around me—and it nearly takes my breath away. The scent of his laundry soap and shaving lotion pulling me in.

When I finally open my eyes, I can tell it's late. The sky is dark outside the windows and the fire I'd heard Huck fixing up earlier is mostly embers. I shift inside a pair of arms, feeling more awake by the second.

I consider sneaking out from his embrace and maybe building up the fire again. Or pouring myself a glass of wine. But every inch of this man is pressed against me, my back to his front, and every last one of those inches feels really, really good. Too good to rip myself away from, so instead, I press impossibly closer and spin in his arms to face him before covering his face in slow, methodical kisses, curling his wavy hair around my fingers at his nape and tugging with the slightest pressure. Then I gently nudge my thigh between his, sliding along his rising erection. I'm making a wild guess here, but I'm thinking he won't mind waking up this way.

A breath later, his hands are inside my shirt and slipping skillfully underneath the cups of my bra. We start making out to the sound of embers popping like we're two teenagers on a couch in his parents' basement, ramping up heartbeats and chasing the sparks zipping through our bodies. Over clothes, under clothes, I haven't even taken off my clothes and I'm nearly there just from the delicious friction of his body against mine.

Huck catches my gasp in his mouth and slides his hands from my breasts, gripping my waist in one and pressing a finger to my lips.

"Don't you dare. Not yet."

I whimper and his lips quirk in a happy grin, his eyes tender. He surges up and over me, standing. His hand reaches for mine.

"C'mere, darlin'." And he's leading me to his room.

"Oh, but you spent all that time setting up . . ."

He raises an amused brow. "It was barely five minutes, not that you'd know, Sleeping Beauty. Besides. A man can change his mind, and right now this man wants you naked in his bed."

"Oh, well. All right then," I agree, following behind him, his hand tugging me along. "That's a good idea."

"I'm full of them," he teases. We make it to his room, which is a healthy mix of masculine and neat, his bed made, his clothes put away.

"Did you do this when I was sleeping?"

He pulls on the hem of my shirt, peeling it up inch by teasing inch and shaking his head. "I'm tidy," he says in between following the path of his hands with his mouth. "Melissa's fault," he continues in between kisses. "She told me back in high school that I'd never have sex if I didn't have clean sheets and a made bed."

I whip off my shirt the rest of the way and grasp his stubbly face between my fingers. "Bravo, Melissa. Remind me to bring her an expensive bottle of wine the next time I visit."

"Absolutely. As long as you swear never to say my sister's name during sex ever again."

"You started it." He nibbles in between my cleavage and I give a yelp that he answers with a lick. That might leave a mark.

God, I *hope* it leaves a mark. Just a little one. I never wanted to be marked before. It always felt misogynistic or something, but the idea of being marked by Huck . . .

Whew. Can your entire body flush? Because my entire body is aflame.

I pull off his shirt and soon we're shedding pants and diving onto his bed.

"Are you going to get mad at me if I go down on you again?" He waggles his brows and I smack his chest lightly.

"Get the fuck out. Are you gonna let me repay the favor this time?"

"I'm gonna insist."

Hell.

"Thank god." I push him back on the mattress with a bounce and bite down gently on his raised nipple before placing open-mouthed kisses across his chest and down down down to where I've wanted to be for ages.

Huck is a dream. He's considerate, confident, sensitive, and a hell of a lyricist. He's down-to-earth, patient, and soulful. He's handsome in the maddeningly interesting way that he could not care less how he looks except to make an effort for you.

All of that is enough. It's too much, honestly, and I haven't come to terms with how I feel about it all, but for the moment, I'm just gonna thank all the gods for his thick cock and swear it was made for me. I take him between my lips, slowly inching toward the base and wrapping my fingers around him to make up the difference when I reach my limit. I twirl my tongue around the head, dragging it along the slit before plunging down again. I grip his hip with one hand to steady myself while tightening my hold and sucking hard, hollowing my cheeks and making him rasp out and buck his hips off the bed.

"Lorelai," he warns with a practical yelp, and I grin around his cock, my eyes seeking out his and answering him with a low, questioning *hmm?* that has him panting. Eventually his hands find my hair, but they're gentle. "I'm already so close. I've been close."

In response, I dive down again, this time with even more enthusiasm. There is nothing I want more than to feel him come apart on my tongue. To have that power over him. To make him feel *that* good. I grip harder with my hands and hum my encouragement, making my mouth as tight as I can before he stops me.

"Oh god, Lorelai, you have to stop. I give in. Whatever you want. But please let me finish inside of you. I need to watch you come with me inside of you."

How can I say no to that?

So I climb him like a fucking tree, and he hands me a condom. He props himself up with a pillow as I rip open the foil, rolling it along his length before straddling him and taking him inside me, stretching and filling me with the most exquisite friction all . . . the way . . . down. I moan and probably would be embarrassed at how loud it is, but oh god, I don't care—this feels better than anything I've ever felt in my entire life. Well, until he moves his hands, cupping me, his thumbs plucking at my nipples and pinching just enough to make my eyes roll back and my head drop, my muscles completely useless.

He removes his hands and I want to protest, but then his hot mouth is there instead, sucking and biting as his talented fingers find my clit. I'm drenched and quivering, my blood is on fire, and everything is so, so much. So fucking much I can barely breathe, my breaths coming in pants and moans as he's whispering encouragement and pulling me to the edge of the cliff until he says, "Now, Lorelai."

I start rolling my hips, grinding against him and gripping him from the inside out, and he's lifting off the bed, thrusting inside me until I feel myself seize up, curling in and pressing down, my walls fluttering and clamping, and I sob with relief as wave after wave of near-unbearable pleasure overwhelms me.

Huck's grip on my hips tightens to an almost painful degree as he groans against the base of my throat and comes hard inside of me. We stay like that, wrapped tightly together, so tight I can't tell which limbs are mine and which are his, for a long time, inhaling each other's breaths and matching heartbeats and I know I'm fucked. I mean. Clearly in the literal sense, but also in the figurative sense.

Because there was nothing *friendly* about what we just did.

. . .

In effort to restore factory settings on our friendship, I don't stay the night and he doesn't offer. To be clear, he doesn't *not* offer. This isn't like the last time where he packed up leftovers and shooed me out after the orgasm. For one, we both orgasmed this time. Actually, is there such a thing as a double orgasm or maybe just a really, really long one? Because if there is . . .

I need to call Shelby.

Anyway, factory settings. Dinner was never part of the deal. So what if we fell asleep together on the couch first?

FACTORY SETTINGS. I used his bathroom and cleaned up, and by the time I was done, he was back in his clothes. Like a hookup. A really fucking solid hookup. Just friends. Really good friends who are really good at sex. Because even if I wanted more, and I don't, I can't. We can't. I can't fall in love with him. If I thought Drake destroyed me, Craig—Huck—well, I just don't think I could handle losing him, too. Because eventually he's gonna have to let me go. I'm still a cussword in this town, after all. But he won't be taking my heart with him when he does. So no. That's not this. This is best friends who have really hot sex and keep their hearts protected because they are smart.

I walk back down the stairs to my apartment and text him good night before stripping off my clothes and crawling into bed, still smelling like him. Still feeling his hands on my skin. Still tasting him on my tongue. Still hearing him in my dreams.

Greatest friends' hookup ever.

23

LORELAI

MY TEARS RICOCHET

I woke up this morning feeling like the Queen of My Own Orgasmic Fate, but that was quickly overshadowed by how, similarly to my (happy) vag, my career is royally fucked. It's been three days since the disaster of an apology tour wrapped with me salting, then gratuitously razing any ground I'd gained, all before firing my agent.

It's probably too early to call my comeback a colossal dumpster fire, if only because that feels disrespectful to Huck and Coolidge after working on the duet together. If nothing else, I know I can be proud of that particular song. Even if it only boosts Jefferson's career, I'll be thrilled. The kid deserves everything good, and I'd be proud to be a part of that.

And Huck and Arlo are too talented at what they do for a connection to me to mess with the outcome of their work.

I might be persona non grata around country music, but my thirty-three-year-old vocals are like the finest vintage. Aged to perfection. I'm at my peak, baby.

Anyway, hell, I need to get some air. I need to get out of Nashville and away from everything that reminds me of what a mess my life is. I pack a day pack, including ropes, harnesses, chalk, and carabiners, as well as a couple of protein bars and two bottles of water, one to throw in my pack and the other for the car ride home.

Two hours and forty windy miles out of town later, my forearms burn and something warm is trickling down the back of my leg. I don't know for sure if it's sweat or blood, but I don't care. The sun is blazing, but under this shallow rock shelf, there's cool relief on top of the sweet release of being too busy keeping from falling and breaking my ass to care about anything else. I hold my position, shifting my foot from an outside to an inside hold, so that I can release the fingers of my right hand to shake them out. At first I feel the sting, but soon it's calmed to a dull ache and I repeat with my other hand. Then I wipe at my forehead and lean back to think, relying on my harness, and peering over the shelf at what lies ahead.

It's only five more feet to the top of this cliff, but the shelf makes those feet feel impossible. My shoulders are annoyingly stiff. I barely make it out on my own anymore, and while I run nearly every day, rock climbing challenges my muscles in a unique way. Between Shelby and Cam's wedding and Jen's apology tour and trying to find validation in a town that doesn't want me . . .

Well, I've lost touch with me. Not the Nashville Darling version and not the Pissing Mad Woman version.

I'm missing the *real* Lorelai. She's been fading in and out like a firefly dodging jars in June. A few months back here and I'm turning into the bullshit scared girl who let country music execs run her out of town. I've got Drake showing up at my doorstep, making gooey eyeballs like he's the fucking hero, and strangers online judging my every move, getting in my brain and making me second-guess my own name. I remember last year when Shelby's ex Lyle was fucking around with her in the press and creating drama for the sake of whatever gets narcissistic jackholes like him off. My best friend finally got fed up and made the ballsy move of taking control of the entire narrative. She and Cameron fought back, using happiness and a big old dose of refreshing honesty.

I stare off into the distance at the rolling green hills upon green hills upon rocky outcroppings like the one I'm climbing and close my eyes, letting the early autumn breeze cool my face and whip away my morose thoughts.

Nothing for it. I can't hang here any longer. Every minute that passes has got my muscles seizing up, and I can't afford to be shaky on the shelf or I might as well just belay back down. Up to this point, I've always climbed alone, taking every possible precaution and preventive measure, while also pushing myself. But I'm out of shape. I've been spoiled by gym rock wall climbing and meandering hikes.

I make a vow to return next weekend, mentally carving out time for myself, and work to wrap this up as safely as possible.

As I do so, it occurs to me that maybe I don't have to do this alone. Climbing, yes, but in other ways, too. After "Ohio," I left town by myself. It was me versus the world. I'd been abandoned by everyone who was supposed to care.

But now I wonder if maybe I hadn't been. After all, Craig found me.

And five years later, he keeps finding me.

I shove off in a rocking motion from heel to toe and make a grab for the top of the rocky ledge. Before gravity drags me under, I swing a leg up and over in one motion while curling my biceps. I'm too close and clumsier than I used to be, though, and scrape my collarbone and breastbone as I pull up, leaving a piece of me behind on the sharp rock.

I make it to my knees and stifle my groan, holding a hand to my chest to soothe the sting, but also to relish the pain. It feels familiar and real and possibly like the start of something better.

· · ·

(EIGHT YEARS EARLIER)

It's one of those rare nights when the stars align and Drake and I are in the same town at the same time. His most recent tour wrapped over the weekend, and I leave for mine in three days. It's not enough time to travel anywhere and get away from it all, but it's enough time to hole up inside his small apartment for some nostalgic songwriting and long-overdue lovemaking.

If he was here, anyway.

I check my watch again, holding back a sigh, and Huck grunts over his notebook, making a note in his chicken scratch before sticking his pencil over his ear with a sly smirk. "Relax, Lorelai. I can practically hear your repressed hormones from over here. You know Powers always needs to debrief the minute we get home from a tour."

"For hours?" I scoff. "It's been at least four, and anyway, you're here. Doesn't he need to debrief you, too?"

Huck lifts a shoulder, strumming once, a loud discordant sound, on his guitar. "Nope. Just the talent."

I roll my eyes. "Fuck off. You know you're as much the talent as he is. He knows it, too."

Huck raises a single dark eyebrow.

"Even if he won't admit it out loud."

The other brow goes up. Another loud strum.

"Even upon threat of death."

He snorts.

My phone buzzes with a text alert and it's embarrassing how quickly I reach for it.

DRAKE: Don't wait up, baby. Need to schmooze some bigwigs from the label. Promise I'll make it up to you tomorrow.

Fucking hell. I haven't ridden a dick in months. Even phone sex has lost its appeal, and I'm supposed to leave for another four weeks.

This was the dream, Lorelai. Always. You are living the dream. Right now. The sacrifice to your vag is worth it.

"Thank you for your service," I mutter under my breath to my poor neglected vag before typing a response.

LORELAI: You better. You have a lot of ground to cover and only two days to do it.

He gives my text a thumbs-up and I throw my phone down with a growl.

"I'll give you a thumbs-up."

I scramble to my feet, brushing my hands down my jean-clad thighs. "I need a drink. What do y'all have around here?"

Huck tilts his head to the side. *"Pretty sure there's beer."* I frown and he laughs. *"Too good for beer these days. Okay, I think there's some tequila we got from some fancy exec type. It's for sipping, though. Which is why we ain't opened it . . . ever."*

I find the bottle in question and spin around, waving it at him.

"Get drunk with me, Huckleberry, and let's write something good."

. . .

An hour later, we're sauced and the bottle is three-quarters empty. Turns out, Huck and I suck at sipping.

But we're not half-bad lyricists.

Our knees are practically touching as we sit cross-legged across from each other, our guitars cradled in our laps. Huck's working through a bridge of one of those merry "this is my hometown dive bar" kind of country songs everyone loves and Drake is known for. I'm trying to power through the third stanza of an emotional ballad about my parents' divorce. It's not my usual fare, but this is my second album and I'm hopeful I'll get a little more rein to write something with some emotional heft.

We work perfectly together, swinging back and forth between his song and mine, flipping the switch flawlessly. It's always been like this with Huck. I said magic and I wasn't exaggerating. It's unlike anything I've ever experienced with someone else. His creativity is the other half to mine.

Or something like that. Tequila always makes me feel . . . more.

So does Huck.

"Hmm?" he says, looking up from his notebook.

"Hmm?"

He grins, and it's a loose, happy-filled kind of thing. Like I said, more. "You said 'so does Huck.' What do I do?"

I sink back, startled. "Oh. I forgot already. I think the tequila is getting to me."

He lifts his own tumbler and takes a long sip and I'm drawn to the way his tongue reaches out to lick his lips as he puts down his glass.

"I was actually just thinking that this is my favorite," I tell him half honestly.

"The sipping tequila?"

"Ha. No. You were right about that. It'd be better in a margarita with some salt around the rim." I push my hair behind my ear, feeling flush, but also brave and more than a little fond of the man in front of me. "I mean writing with you. Sitting around getting drunk and writing songs. It's magical, you know?"

Huck's head dips to the side and his blue eyes crinkle in the corners as he takes me in. He nods slowly. "Yeah, it is."

"I don't have this with anyone else. It's special."

Something flashes in Huck's gaze and he continues to meet my eyes. Eventually he says, "It is."

From somewhere, my familiar text notification chirps out and I straighten with a blink. I clear my throat, feeling uncertain. Something just happened, but I don't know what it was. "That's probably Drake."

Huck nods, returning to his paper. "Probably."

I bite my lip, watching him, but he's focused on his notes, and I give up. The moment is broken. The magic is gone.

24

CRAIG

LIKE A WRECKING BALL

Drake never understood that the key to creating good music is to listen to everything. The man refuses to listen to anything but contemporary country, out of fear of contaminating the creative well or whatever. But that, along with so much else Colter subscribes to, is such bullshit. You go stale and lose your sense of what culture is reacting to in the moment. What's hitting the hardest. What is striking the proverbial chord. Whatever is making people feel. Not to mention, the history of the thing. Decades of hard-won wisdom and creativity all lost because you don't want to come off sounding "too folksy."

Clichéd as it may sound, I've always used music to get in touch with my emotions. I don't have a name for something until I hear it. The more I listen, the more feelings I have. The more feelings I have, the better a songwriter I become.

Sometimes it's the words, but not always. That's why

cover songs are so impactful. Nine Inch Nails' Trent Reznor wrote the song "Hurt" and it was fucking genius. But I didn't weep until I heard Johnny Cash's wizened baritone sing the lyrics. Eddie Vedder's "Just Breathe" is grunge perfection. It defines an era of grimy ballads. Still, it wasn't until Miley Cyrus sang the chorus that I fully felt the gutting pain of holding back.

Drake never understood any of this. It's like he sees making music as a multiple choice quiz when it's actually been an essay test the entire time.

Multidimensional, multifaceted, nuanced. Open to interpretation.

It's a shame he never took the time to figure it out. If he had, maybe he wouldn't be freaking the fuck out that my "cover" of "Jonesin'" has flown up the charts in the weeks since Arlo helped me lay it down all official like.

He wouldn't have teams of legal advisors combing through the online speculation about the extra verse. Wouldn't need to double and then triple down on his efforts to get me to sign away my cowriting rights weeks before the final decision on Best New Song nominations goes live.

If only he'd stopped at "Jonesin'."

I don't feel guilty anymore. After all, he brought this upon himself. I gave him plenty of notice. Too much, even.

But that doesn't mean I feel good about it. Knowing I'm the subject of so much outside conjecture about things between me and someone I used to call a friend is uncomfortable, to say the least. Also, I'm sleeping with his ex-fiancé. Sure, it was years ago that they were together, and he was the asshole who walked away, but it almost feels like

I've won the lottery out from under him, and when the rest of the world finds out, it's gonna look . . . complicated.

If there is one thing Lorelai and I have never been, it's complicated. Easy as Sunday morning, more like.

So it's a good thing I'm picking her up on my bike and taking her to this new place out of town and away from prying eyes. Not that there's anything for people to pry into aside from multiple (friendly) orgasms over the course of a few weeks and the nearly complete duet I wrote for her and Coolidge. Even if I wanted more, which, let's be clear, *I do,* that would definitely fall outside the purview of "friends with benefits."

Arlo gave me a sort of litmus test of what constitutes "FWB (friends with benefits)" behavior. It goes something like "If you met a woman in a bar and took her back to your place, would you then also . . ."

It's not a great test, honestly, because Lorelai and I have been close friends for a long time and we also live at the same address. So obviously we don't act like strangers in a bar, but Arlo's explanation was "maybe so, but you also don't *date* your friends, so that's where to draw the proverbial boundaries," and I'm trying to remain true to the spirit of the thing. Take tonight, for example. Yes, I am taking her out to dinner because *we already made plans* and need to eat anyway, so who cares if we do it together? But I'm taking her on the back of my bike, so it's not like we can hold hands or talk about our days or whatever. And the restaurant is a hole-in-the-wall barbecue joint. In fact, calling it a restaurant is even a stretch. More like a roadside stand with a couple of weathered picnic tables and plastic baskets full of wet naps. I would never take a real date there.

After, if we end up at my place or hers, and more orgasms ensue, great. Fine. Excellent. I'm not *planning* on it, though.

LORELAI: What is the dress code for tonight?

I bite back a sigh and make a mental note to have Arlo explain his litmus test to Lorelai.

CRAIG: I'm picking you up on the bike. So whatever that means.
LORELAI: I was hoping you'd say that. The shortest skirt I own, then.

I can't tell if she's kidding, so I let it go.

CRAIG: And before you ask, we're just getting BBQ. Nothing fancy.
LORELAI: At that little shack outside town you keep going on about? FINALLY. I've been waiting for-the-fuck-ever for you to take me!
LORELAI: Speaking of taking me . . . I have this fantasy about you, me, and that bike and a deserted back road . . .

I groan, dropping my phone on my desk and burying my face in my hands, working to dispel the image that's instantaneously and inconveniently branded on my brain.

"Everything okay, boss?"

I scoot closer to my desk, making sure any evidence of my reaction to her text is hidden, but Arlo is already sauntering over to the incriminating phone still lit with her message.

"I'm gonna need to you to explain your litmus test to Lorelai. She seems blurry on the details."

Arlo's reach halts inches from the phone and he throws his head back with a whoop of ringing laughter. "I'll schedule her in for a one-on-one next time she's in to record."

. . .

Just before I'm about to leave for the day, my Mac pings with an alert that I've received an email from the agent of the pop princess looking to go country whom I've been in the early contract stages with. She's decided to pull out over "a difference of visions," but attached to the email is an article from some industry insider magazine reporting on Lorelai's "disastrous" (their words, not mine) apology tour that wasn't.

I skim through the article, out of morbid curiosity, but it's the same old shit-for-brains nonsense as all the others. I read the email again, gauging my response. Honestly, I'm not surprised, nor am I really that upset. I mean, I don't want to lose business, especially only a few years in, but I get it. If she was trying to make the transition to pop, it might be different, but if she's trying to get on the good side of the industry and worm her way in, aligning with On the Floor Records is probably not the way to do it.

"Knock knock!"

I look up and see Lorelai in a tiny flowy skirt, a denim jacket, and her cowboy boots. "Hey, gorgeous . . . er, *friend*."

She raises an eyebrow, amused. "You okay?"

I close the lid of my laptop with a slap and get to my feet, stretching. "Yeah. Long day, but I'm much better now," I assure her. "Let me just grab my helmet. Did you walk?"

Lorelai holds up her helmet that I somehow missed. "Yeah. I didn't get my run in this morning, so I took a meandering stroll."

"Hey, boss, did you see that email from Star Olympia's agent? Can't say I'm shocked they backed out, but that commission would have been—" Arlo's voice echoes through the hallway until he leans around the doorjamb. "Oh. Hey, Lorelai! I didn't realize you were here."

"I let myself in. You looked busy. What's this about Star Olympia?"

I wave a hand, purposely casual while throwing Arlo a meaningful look. He takes my cue and blows a loud raspberry. "Eh. Nothing. She was maybe considering recording a country album with us, but honestly, it was barely a thing. You know pop stars. Flighty as fuck. Good riddance if you ask me. Who wants 'em or their money. Not us!"

Okay, so he might have laid it on a little too thick. I throw him an exasperated glare before Lorelai turns to me, looking worried. "She backed out?"

"No. She never had a contract. We met once to consult." After which she was ready to sign the papers and hand us total control, but I figure that part's best kept to myself. I grab my helmet and start to shuffle everyone toward the door. The sooner we get to my bike, the sooner it will be too loud for Lorelai to ask me any more probing questions.

"It was because of me, wasn't it?"

"No, darlin'. It was because of me."

"Huck. It's because you're working with *me*."

"Can you lock up behind us, Arlo?"

"For sure. Have fun, you two!"

We make it out the door and around the back of the building, where I'd parked my bike in the shade earlier this morning. I straddle the bike and look expectantly over my shoulder at Lorelai. "I don't have a sidecar, Jones. You're gonna have to hop on and hold tight."

She presses her lips together and I know she wants to ask me more questions but there's no point. I'm more stubborn than she is. Eventually she relents, pulling her helmet on and getting on behind me. She wraps her arms around my waist extra tight and we get out of town.

. . .

One of the perks of not dating, I suppose, is that no one feels the need to wait for romance and flowers and soft music to get naked. No arbitrary third-date deadline to keep things proper. Just sex. When you stop by her place to drop off work and she's dressed for a run and you suddenly realize you have a previously unexplored interest in the slippery thin material of athletic wear, sex. When you're pulling together an album at work, and she comments on the convenient height of your desk and how hot you look in reading glasses, sex. When you watch the video of her telling off the douchey radio deejay for the fifteenth time and need her to know how amazing she is, sex. When she sends a quick "hopping in the shower" text followed by "left my front door unlocked better hurry before someone kidnaps me," shower sex.

And when you're cruising on your motorcycle, her and your stomachs full of Nashville hot chicken and the "best slaw this side of the Smokies," and your friend eagerly sticks her hand down your pants, practically causing you to crash said motorcycle into a tree before you safely park down a deserted dirt road, pull her onto your lap, roll on a conveniently packed condom, tug her panties to the side and plunge so deep inside of her that you're pretty sure you'll never stop seeing stars . . . well, motorcycle sex.

I'll be honest, sitting here, still mostly dressed, clutching my beautiful, sexy, wrung-out friend against me, slowly smoothing my hands up and down her muscular thighs (because of course she really did wear her shortest skirt on our non-date) and listening to the sound of our heartbeats making a thudding return back to normal . . . I can't say I'm not enjoying this. Immensely.

And in these moments, when we're connected in this way—as close as two people can possibly be—it's almost enough. She's with me and I'm with her. That's all that should matter. Anything else is over the top.

But then I press a kiss to the space where her long neck and shoulder touch and we reluctantly pull apart. The connection is broken and that's all it was: a meeting of bodies. A temporary link. Shared air, and now that we're apart and she's adjusted her straps and I've zipped up my pants, the air is only air.

25

....

CRAIG

YOU AND TEQUILA

Thirty minutes later, the sun is starting to slip in the sky when I pull up to our place and cut the engine. Lorelai unfolds herself from the back of the bike and turns to where I haven't moved yet. I tug off my helmet and hold it in front of me but stay on the bike.

"Nightcap?" She bites her lip.

"I better not."

Lorelai's eye flash with obvious hurt and I bite my tongue from saying what I really want, which is "I brought my toothbrush, how about you just give me a drawer?"

"Yeah. You're right," she says instead. "If anyone saw . . ."

"Christ, Lore. You know I don't care about that."

"You should," she insists hotly. "I'm poison. Drake's a—"

"Fucking idiot," I snap, exasperated. "Don't you finish that thought."

She ignores the warning in my tone and shifts her weight,

looking like she's itching for a fight, which is crazy. Lorelai and I never fight.

"You're the idiot. It's like you don't even care about your business, attaching yourself to me. I'm poison in this town, and you know it."

What is happening?

I get off the bike and reach for her arm, tugging her to her steps and holding out my hand for the key. She narrows her eyes at me and slaps them in my palm.

Once I unlock the door, I lead her inside and shut it behind us. "What are you even talking about?"

"You! You're constantly putting other people ahead of yourself. First Drake and then your clients and your family! Even me! I can't let you do this anymore."

At once, I feel light-headed. "Let me do what exactly? Record your music? Make your albums? Or is this about the sex?"

"I never said anything about the sex," she huffs, and I want to strangle something. Instead, I walk her back until she's against the door. I put my hands on either side of her, close, but not touching. I lean forward until her lips are centimeters from my own.

"Of course not. Because this." I flex my hips against her, knowing I'm hard as a rock, despite the acrobatic motorcycle sex only a half hour ago. Her breath hitches and I do my best to look unaffected. "This is casual, right? Just fuck buddies. So if I'm understanding this right, you don't think I should produce you, but I can *fuck you* whenever I want." The words taste bitter and crass on my tongue. It's not like that. For me, it's never been like that, but maybe for her it has been?

"I'm saying your reputation will suffer by being seen with me."

My voice strangles in my throat. It's like she doesn't even know me. "How many different ways do I have to tell you I don't care?"

Lorelai's fingers trace delicate patterns into my collarbone beneath my T-shirt. "You should care."

I can't help it. I'm fucking hurt. I knew this was casual to her and I went along with it, but I thought she at least knew where I stood in our friendship. I thought she knew I wasn't like Drake. That I didn't care about the same stupid shallow bullshit. That I love her.

I know I haven't said it, but hell. It's written all over my face and every fucking thing I do.

I step back and Lorelai's hand remains extended between us. This time she's grasping for air.

"I can't do this. I'm sorry. I thought I could, but it turns out, I'm not built for casual."

Her fine dark brows draw together. "I understand, but . . ."—she steps into my space and presses her body to mine—"that doesn't mean this can't . . ."

"You're not hearing me. I'm talking about this." I gesture between our bodies, my straining erection, her flushed skin. "I can't do casual between *us*. I'll still produce you. You're incredible and it kills me that you don't see what I see. Your potential. Your gift." I release a harsh breath, putting another step between us, my heavy boots thudding in the silent house. "You better be at the studio bright and early tomorrow. But the sex. It has to stop."

"But it's been so good. I know I'm not alone in this, Huck. We're perfect together."

I reach for the door and nod, feeling like a sap, running out before I change my mind and rip her clothes off, throw her on the bed, and make her come on my tongue.

I lift a shoulder and speak at the wood grain in front of me. "I know we are. I'll see you tomorrow. We can do this, Jones. We've slept together and gone back to being friends before. It'll be just like last time."

And then I walk out the door and get on my bike and ride away, because there's no way I can stay under the same roof as her right now.

. . .

Two days later, and Lorelai hasn't shown up in the studio. I know she's in town. Her car is out in front of our place, and as far as I can tell, it hasn't moved. I heard her shower kick on last night.

So she's avoiding me.

I let it go yesterday because honestly, we both needed the space and I needed a day to lick my wounds. I know it's ultimately my own damn fault. Doesn't mean I'm not mad about it.

But she didn't turn up today, either, and that won't do. I'm not about to let what happened between us derail her comeback. We can be professionals. *I* can be a professional.

When I get home, I don't even bother with my place. I knock on her door. I wait, listening. Nothing. I knock again, louder this time.

"Lorelai," I say loudly. "Answer your door, Jones."

No answer. I dial her number. It rings, but I don't hear her pick up.

Fear turns my blood to ice. What if something happened? What if she didn't lock her door and someone came in and . . .

The door swings open.

"Thank God . . . Shit, are you okay?"

Lorelai doesn't answer, just leaves the door open behind her and shuffles listlessly toward her couch, where she collapses on the cushions, curling on her side. I follow her, closing the door and taking in the scene. The TV is on some vampire movie, but it's on mute and she's buried herself under the oversize comforter from her bed. The window shades are pulled, and it's dim as night in here.

Oh no.

"The Nashville chicken?"

She nods. "Must have been. Or the fryer. I checked the website when I got home. It said GF, but the fine print was 'gluten friendly,' not 'gluten free.'"

I move to squat in front of her. "What the fuck? I'm gonna call them."

She winces and I lower my voice. "Sorry." Up close I can see the dark circles under her eyes and the gray pallor of her skin. Her brows are drawn tight, a clear sign that she's in pain, and I sigh.

Lorelai was diagnosed celiac about six months ago, and her doctors told her the longer and more strictly she avoided gluten and dairy, the more sensitive she would be to contamination. Gluten friendly wouldn't be enough. Not for her.

This is my fault. I read the site ahead of time, but I didn't read carefully enough.

"Hell, Lore. This is my fault."

Her expression is dazed, but she manages to roll her eyes.

"Okay," I whisper, standing and removing my jacket, hanging it over by the door and rolling up my sleeves. "First things first." I walk into her kitchen and fill a kettle with water, setting it on the stove to boil. I grab over-the-counter pain meds from the cabinet and a bottle of water from her fridge and make my way back to her.

"Migraine?"

She nods and I shake out two pills.

"How about your back?"

"On fire," she croaks.

I shake out a third and pass them to her along with the water bottle. "Start with these."

She takes them and puts the water bottle on the floor before slipping down onto the couch.

"When was the last time you ate?"

She shakes her head. "Can't keep anything in me."

The kettle screeches and I rush to turn off the flame. I pull out a little plastic bag of peppermint tea Lorelai got for her migraines and pour the boiling water over it to steep. After a few minutes, I nudge her.

"You need more fluids. This will help. I'm gonna run out, and by the time I get back, you need to drink this whole cup."

She blinks but doesn't argue, and I stifle the guilt roiling in my gut before leaving her alone on the couch. Once I get outside and clear of the door, I curse, swinging uselessly at a low-hanging tree branch and startling a neighbor. I ignore her tsks

---

and fling open the garage door with a loud bang before climbing on my bike and revving the engine louder than necessary.

You fucking idiot. Thinking you were giving her space because she was upset over you cutting her off and instead she's in incredible pain. Such an asshole. God.

Five minutes later, I'm marching through the automatic doors of the grocery store and grabbing a basket. I fill it with essentials: blue Gatorade, hot water bottles, Epsom salts, several cans of gluten-free chicken soup, Ben & Jerry's dairy-free Cherry Garcia because even when she doesn't feel up to keeping anything down, Lorelai wants ice cream.

I text Arlo from the checkout line.

LORELAI GLUTENED. I'LL BE OUT TOMORROW.

He responded before I even got the items on the belt.

GIVE HER A GENTLE HUG FROM ME AND DR. JOSH. BTW DR. JOSH SAYS START WITH BONE BROTH.

"Shit," I curse under my breath and turn to the elderly woman behind me in line. "Can you watch this for a second? I just need to grab something else real quick."

She smiles knowingly. "First time with a sick wife at home?"

I don't correct her. "Yeah."

• • •

I return with my spoils and don't bother knocking, unlocking the door with my master key. "I'm back, Lore. Got you ice cream."

"Cherry Garcia?" she asks from her pile of blankets.

"You know it."

I put away the groceries, filling the kettle again, and start up some bone broth in a pot. I pour boiling water into the hot water bottles and put the soup in a large bowl on a tray before walking it over to her couch.

"Okay, Princess and the Pea," I tease gently, using the nickname she gave herself after realizing how tender her body would get from glutening. Even her skin aches. "It's time to feel better. I need you to sit up, though."

Lorelai rises with a wince and adjusts herself on the cushion. When she's settled, I place the hot water bottles behind the small of her back and around each hip. Her eyes close with relief. "Thank you. I know it's still hot outside, but it cannot get warm enough in here for my bones."

"Which is why," I say with a grin, passing her the soup, "I'm gonna run you a hot bath with some Epsom salts next."

"I don't have any—"

"It's okay. I bought some. I read an article about Epsom salts a little while ago. A bath with them will help soothe your muscles. I know it's your bones that ache, but lying there all tense like you are is hard on your muscles, too. Besides, the warmth will help."

She blinks, her expression unreadable. I can't tell if that's because she thinks I'm being nosy and overbearing or if it's the gluten. Both, probably.

"Bone broth," I tell her once she takes a sip of her soup. "Dr. Josh suggested you start with it."

Lorelai takes a few more sips before putting down her spoon. "You told Dr. Josh?"

"I told Arlo," I clarify. "Because I'm not coming in tomorrow. He told Josh."

She pauses mid-sip. "What? You can't miss work. I'm fine."

"First of all, I'm the boss. I can do whatever the fuck I want. Second, you're not fine. You look like hell. Third, this . . ."—I gesture to her listless form, hunched over on the couch—"is my fault. I'm the one who didn't research the barbecue stand carefully enough."

Her eyebrows scrunch together. "Huckleberry," she says softly, "you can't fight all my battles for me."

I bite down on a response, because I know she's not just talking about gluten. And because if she let me, I'd never let her fight another battle alone for the rest of her life.

. . .

After running her a bath, I get to work straightening out Lorelai's bed with fresh sheets and her trusty comforter. I refill her hot water bottles and place her pain meds and a glass of room-temperature water on her nightstand. My gaze snags on a picture there and I lift it to my face. It's an old one. From when Lorelai was still the darling of country music and I was still playing backup with Drake. It's of the two of us. My hair is long and shaggy and my hands are in my pockets. Lorelai has her arms flung around my shoulders and she's pressing a kiss to my flushed cheek. Honestly, we might have been a little stoned in this picture or maybe drunk.

Or maybe we were just us. Two happy idiots before fame complicated everything. I put the frame back down and make my way over to Lorelai's dresser, digging out a pair of flannel pants, an old tee, and a pair of fleecy socks and completely ignoring the top drawer where I know she keeps her lingerie.

Not today.

Then I remember our argument.

Not ever.

I hear the telltale sound of Lorelai getting out of the tub and I lay the clothes on her bed with a handwritten note telling her I'll be back in the morning before ducking out and climbing the stairs to my apartment. A few minutes later, I flop on my bed, fully clothed, alone except for my asshole cat, Waylon, who gives me a death glare.

"Yeah, buddy," I mumble as he turns and starts licking his butt on my duvet. "I'm mad at me, too."

26

LORELAI

WE'RE NOT FRIENDS

A week after Huck ended things, then did an abrupt turn and took care of glutened-me for two days straight, navigating the biggest emotional minefield between us to date, I get a text from my new friend Annie Mathers inviting me out. She asked me to join her at a tiny little-known bar way off the main Nashville drag to watch Coolidge and the gang play.

I feel kind of weird because the group is quite a bit younger than me, but also I could use a friend in town and who am I to be picky? I am quite literally at their disposal. I have one best friend here and I could swim laps in the mixed signals and wrong turns between us. We've been back in the studio the last few days, and when we're there, wrapped in song notes and speaking lyrics, things between Huck and me are the same as ever, but outside? Things are extra strained. I know we slept together years ago and were able to remain friends after, but this feels different. It wasn't just a tipsy one-night stand. It was weeks of hooking up in every way imaginable. And also unimaginable ways. Just so many *ways*.

We know too much.

If I'm honest, and full disclosure I'm not being honest with anyone right now because it fucking sucks . . . this thing between us? Didn't ever really feel casual. And my whole plan of guarding my heart by insisting it *be* casual backfired spectacularly because apparently hearts don't take directions well. Hearts just do whatever the fuck they feel like, and mine felt like loving Huck.

And now that's done. So bravo, Heart, you bitch.

At eight o'clock, I'm locking the door behind me and slipping out in my favorite ripped jeans, tee, and baseball cap, tucking my keys and phone in my back pocket. I'm not hiding, but my name finally stopped trending on Twitter, and after all the hard work and energy Craig and Arlo put into my album this week, I don't want to blow it up by reminding everyone I'm still in town. They can't afford to lose any more contracts.

Another point of contention to add to the pile.

I arrive at the bar and spot Annie's famously wild golden-brown curls in a booth near the very front, along with a statuesque blonde and a small-framed dark-haired woman who looks familiar. Without making eye contact with anyone else, I make a beeline for their booth and sink into the open seat before beaming up at the trio.

"Lorelai!" Annie shouts, her sweet-as-pie megawatt smile on full display as she throws her arms around my neck. I hug her, a relieved laugh caught in my throat, already feeling every eye in the entire bar on us.

"Hey, girl," I say, pulling back, "thanks for the invite. I'm Lorelai Jones," I say, holding out my hand to the dark-haired woman. Her grip is strong, and one glance at her cut arms in her stylish tank confirms my suspicions just as she's saying her name.

"Kacey Rosewood."

I nod at Annie's cousin and fiddler, feeling a little starstruck. "I'm a massive fan. You're so fucking talented."

"More talented than my husband?" She quirks a nod toward the stage, where Fitz Jacoby is accompanying Jefferson. Tonight he's on the fiddle, and he's of course dazzling. Even still, Kacey Rosewood is a prodigy, and I'm not ashamed to admit I'm inclined to root for my fellow females in a male-dominated industry.

"I'm biased, but obviously, yes."

She laughs, dark eyes sparkling. "Fair enough."

"Trina Hamilton," the blonde says, her hand extended, her matte lips pressed in a firm line. "I manage Coolidge."

"Oh!" I say, startled. "Um." My eyes dart to Annie and I lower my voice. "Is it okay that I'm here?"

Annie's brow furrows over the rim of her drink. "Of course. Why wouldn't it be?"

"Well, I don't know if you heard my interview—"

"Fucking idiots," Trina cuts in, pretending to swat at a particularly stupid mosquito.

"Which ones?"

"All of 'em," she scoffs. "Jennifer Blake, to start. Putting you in front of the fucking firing squad with nothing but a piece of tinfoil over your heart. Christ. What on earth were you even doing there?"

"Apology tour? I guess? Doesn't matter. I fired her," I say quickly.

Trina's eyes flash with approval, and despite being a grown woman who kicks ass on a regular basis, I immediately warm. She reaches her manicured hand for mine, and with her other, motions for a drink. A server approaches and faster than I can blink, I'm ordering a G and T and scooting closer to the trio in the booth.

"Listen, Lorelai," Trina says in a low drawl, "you were young, you were angry, and you used the platform they gave you, and when you did, they got their dicks in a Celtic knot."

I choke on air, skeptical. "You don't think I was in the wrong?"

She rolls her eyes. "Christ, Neil Young? There are a thousand other songs I would have chosen over 'Ohio' to get your point across." Annie snorts into her glass with a rattle of the cubes and exchanges glances with her smirking cousin. When Trina levels her with a look, she lets out a full-bellied laugh.

"Sorry, Trina, but you say that like Neil Young isn't a legend of protest rock and therefore a brilliant choice for actual protesting."

"Neverthe*fucking*less, there were better ways to do what you did, and shame on your management for not supporting you."

I'm so shocked by her enthusiastic defense, any response evaporates straight out of my brain, so I just nod my thanks and take a grateful pull from my newly arrived gin and tonic.

"Well, Trina would know," Kacey says with a secretive grin. "She's been supporting those idiots up there for the last half a decade."

"And the Lord knows how they try me," the older woman mumbles under her breath, but it's softened by the proud way she watches the three men on stage.

The music is excellent, and it feels good to be around other female artists. It's not that Shelby and Maren aren't incredible women. They're the actual best. But there's something about being around women who get it. Get *this*. This overwhelming urge to perform and put yourself out there time and again. Why I can't just give it up and go back to teaching. Why I want this so fucking much.

I eventually let Trina buy me another drink, this time a double, and start to relax. Before I know it, our table's collected a number of empty glasses and bottles. By the time Coolidge takes a break, we shuffle around to make room for the three men.

"No Boseman tonight?"

Annie answers for me. "Ladies' night. I only invited Lorelai." She looks at me. "I didn't even think. Is that okay? Do you want to call him up?"

"Totally okay. I needed a ladies' night in a bad way."

"Craig Boseman?" Trina asks idly.

"Yeah—" I start to answer, but Fitz chimes in.

"Talk about a power couple, right?"

"Oh, well." I can feel my cheeks warm. Damn gin. "We're not actually—"

"There he is!"

Coolidge grins apologetically at Annie and then at the rest of us. "I texted him earlier. Sorry. Didn't get the memo about ladies' night."

We all turn, and I try not to stare as Huck weaves through the crowd, making his way over to us. He's dressed in well-worn jeans that hug his glorious hips and a faded Tom Petty T-shirt. A perfectly normal pair of clothes. Underdressed for a bar, even.

So why am I sweating? Probably just the lingering effects of my glutening.

His eyes meet mine across the sea of people and his lips curl in the smallest grin only for me and I cross my legs, squeezing them together and taking a long, fortifying sip from my straw. He saunters up and is shaking hands with the men and Trina when Annie jumps up and gives his cheek a loud smacking kiss before swiping at her eyes.

"I'm sorry, it's just that I'm so happy you're working with Jefferson."

Coolidge shakes his head as if she's the most adorable thing he's ever seen, and honestly she might be.

"Sorry, Boseman," Jefferson apologizes with an easy, loping smile. "She's not much of a drinker, so when she does let loose, she turns into a giant sap. The first time we drank together, she basically adopted me. No getting away now."

Huck laughs low, settling into the back of the booth, his shoulder brushing mine and sending a frisson of awareness along my skin. My heart gives a throb in my chest and I take a sip from my glass, the ice clinking clumsily against my lips. His eyes dart toward me and away before he turns to Coolidge, who is waving a server over.

Jason starts showing them something on his phone and Huck takes the opportunity to lean close and whisper in my ear. I ignore the way his breath electrifies my skin. "Is it okay that I'm here?"

"Yes!" I blurt before softening my voice to match his. "Annie invited me," I explain unnecessarily.

His eyes flash with humor before zeroing in on my mouth, and he's so close I can practically taste his toothpaste on my tongue, and I can't really breathe. I feel like I might pass out. Or spontaneously orgasm. Or both.

It's been like this all week. Well, once I got over feeling like death. Even then, it's hard to ignore a guy who runs you regular hot baths. For me anyway. Huck appears unfairly unaffected.

"Another round for the table!" Kacey suggests, interrupting our staring contest.

We get our drinks, and everyone is talking over one another, laughing and teasing, and it's clear these two bands and Trina are close. I try not to think about how much fucking talent is sitting around this table right now and how much attention we have to be attracting by default.

"'Independence Day,' Martina McBride," Huck says, raising his brow in a familiar challenge, and I grin, taking a steadying breath and feeling the world around us right itself ever so slightly.

"'The Night the Lights Went Out in Georgia,'" I counter.

"What's this?" Coolidge asks.

"It's an ongoing game Lore and I have played for what? A decade?"

"Roughly, sure. One of us will name a song and the other has to name a better song until we agree on the best one of the bunch. It's kind of an honor system, really. I mean. You can't just be like, 'Achy Breaky Heart,' when everyone knows that's a terrible song. Anyway, stop stalling, Huckleberry."

"How about we make it interesting?" He smirks.

"Ooh! A bet!" Annie cries out gleefully.

"Like what?" I ask, bemused. We've never done a wager before.

"If you win, I have to get up there and sing."

"Done," I say, without hesitation.

"And if I win, *you* have to."

I hesitate for a beat, only because I don't know if I am up to hearing the inevitable boos tonight, but I'm positive I'll win.

"Fine. Stop stalling and give me your next song."

"'Fancy,' Reba."

A chorus of *Oooooooohs* breaks out around the table. For good reason. "Fancy." Fuck.

I scramble my brain for something similar. "'Ol' Red,' Blake Shelton."

"'The Devil Went Down to Georgia.'"

My jaw drops, because like the devil, I know that I've been beat. Huck knows it, too, from the glint in his eye. He remembers I was raised on Charlie Daniels and I've forgotten. Alas, I'm honor bound to cave.

"That was sneaky, Boseman."

He folds his arms over Tom Petty, inordinately pleased with himself. "All's fair, Jones. What're you gonna sing?"

"A cappella?" My stomach flutters with nerves. I mean, I can do it but . . .

"With a full band," Annie pipes up. "Or at least a fiddle player and a backup singer."

"I know just the song. I've been practicing the strings in 'Toxic,'" Kacey says, getting to her feet. "How are you with Britney Spears?"

I'm so touched I could cry. I mean, obviously *won't*, but my smile is full-blown. I don't know what I did to deserve the loyalty of these insanely talented people, but I'm not gonna question it tonight.

"I fucking love Britney. Let's do it."

27

LORELAI

FOLLOW YOUR ARROW

Minutes later, we're situated on the small stage and Jefferson is introducing us. "Esteemed patrons! We're gonna have a special treat tonight because these three exceptionally fine ladies who shall remain nameless, but I'm betting you'll recognize, have, well, not prepared per se, but are gonna perform a little ditty for us anyway. So put your hands together for . . ."

Annie stage-whispers from behind me, "Neil Young's Bitches!"

"NEIL YOUNG'S BITCHES."

With that, Jefferson jumps off the stage to join the rest of the guys and Trina at the table and I remove the mic from the stand, thanking the good lord I drank that third gin and tonic.

One gin to remember, two to forget, three to sing Britney like your heart depends on it.

Kacey drags her bow across the strings with a powerful motion, somehow pulling out the very familiar melody. I let her go a few counts. Long enough that the rowdy crowd starts clapping and stomping along with me and Annie, giving us a nice little backbeat to work off of.

I lift the mic and strike a sensual pose before allowing my mouth to fall open, and then I sing the first line to uproarious applause. By the time we've made it to the familiar chorus, Annie and I are both center stage swerving our hips and channeling our inner pop stars. If pop stars had souls made out of three chords and the truth twisted with twine. Really the star of the show is Kacey and her biceps.

I've nearly made it to the end, the final repetitious chorus, and the adrenaline is starting to wear off a little, but that's when all my earthly focus narrows to a single point. One man and a wolf whistle piercing the air. He sustains me.

The entire bar is on their feet when we strike our final pose and take our bows before dragging Kacey to the forefront and clapping. She jumps off the stage onto Fitz's back and we make it to our table amidst the glow of smartphones and cheers.

Even still . . .

I try to hold on to the fizzy, happy feelings of being onstage and performing to a rambunctious crowd, but it's tricky. Like trying to hold on to bubbles: the ones that don't burst immediately float away until you can't follow them any longer and you're left empty-handed with soapy fingers.

Even after I was canceled from country music, I never actually believed that was it for me. That I was done. In my heart, I knew I had more to give and I'd be back, and things would eventually right themselves once more.

But hope is hard to come by these days and . . . I don't

know. Maybe that *was* it for me. Maybe Craig was right when he said what happened to me paved the way for today's young artists. But that doesn't mean I get to make a return. It just means I was a cog in the collective efforts. A valuable piece, even, but the patent's expired and I have a classroom waiting for me in Michigan.

"Uh-oh. What are you thinking?" He's looking at me, his blue eyes narrowed, and it's as though everyone else fades away.

I sigh and my voice is soft, but I know he hears me. "What if this is it, Huckleberry? What if this is all I get?"

He shakes his head. "It's not. This is only the beginning, Lorelai. We're just getting settled at the start."

I'm wrapped in strong arms and held for a long moment as his fingers smooth up and down my spine and my chin tucks into the pocket formed by his collarbone. I inhale his familiar scent and let my eyes fall shut and I'm struck with the insane thought, in this devastating moment, that despite all of it, this *could* be enough. Being held by this man is enough.

The moment ends when someone accidentally knocks into us and Craig steers us toward our booth. We scoot inside and I ask a server for an ice water and run my hands down my jeans, feeling off-center.

The questions, the revelations, the rise and fall of adrenaline. The gin and tonics from earlier slosh in my gut and I wonder if I should go home. But Annie and Kasey are fired up after our performance, and Jefferson, Fitz, and Jason are heading up to the stage to finish their set. I shouldn't leave yet. Besides, what am I gonna do? Rush home so I can pretend not to listen to Huck move around his apartment while pretending not to check social media for what bullshit people are saying about me today?

Trina leans in. "You said before that you fired Jennifer—"

Huck raises his beer. "Thank God."

Trina smirks in agreement. "I like him," she says to me, and then to him she adds, "I don't like most people in this town, but you, I like."

He tips his bottle against hers. "Cheers, Hamilton."

"Anyway, as I was saying, you fired Jennifer. So presumably you're without representation currently. Is that correct?"

I frown. "Well, yeah. But I figure at this point no rep is better than a shitty rep and Huck's been helping me to reinvent—"

"You misunderstand," Trina cuts me off. "That wasn't me judging you. That was me offering you representation."

My jaw drops open and my brain flip-flops for the third time in an hour. "Are you serious? That's a terrible idea. I'm a fucking shit show."

"What? You are not! You're incredible," Annie breaks in. "That's an awesome idea!"

"I'm basically a pariah in this town—"

Craig's warm fingers reach out and cover my lips, and as out of control as this all is right now, I still fight the urge to lick him.

"Stop talking the nice agent out of representing you."

Trina waves him off. "Look, Lorelai, I'm no stranger to tough cases, but I know what I like, and I like what I see in you. You've got stage presence, you're down-to-earth, your range is sultry and sweet, and you have a good head on your shoulders. You also come with a built-in fan base and a record producer who knows his way around lyrics and composition."

"Trina." I try to instill reason. "Let's be real. I'm more than a tough case. This town hates me."

"Bullshit. From what I saw, they love you."

"Here, at a bar, sure. But radio and record companies? Square just canceled on me, and as of last week, my name was still trending on Twitter, and not in a good way."

Trina presses forward, tapping the table with her long red fingernails. "Okay, I'm gonna be real transparent with you. Annie didn't invite me along tonight."

Annie starts to protest, and Trina rolls her eyes. "Yes, yes, I know I'm always invited, but honestly, you kids exhaust me most of the time. Anyway, she mentioned she was inviting you and I tagged along because I've been following your career since you first hit the scene, a cute little southern belle with terrible highlights. I wanted to meet you and see what you were like. I've long suspected you were impressive, and you've proven it tonight."

"God," I groan. "I wouldn't have drunk so much. I'm acting like a twenty-something. No offense," I say to Mathers.

"None taken!" she replies cheerfully.

Trina scoffs. "Fuck's sake, Jones, I bought your drinks. I have no interest in polish. I just want to know you're the real deal, and everything I saw tonight proves that. You don't have to tell me right now. Go home, sober up, talk to whoever you need to talk to," she says, obviously eyeing Craig, "and get back to me." She passes me a business card.

I take the card and immediately slip it in my pocket. "I will. Thank you."

. . .

Oops! She Does It Again!

By Alice Britton

Oh, what company they keep! Spotted this weekend at a downtown club in Nashville, country music's most infamous former starlet, Lorelai Jones, drinking cocktails with none other than country music's darling, Annie Mathers, while the pair watched Jefferson Coolidge (né Clay Coolidge) play a set on stage. While it's unclear whether the pair of crooners were trading industry secrets or kisses, they did surprise the busy Saturday evening crowds with a last-minute rendition of Britney Spears's "Toxic," even, one insider shares, calling themselves Neil Young's Bitches, no doubt a tongue-in-cheek reference to Jones's fall from grace after singing Mr. Young's "Ohio" some years . . . (cont.)

Comments (2354)

chickenLIL I was there! Their performance of "Toxic" was brilliant and I'm pretty sure Annie Mathers is dating Jefferson Coolidge still, NOT Lorelai Jones. Though I would love that.

Fabriceducation Free Lorelai!

LlamaLlamaMelodrama Wonder where Drake Colter was?

JesusISourLordandSavior Repent, sinners!

SharkWeekIsMyFave My cousin was there and he said Lorelai was seen hugging Craig Boseman.

ChestertheInvestor I was today years old when I realized "Jonesin'" was written by Craig Boseman and not Drake Colter and now Boseman and Jones are being seen together?!

JunieB Not only that, I heard he's producing her next record . . .

MusicFirst Promote this @jaslkn45

28

CRAIG

ALL I SEE IS YOU

We finish recording Lorelai's album, titled *Avalanche*, late Wednesday night. One of the hottest nights of the summer so far. It's a whopping sixteen songs, but there was a method to my madness. We recorded twelve new tracks, almost all written by Lorelai or at very least cowritten, as is the case with the duet we teased first that's being featured on both Lorelai's and Coolidge's "debuts." We also included a couple of popular stragglers, officially releasing them this time, as part of the entire collection of Lorelai's solo work, including "What They Have," which she wrote for Shelby and Cameron, and a rerecorded studio cut of "Ohio."

The way I figure, after a lengthy meeting with Lorelai and her new boss-manager Trina Hamilton, there are only two options forward if she wants to reinvent herself. One, the bullshit apology tour where she was forced to pretend she was someone she wasn't, who was sorry for something she wasn't sorry for. (The route exactly no one wanted to go down again.) Or two, embrace what happened, stand proud, and hold tight to your principles, then create a fucking brilliant piece of art that no one can argue against.

Honestly, it was the easiest album I've ever worked on. Even if I didn't miss the hell out of seeing her naked, I would still jump at the chance to record all her records. She's a professional through and through and primed and ready to take back what's been owed her.

I don't know if country music radio will accept her. They'd be fucking idiots not to, but that's out of my control. What I *do* know, with absolute certainty, is it won't matter in the end. Because everyone else will accept her.

. . .

I'm closing up the studio alone. Lorelai is headed to the airport to pick up Maren and I've already sent Arlo home for the night. He and Dr. Josh have started their prenatal parenting classes at the hospital so they can learn how to change diapers and . . . well. Other important stuff, I'm sure.

My phone rings and I grin, answering right away. "Hey, D, what's up?"

My nephew hedges, "Nothing much. Just felt like calling to say hi."

I turn off the lights to the studio and lock the door behind me before heading for my still-lit office at the end of the hall. "Everything okay? You sound a little down tonight. Too much Fortnite?"

"Maybe. I'm bored."

I bite back a snort. Oh, to be bored. What *that* must feel like.

"Ah. Let me guess. Your mom told you to hit me up for entertainment."

My sister's muffled voice in the background confirms it, but I don't mind.

"Kind of. I was watching this show on TV and they do pottery and stuff and Mom said you have a studio. I was thinking I wanted to try it and maybe you could teach me."

I sink into my chair and work to swallow around the tightness in my throat, a little baffled at my own reaction. Then again, wasn't this exactly how I was twenty-five years ago? Calling up my great-uncle and begging to go out to the cabin with him? It was about art, sure. But it was also about wanting to spend time with a man I admired. Besides, what I lacked in pottery skills I made up for in fishing, and Uncle Huck never cared.

Fucking a. I swipe at damp eyes and clear my throat. Hell, it's been a long month.

"Yeah, D. I do. It's pretty rustic out there, though. Like camping, basically. You sure you don't want to try a nicer place in the city?"

"Um. Well. I guess I don't care, but I don't mind camping," he offers, sounding excited. "That could be fun."

"Okay then, I'd love that. Let me check my schedule for the next couple of weekends and I'll call up your mom to let her know I'm kidnapping you."

"Okay, but just us, though, right? No girls."

This time I snort aloud. Preach it, kid. "No girls, my

dude. And no moms," I clarify, just in case. "Just us and the kiln and the lake and the bears."

"Are there bears?"

"Only if we're really lucky."

"Thanks, Uncle Craig."

Christ. It's like my throat is swelling up. I swallow hard and clear it once more. "You got it, buddy. Thanks for asking. I can't wait."

I hang up the phone and drop it on my desk, shaking my head and staring at my calendar. The next few weeks are pretty busy and I'll have to rearrange some stuff, but I'll figure it out. My sister is an amazing single mom who's raised a household full of respectful and smart kids. But D's the youngest by a lot, just like me, and the only boy. He's probably getting to the age where he's going to need a masculine presence in his life for some things.

I should step up more. Prioritize him.

A knock startles me out of my reverie and I look up to see Drake Colter standing at my door.

I sit back in my chair and gesture to the seat across from my desk. "I was wondering when you would show up. Figured if I ignored your lawyer's emails long enough, you'd find your way eventually."

"You won't sign off."

"Nope."

Drake presses his lips together and runs a hand through his glossy magazine-mussed hair, agitated. I'll tell you what. This guy's never been to Burl the Barber. "Are you gonna tell everyone about the other songs, too?"

I cross my arms over my chest and bounce lightly in my chair, letting it creak in the silence. "And what would I tell them exactly?"

Drake huffs impatiently, shifting in his seat. "Fuck off, Boseman. Are you going to out me or what?"

"Are you going to add my name to 'Best Worst Case'?" I counter.

"You know it's too late. The nominations are already up."

"Interesting how you sat on that for *months* until it was too late to add my name. I think I'll just wait and see how this all plays out. But I know one thing for sure. You won't be using any more of my songs after this. You're on your own now."

"I can't write. You know that. Not like you do." His jaw clenches and he narrows his eyes. "I'll pay you for them. I know you're writing for other people now. Lorelai and that fucker Coolidge . . ."

"I am."

"So write for me. I'll pay you. Give you full credit from this point on."

"No."

Drake sputters, leaning forward, his hands on my desk, and like several other times over the last few weeks, I try valiantly not to think of the way Lorelai looked, bare naked and spread out across it. The thought of his hands touching where her body had been—

"No," I repeat more firmly. "I'll be damned if I write one more word for you. You're an entitled bastard who takes everyone who cares about you for granted. Fuck that, I'm done," I spit out, slamming my fists on the desk and dislodging his. "You can write your own music or pay some other ass-hole to do it, and when the critics hear your new songs and speculate about how different they sound, or they question how your old songs sound like my new ones . . . and when they put two and two together that you're a fraud, *then I'll be paid*. And Lorelai will get paid, too. And you know what? Even Coolidge will get paid. And every other person you've kicked and stomped on and thrown off on your way up the ladder to where you are today."

"You're not suing me?" he asks, disbelieving.

I lean back into my chair, casual once more. "Not today."

"But will you?"

"I can't say for sure. Guess I'll see how things pan out in the future. The industry is fickle, as you well know, and I'd hate for something like a ruined reputation to bring you down after you've worked so hard. Wonder what that would even look like? Would your label drop you? Your friends? Your agent and team? Would they cancel *your* tours?"

He leans back in his chair with a sigh. "So this is about Lorelai, then? She get under your skin? You guys together?"

I shake my head, nonplussed. "This is about the way you treat people. Lorelai, sure. You fucked up big-time on that one. She wanted to marry you and you let her go." I shake my head, laughing humorlessly. "Which is just unreal to me. But I was actually talking about me. Which was always the problem. You kept forgetting about me. Disregarding the long hours I put in for *years* to help you get where you are. Writing your songs, playing in your band, smoothing things over with your fiancée and your family and the press and your agent and whoever the fuck else. Don't worry, *Boseman's got it.*

"Well, man." I spread my arms wide, grinning and gesturing to my little empire. "It's not a lot, but it's mine. Look around. I got it. And now I want you to get *the fuck* out of my studio."

. . .

After shaking off my encounter with Colter, I was too wired to go home to my empty apartment. Things with Lorelai have been a little warmer after finishing up the album, but they're still different. Awkward. With Maren in town, I figure it's best to let her have her space and spend time with her friend without my crashing their party.

So I head out on foot toward downtown. It's been a while since I wandered the streets of Nashville alone, taking in the sights and sounds. The smell. The intensity, desperation, and unrelenting hope of it all. No set direction. Just absorbing it into my pores and trying to remember where it all began for me. Why I'm still here, doing what I do, despite the bullshit.

I know I'm being immature when it comes to Drake and the songs. Petty, even. I should just sue him and put him out of his misery or sign the nondisclosure and put myself out of mine. I'm an adult and a businessman. But somehow, weighing both of those "more mature" options feels like caving into a part of myself I'm not interested in feeding. Signing the nondisclosure feels like bending over to Drake. Still. Again. Allowing him to use those songs to further himself. But suing him might feel worse. Initially, I didn't get into this industry for the credit. I avoided the fanfare, happy to play backup and write behind the scenes. Money and popularity were secondary to the art. I know more now, obviously. Of course you need money to survive. That's a nonstarter. And popularity might be secondary to art, but the more recognition, the more art you get to make. And I'm also aware of my privilege. I've inherited enough money to start my own label. It's easy to be like, "I'm in this for the art," when I don't need to worry about paying my electric bill. Which is sort of the point, I guess. That same privilege also means I don't *need* to seek out more money just to stick it to someone who used to be my friend. Choosing to do so would be simply for the principle of the thing, and that doesn't sit well with me.

It's convoluted, but my gut says I'm making the right choice by not making a choice at all. Maybe it's immature, or maybe it's a temporary stopgap that's gonna bite me in the ass cheek later. Probably will, but I have to live with myself in the meantime.

I eventually stop in one of the bars, order a beer, and sit on a patio at a small table by myself, watching the people passing by on the sidewalks and listening to the echoes of at least three different songs being played in three different open-air bars on this very corner. I'm nearing the bottom of my glass when a familiar face settles in the chair across from me.

"Ms. Hamilton," I say with a nod to the tall blonde.

"Please, call me Trina. Ms. Hamilton is what I make Coolidge and Jacoby call me when they piss me off. Craig, this is my wife, Melody." She gestures to a pretty redhead with bold glasses. "Mel, this is Craig Boseman, one of the most talented producers about town."

"Ha," I say. "Pleasure to meet you, Melody. That's an embarrassing exaggeration, Trina, but I'm not above flattery. Can I get you ladies a drink?"

Trina's already shaking her head, waving a server over. "Ordered at the bar and told them where to find us when I saw you out here. You alone tonight?"

I nod, taking a long sip from my glass and motioning for another. "Yeah. Had an unfortunate encounter with an old partner this evening and found I needed to decompress."

"Maybe he'd rather be alone, then, Trina—" Melody says with an apologetic smile.

"Nonsense," Trina says, waving off her wife before nailing me with a look. "Drake Colter's a fraud. You know it, I know it, everyone in this town ought to know it if they've been paying attention."

I shake my head. "You are an uncanny woman, Trina Hamilton."

"You don't get to where I am in life without picking up on a thing or two."

"Clearly," I mutter into my fresh beer before lifting it to my lips.

"So listen up close, because I don't dispense this wisdom on everyone . . ."

Her wife snickers and rolls her eyes in my direction. "She hasn't made it to Antarctica yet."

Trina ignores her, but her glossed lips twitch in amusement. "That song you wrote about Lorelai, 'Jonesin'"?" I splutter and she ignores me, plowing ahead. "What, that was a secret? Jesus fuck, Boseman, don't be embarrassing." I wave her on, coughing. She huffs, clacking her long, manicured nails on the table. "That song that you so very clearly wrote and that Drake Colter so very clearly stole and used to publicly court my client is number two on the charts as of today. Did you know that?"

I shake my head. The *Billboard* numbers dropped this afternoon and I've been a little preoccupied.

"You made your point real good, didn't you?" Trina says. "Unbelievably, I don't think you were even trying, but that's part of your charm, ain't it? You know what song is number one?"

I shake my head.

"The fucking duet."

I sink back into my chair. "No."

Trina grins. "Why the fuck do you think I'm out here with all these people? I'm celebrating. We have done the impossible and it's because of you."

"Have you told anyone yet?"

"Hell, I've told everyone. If you picked up your phone, you would probably know by now."

I check my phone and it's got a dead screen. "Battery died," I tell her. "That's, well—I'm not shocked. I knew when mainstream radio picked it up out of the gate it would do well. And Lorelai and Jefferson are . . ." I grin and Trina beams back.

"I know it. I told you. I can spot these things."

My head is spinning with the news. Holy hell, it's happening. "That's incredible. Thank you, Trina." I get to my feet, quickly downing the last of my beer and placing the empty glass on the table. "I should get. I need to charge my phone and I should call Arlo and tell him the news. And Lorelai . . ." I trail off, thinking.

"Of course." Trina's eyes are dancing with amusement as she holds out her hand. "Thank you, Craig. And congrats on number two! It's been a pleasure working with you and I can't wait to see what the future holds."

I shake it, reaching around and placing a kiss on her startled cheek before turning to her wife and giving her a hug. "Good night, you two." I throw all the cash I have in my wallet on the table. "For my drinks and another round on me. Go wild."

. . .

I make it back to the duplex in silence, feeling strange. I'm elated, of course, but it's surreal, too. I've had hits before. But this feels better somehow—more intense—because I love these people so much. I want only good things for them. I want Lorelai back in the spotlight. She deserves it and I was able to help her with that. It's . . . it's a lot. I'm walking up the drive in the dark when I hear the soft strumming of a guitar and her sweet and smoky vocals ring out. She must be on the balcony with Maren. I don't want to interrupt, so I wait. And listen.

I don't recognize the song. It must be new. It's not something we laid down in the last few weeks, at any rate.

You let me go—
> *Well, that's a lie. You pushed me out the door.*

My heart gives a lurch in my chest. A steady throb. Is she—

> *And slammed it in my face*

You locked it twice.

I didn't—is that what she thinks? That I froze her out?

> *And said I was a waste*
> *   Of time*
> *   Of space*
> *   Of effort*
> *   Of lace*
> *You let me go*
> *And I bet*
> *you wish you didn't now*

I'm frozen in time, stock-still under the balcony in the dark, her soft words finding purchase like little needles stabbing my skin, poking my veins, and bleeding me out. The words sting, but it's her voice. God, it burns from the inside out. She hates me. I did this. I kicked her out. I was her friend and I made her feel worthless. Less than. When she's . . . fuck. She's everything and she's right. I threw it all away.

29

CRAIG

I'M NOT ALONE

I have to leave town. After hearing Lorelai's song on the balcony, I dart up the stairs as silent as possible and call my sister, waking her up, to tell her I want to surprise Dustin with an adventure in the mountains. I'll be there at sunrise, ready to go. To her credit, she doesn't chew me out, much, for the last-minute plans. Either I sound as desperate and unhinged as I feel or maybe she's just ready for a weekend without kids around. Either way, I pack up everything we can possibly need and ignore the intense pang when I hear Lorelai's familiar tipsy laughter ring out through the sliding glass door.

This, right here, is why you don't rent out half your duplex to your friend you're in love with. Christ, someday soon Lorelai is gonna bring a random guy back to our place and I will have to set the entire thing on fire and burn it to the ground.

After sounding the alarm and making sure everyone is out.

And also maybe sending a letter so she moves her expensive stuff out to safety.

And I'll grab my asshole cat, first.

Okay, fine, that's a lot of fucking work. I'll just move out.

And you know what? After hearing that song, I deserve to have to move out. Once that song hits the radio (which it *will* because I will produce the hell out of it. I can already tell it's a banger), disappointed women everywhere will scream it from rafters and I will become the poster boy for fucking up a good thing.

Until then, I have a nephew who needs me (or maybe I need him at this point) and the open air of the Smokies and *no girls are allowed*. Thank God.

I trade my motorcycle for Melissa's more practical Chrysler minivan and we hit the road at first light after the requisite stop at Clark's Mini Mart to purchase our weight in Little Debbie snacks, sugary drinks his momma wouldn't approve of, and pork rinds (they don't really count as meat, they're basically deep-fried fatty air). I can spare only four days, and we plan to make the most of every minute.

I'm not used to sharing my inherited sanctuary with anyone, but I find I'm looking forward to it. It can get a little lonely out there when the sun goes down and the world is asleep. I've packed cheese dogs (for him) and marshmallows, along with some of those long metal pronged sticks to roast them over a fire under the stars. Between that and the fishing we'll do while waiting for our pots in the kiln, I think I've covered everything I can remember from the nights I spent learning about pottery and life at my uncle Huck's knee.

Except by the end of the first day, it's clear I've forgotten a lot of what my great-uncle Huck taught me, and really, the pottery shed has seen better days. There's a bat's nest in the corner over the kiln and neither Dustin nor I are manly enough to scare them off, plus Melissa would murder me if I returned her baby with a rabies infection. So instead, we close the door, locking it up real tight, and I make plans to call one of those exterminators that don't actually exterminate but rather "relocate" the pests.

Good news is I brought my guitar. Even better, I thought to grab a second one for long nights around the fire. So maybe I'm not Great-Uncle Huck, passing on my world-renowned pottery knowledge to a new generation of young artists . . .

But guitar playing is pretty cool, too. Not to mention, D's a natural at coming up with lyrics. We take turns over the bonfire laying down rhyming verses, and I'm itching to write down some of his lines. With permission, of course. And full songwriting credit, for fuck's sake.

We spend the next few days sunning ourselves on the shore, casting lines off the fishing rock, and learning chords at night. We eat fresh fish until we're sick of it, and then I drive us into town, where we drink iced slushies and he gets a burger the size of his head while I end up with a salad the size of, well, a big plate. Because fiber. Long gone are the days I can live on marshmallows and fried lake perch.

And through it all, I barely think of her.

Finally, when our last night rolls around, we decide to sleep under the stars. I aired out an old two-person tent just in case we actually do see a bear, and we sit around our bonfire.

"I don't want to go home," D says, his fingers glued with sugar and chocolate.

"I hear ya. But if I kept you here much longer, your mom would come after us, and that would definitely mess with the whole 'guys only' vibe we have going on."

"I thought that was just for this trip?"

"Why?" I ask, passing him a graham cracker and trying not to laugh at the amount of marshmallow covering his face. "You making plans to bring your dates out here in a couple of years? Because I'll tell you, it's probably more rustic than most girls prefer."

"No," he says, flushing in the light of the fire. Poor kid has his uncle's cheeks.

"Uh-oh. Is there a lucky girl in your life, D?"

"Not yet. I'm only twelve."

I want to tease him, but I make myself stop. This is a safe space, after all. Where we keep our secrets until we don't want to anymore.

"What about Lorelai? Has she come out here yet?"

Apparently not *my* secrets, though.

I pretend to be considering my marshmallow, rotating it this way and that over the embers, buying myself some time when I decide it can't hurt to share.

"I haven't brought her, no. Though we talked about it once. She seemed pretty excited about checking it out one day."

"Why don't you bring her, then?"

I grimace, partly because my marshmallow's on fire and partly because Lorelai.

"Maybe I will one day. But things are pretty complicated

with Lorelai. She's a super good friend, but that's all. And it's not always a good idea to bring your super good friends who are girls on overnight trips to your creepy cabin in the mountains."

"Because you'll want to have sex."

I choke on charred marshmallow, hacking and coughing and inhaling smoke until my eyes are streaming. This kid's straight talk could give Trina Hamilton a run for her money.

"Where did you hear that? Am I allowed to—hell, is that why? Did your mom send you here so I could talk to you about sex?"

If a twelve-year-old could scoff, he does. "Duh, I took a class in school."

"In fifth grade?"

"I'm in seventh grade, Uncle Craig."

I rub a hand down my burning face. "Right. I knew that. Sorry. Okay, so you already know about sex. Good. That's good."

"So is that why you can't invite Lorelai? Because Mom says you're in love with her. And when you love someone, you get to have sex with them."

Holy shit.

Holy. Shit.

Right now would be an excellent time for a bear attack.

I decide the best route is the most direct. Like ripping off a Band-Aid.

"I don't know where your mom got that information from, but between you and me, I guess, sure. Yes. I love Lorelai. Have for years. Haven't told her because I know she doesn't feel the same. So, no more—so, *no* sex," I amend, sweating. "Like you said. You should love someone before you have sex with them. Or at least wait until you're old enough and man enough to buy condoms yourself."

"Does Lorelai know you love her?"

"No. Thank God."

"So how do you know she doesn't love you?"

"She never told me."

"You never told her that you love her."

I blink, staring in the firelight, wrapping my head around his preteen logic and looking for the holes. Or even *a* hole. But, dammit, there isn't one. It's massively oversimplified, sure, but maybe I've overcomplicated things.

Wouldn't be the first time.

"Fair enough. You got me on that one, kid. I'll think about it. For now, though, I think we better get to bed. We have a long ride down the mountain tomorrow, topped off by a side trip to my place to figure out a way to get the marshmallow out of your hair before your mom takes one look and decides to shave it all off."

30

LORELAI

CHANGE MY MIND

Shockingly, Maren makes it three whole days before she corners me about the dismal state of my love life. The diabolical Junior Miss Michigan waited until I was literally hanging off a cliff's edge, my life in her hands, before she brought it up in a maddeningly casual and not-at-all-out-of-breath way.

"So, just how long have you and Craig been sleeping together?"

My grip slips and I thud against the rocky surface with an audible *oomph,* wholly dependent on Maren to steady me and my harness before I find my handhold and footing again.

I make a grab for another hold and pull myself up before answering. "We aren't sleeping together."

"Maybe not right this second, no, but you are definitely sleeping together."

"Okay," I concede with a soft huff, straightening and letting my one hand loose and shaking it out. "Allow me to rephrase. We are no longer sleeping together." And because

I know she won't let up until I tell her every detail, and because I *need* to tell someone, I signal that I'm going to belay down. Jumping down the cliff's surface in long, careful leaps, I'm back on the hard ground within seconds.

"It's always so unfair how it takes such an enormous amount of time getting up the cliff and only seconds to get back down. The fun, easy part should last longer."

"I feel like there's a metaphor in there somewhere," Maren says, her expression shrewd.

I snort. "Probably. It's probably one of those obnoxious ones that's supposed to teach a lesson. Let's not try to figure it out today, hmm?" I walk over to where our packs are sitting in a pile near several stacked boulders and pull out a couple of granola bars, offering one to Maren and twisting the cap off my water.

We drink and snack in silence for a few minutes, idly watching a couple of other climbers ascend a far more dangerous route farther away on the cliff. Maren doesn't ask me her question again. It's not as though I've forgotten it. She knows I'll share in my own time. Finally I sigh and settle on the top of a boulder, gesturing for her to join me, and lean back on my hands, letting the sun freckle and warm my skin.

"Short story short, we decided, consensually, to try that precarious friends-with-benefits situation I mentioned weeks ago, because we suspected—well, okay we *knew* from some experience that things between us can be very, very good. And it was exceptional. Like." I fan myself and I'm not even being dramatic. I legit feel sweat slip between my breasts. Sure, I've been climbing a mountain in the midday sun, but this sweat is all Huck.

"A lot of sex, Mare. Sex in our apartment, in his office, on his motorcycle . . ."

"Okay, we'll circle back to the logistics of *that,* because I am definitely curious."

I grin, and I am one thousand percent sure it's straight-up dopey. "And then, I don't know, I blew it, but I'm not exactly sure how. Jennifer had me do that apology tour and the final interview basically exploded in my face and my name became this cussword in country music all fucking over again and I was just trying to protect Huck, you know? He has this brand-new business and he's so talented at what he does. He deserves success and, you know, all the good things that come with that. The studio should be everything to him. He doesn't need an association with me to mess it up."

Maren's brows pull together in a tiny crease. "Did he say that?"

"No, but come on, Huck would never. He's too nice. And that was my point! He lets people take advantage of him and his good nature time and again, and I wasn't about to be one of those people."

"So, let me see if I understand this. You think having sex with Craig was taking advantage of him?"

"No!" I practically shout, scaring a couple of birds before lowering my voice to a more reasonable level. "Okay. The sex was a separate thing. I haven't gotten to that part yet. I told him we shouldn't be seen in public or at his studio together because he would be tainted by association. I'm protecting the asshole. But he got all pissy about it, saying he wasn't Drake and I should know he wouldn't care about that, which again *proves my point.* But anyway, then he said that he couldn't keep sleeping with me because he can't do casual anymore."

"So then you aren't working together anymore?"

I sigh and brush my fingers together, clearing them of dirt. "No. Obviously we're still working together. He insisted on that part, actually. He was like, 'You better be in the studio in the morning,' so I was. Well, eventually. First I got glutened. But anyway, after that, you know what happened from there . . ."

"The duet goes number one."

I nod, still feeling the flip in my belly at the thought.

"So, objectively speaking, being associated with you professionally did not ruin his business at all."

I press my lips together and nod again.

"All right. And just to recap, you said he should stop being seen with you professionally and he refused (again, thankfully), but then he said you should stop sleeping together, instead."

"Yeah."

"So he reinstated the original boundaries."

"Apparently."

"But the sex was good."

"It was out of this world."

"Lorelai." Maren's face is pinched, though she still manages to look pretty. "He's in love with you, you idiot."

"He's not. He's Craig!"

"That's his name, not his feelings. And furthermore, you're in love with him."

"God, Maren, I'm a mess. Admittedly this week was amazing and the duet is doing well, but personally I'm still a shit show in this town."

"That's your *status,* but again, not your feelings." Maren's soft grin is maidenly triumphant. "Face it, Jones, you've been in love with Craig for a long while now. You just confused it with lust."

"Oh, I definitely lust . . ."

Maren rolls her eyes and crumples her wrapper between her fingers, tucking it in her bag to toss later. Ever the park ranger.

"Look, as far as I can tell, as a very much nonexpert in relationships, people in love turn into idiots for each other. So because you love Craig, you are concerned about his career on his behalf."

I frown to myself. That makes some sense. I mean. Of course I love Huck. Of course I care about him. But am I in love with him?

My heart lurches in my chest at the very thought, as if to say: YES, BITCH, OBVIOUSLY.

Maren is plowing along. "And because he loves you, he refuses to abandon you just because of some deejay assholes, which by the way, Shelby, Cameron, and I fully support him in that. And he can't stand the thought of casual sex instead of a relationship."

"You're saying he loves me and wants a real relationship."

"I'm saying you love each other and you deserve a real relationship."

"Well."

Maren narrows her eyes, her head tilting to the side and

her ponytail swinging over her bare shoulder. "You really are surprised by this, aren't you?"

I can feel my face get hot under her scrutiny. "Well, yeah."

"Fucking Drake Colter. I'm sorry, but I wish I had been around back then, because I would have kicked him in the ball sac and ruined his singing career. Drake is one guy. He was the wrong guy, but that wasn't your fault."

"I know that," I insist, feeling annoyed. "Deep down, I do. I'm working through it."

"I know you are. So what are you going to do?"

I glance up at the mountain. "First, I'm gonna make you climb this entire thing while I think good and hard about some revealing question to ask *you* when you least suspect it."

Maren smirks, eyes crinkled in amusement. "Fair enough."

"And then I'm gonna consider what you've said and also what to do about it if it's true."

"It's true," she insists, getting to her feet and tightening her harness. "And while you're thinking about how you plan to interrogate me, maybe you can lead off with some of the more pertinent details regarding that motorcycle sex. For starters, kickstand up or down?"

"Which one?" I ask her with a wink.

. . .

While Huck's been busy fine-tuning *Avalanche* and working hard to make Lorelai Jones a household name once more, and Maren (plus Shelby via FaceTime) has been preoccupied with renovating the shambles of my nonexistent love life, my new agent slash manager slash PR miracle worker, Trina Hamilton, has been chipping away at my disaster image. If it wasn't for the fact that the woman wears prickly like a pair of fucking Luccheses, I'd be concerned she was taking me on as a pity project.

Admittedly, I've calmed down a bit on the pity party since the duet released to acclaim. I'm not a complete lost cause, but scars run deep, and mine were stitched together in a rush job the first time around.

But I've seen Trina chew out a (probably) well-meaning barista for asking if she wanted to change her latte from full fat to skim, so I know for certain she doesn't have a soft bone in her body. Even her cartilage is reinforced with titanium.

I fucking love her. It's been too long since I've felt confident in my own skin around anyone besides Huck and my friends in Michigan. I let this place humble me. More than that, I let it shame me and for what? Because I had principles? Principles, mind you, that are shared by a significant portion of the population. It shouldn't have been shame on me. It should have been shame on them all along. Trina Hamilton and her pointy heels and pointy manicure and matte lips and big hair reminded me of that.

Reminded me of who I was.

Thank God.

"So here's the scoop, Cheetah," she tells me, using her new nickname because she's up to her microbladed eyebrows in Glennon Doyle's *Untamed* and now calls everyone with a uterus, physical, spiritual, or otherwise, Cheetah. Her fingers tap on her phone screen in front of me, and I settle back in my chair, folding my napkin and pushing the remnants of my giant Cobb salad to the center of the table. "I've gotten you an early morning appearance on *The Good Morn-*

ing Show in three days. I know it's a tight turnaround, but Amy Anderson is a massive fan of yours, not to mention angling for the Enlightened News Anchor of the People Award or some other made-up bullshit recognition. Whatever it is, she practically fell out of her chair at the chance to interview you on camera."

There's a loud buzzing noise in my ears that kicked in somewhere around the words *The Good Morning Show.* "Holy shit, can you repeat that?"

Trina rolls her eyes lightly, but I see the subtle beginnings of a pleased smirk around the corners of her painted mouth. "Amy Anderson. *The Good Morning Show.* Three Days. You."

I take a long draw from my iced tea and fan my face, looking around, a little unnerved to notice everyone else just going about their day. No one else looks like they've just received the shock of their lives. Only me. We're sitting in a wide-open street café on Broadway on a Tuesday in full view of God and country. Another change that I'm getting used to. Trina refuses to strategize in private. *No more hiding like you got caught lip-synching at the Super Bowl. You are a goddamn cheetah, Jones.*

"You're completely serious."

"I don't lie about business," Trina says, before tilting her head to the side and taking a short sip through her straw. "Well, mostly."

"What's the angle? How do you know they aren't hoping to burn me on national TV?"

"I'm ninety-five percent sure they aren't. But even if they were, it's a calculated risk that I'm encouraging you to take. This is your chance to share your side of things. To change the narrative. Plus, *TGMS* has a national reach in several different times zones. I've also arranged to have you perform a song."

I choke on my tea and Trina barely misses a step, passing me a clean napkin. "The world needs to be reminded of what you bring to the table without all the gatekeeping and drama. Underneath the moral panicking, there's a hell of a talented singer-songwriter. You're gonna show them that."

"Three days isn't a lot of time to coach—"

"I'm not turning you into a robot, Lorelai. This ain't no Eliza Doolittle shit. There's nothing wrong with the way you are. Your only mistake was in trusting the wrong people, who advised you to turn tail and be ashamed of yourself. We're not doing that, Cheetah. This time you're embracing it. Will you lose some folks? Sure. Though you could lose them just as easily for gaining or dropping weight or having a bad haircut or sleeping with a married man."

"So to be clear, you want me to be myself on national television?"

"A hundred percent you."

"No matter the consequences."

"Can I be candid, Jones?"

"Do you have another way?" I ask wryly.

She doesn't even flinch. "You're interesting as hell. I researched you and the whole *HomeMade* drama with your friends up in Michigan. You stepped back into the spotlight for them, and your fans showed up. Some people step away for six months and can never crawl their way back. You left for nearly half a decade and people were clamoring for more. More you, more Shelby and Cameron, more Craig

Boseman, even more Drake Colter, though the piece of shit doesn't deserve it. All of that, or at least a large part of that, is because of *you*. People are fascinated to see what you'll do next. Even the radio show—"

"I thought you said that was a mistake."

"Not because you did anything wrong," she clarifies sharply. "It was a mistake for you to lower yourself to their level. To pander to those small-minded idiots. They were never gonna welcome you back. Jennifer Blake offered you up on a platter with a side a grits."

"Well okay then," I say, resolved. What's the worst that can happen? They cancel me on a national level? Been there and done that. Gave back the fucking engagement ring.

"Excellent." Trina slips her shades over her eyes and rubs at her temples. "I hate pep talks. I know they're necessary, but they give me migraines."

"Being nice gives you migraines?"

Trina raises her hand to signal for the bill. "Believe me, this is a breeze compared to the days I spent paying bail on Coolidge. But yes, being nice gives me migraines. It's my trigger. Like chocolate and the smell of antiseptic."

"Thanks, Trina."

She grins, accepting the bill and signing off on it with a flourish. "You're welcome, Cheetah. I'll have my assistant send over your flight and hotel details before tonight."

. . .

Two days before I'm supposed to fly to L.A. for the interview and I'm sitting on my balcony with Maren, pouting. It's obvious why. Because on the one hand, literally everything is going right for me. Or at least better. I have an agent in my corner. I have the once-in-a-lifetime chance to share my side of the sordid tale. My best friend is visiting. The album is gorgeous and the duet is sitting pretty at number one.

All these things are the very best. Opportunity knocking and second chances blooming left and right. I can't hardly believe my luck and I'm fucking miserable about it.

Because I don't have Huck. I miss him. I still see him, of course. Regularly, and if you were observing our conversations, you might not even notice anything has changed. For example, the other night I texted him "Black" by Pearl Jam, and he responded within seconds with "Heart-Shaped Box" by Nirvana as if he'd just been staring at his phone, willing me to reach out. Like always.

But it's different. It's more stilted. Forced. Not forced like we're pretending we like each other but forced lightness. As if we're pretending not to like each other so much. He's stopped writing his poetry. I've been checking twice a day, and nothing. And he hasn't made any more claims to "Jonesin'," or any of Drake's supposed other songs, for that matter.

The nominations for Song of the Year were posted and Drake was there, claiming "Best Worst Case" as his without a cowriter. Though I did notice Drake didn't post anything on his socials about the nod and he didn't issue a statement. In fact, he's basically gone dark in recent weeks. Knowing him the way I unfortunately do, I'm positive Old Drake would be crowing from the rooftops about his songwriting prowess. His "spending time locked away in the studio" vague posts mean something came to a head.

And I'm dying to ask Huck about it, but after wrapping on the album, he left town. Arlo said he took his nephew to his cabin in the Smokies. Which sounds planned, so I'm trying not to spiral on the implications, even though he never mentioned it before and also he'd hinted at one point he'd take me . . . Regardless, no one knew exactly when he'd be back and he's completely unreachable. So that's that.

Maren offers to top off my glass and I accept because, what the hell, why not. We're perched on the iron porch railing while Miranda Lambert plays over the speaker. She's singing about a man who done her wrong, and I'm feeling it all the way down to my red-painted toes. Because even though I miss Huck like crazy, I'm still nursing a bruised ego and a neglected vagina and both of those things are capital H, capital F, His Fault.

Even if he was pulling back for the right reasons, which, okay, so maybe he *was*, I'm not sure what I'm supposed to do about it if he shuts down and travels four hours into the mountains where I can't text him.

I know. I hear myself. I'm being a bitch. A lonely bitch who misses her friend, whom she loves.

And his cock. That is attached to him, so it's not like I'm not talking about the same thing here.

Maren is scrolling through her phone, keeping up on emails, and I can tell by the tense line of her slim shoulders that something's wrong.

"Work problems?" Even though I'm headed out of town, I'm leaving for just the one night, so Mare has decided to stay a little longer.

"No, not work. Something else. Just . . ." Her brows draw

together and she shakes her head as if she's dislodging a thought and meets my gaze.

"I need to go to Wisconsin."

I put down my wine and straighten. "Right now? Is everything okay?"

"No, not now." She waves at me to sit and settles in her chair, more relaxed. "But soon. I have to go see some people about a legal thing. It's nothing bad. Just weird. I had an old friend in the North Woods, from back when I led fishing tours, and he passed away. Anyway, apparently he left me some things."

"I'm sorry, Mare. I didn't know you lost someone recently."

She takes a long sip, her gaze suddenly a million miles away. "It was a month ago, actually. I went to the funeral. He was in his nineties and it wasn't unexpected. But I didn't realize he'd left me anything, so I guess I need to go back."

"Was he rich?"

She snickers, relaxing. "Not in the slightest. It's probably a bunch of old fishing poles and fifty-year-old musky tackle."

"Ah."

"Yeah. I'll be sure to take my pickup when I go. So anyway, we were talking about you," she says.

"Were we?"

"Maybe not out loud, but you were definitely thinking about Craig again. Your expression went all sour and we've listened to this album twice through now."

"Did I ever tell you about the time I almost got a tattoo with Miranda?"

Maren's eyes grow huge. "No!"

"We chickened out. We were drunk as two skunks and

wanted to get matching Loretta Lynn quotes. Blake found out and intervened."

"No shit. What was the quote?"

"Turns out it was a Dolly quote, so props to Blake, because that would have been an expensive PR nightmare."

Maren laughs her musical laugh and rests her head against the back of her chair, turning her face toward me. "You gonna be okay, Jones?"

"Always am."

"That's not an answer."

"I know." I sigh. "Yeah, I will be. I need to talk to Huck and tell him how I feel. Obviously. Which scares the everliving shit out of me because I only ever told one man I loved him and he broke my heart. And somehow this feels even more scary, because as much as I thought I loved Drake, I was wrong. I didn't love him. I barely liked him once the dust settled. But I'm head over ass for Huckleberry and he could crush me."

"He won't crush you."

"But he could," I insist softly.

"He won't, though."

"We'll see."

. . .

The next morning, I leave Maren sleeping off a wine hangover and head into the studio early.

"Lorelai!" Arlo raises his head with a start. There is music pumping out the speakers of his work laptop and two empty cardboard coffee cups and a half-eaten muffin beside him on the desk. "I didn't realize you were coming in."

"No appointment."

"Craig's still out, I'm afraid. I'm only in because our surrogate Jessica is due literally any minute and I'm freaking the fuck out. Josh sent me to work, saying I was giving him heart palpitations with my pacing."

"I figured. Hoped, actually. I'm here to see you—if you can keep a secret from your boss, that is."

Arlo's expression brightens beneath his fedora. "I love secrets. Go on."

"I hoped you might say that." I take a deep breath and plop down across the desk from him and pull a piece of paper out of my scratched-to-hell notebook, something I'd worked on late into the early morning. "So here's what I'm thinking, and I'm in a bit of a crunch . . ."

31

LORELAI

NOT READY TO MAKE NICE

I wake up in a swanky hotel room that I barely get to enjoy, thanks to the ungodly time I have to wake up for my interview with *The Good Morning Show*—3:30 A.M. Honestly, they could have put me up in a Motel 6 for the amount of sleep and the accommodations I don't get. I meet Trina and our driver in the lobby at 4:00 A.M., and she passes me a very tall, very hot coffee. The roads are full, either from people who are still awake or, like us, just getting started. Neon lights flash past my eyes, but I'm left to sip my coffee and absorb the caffeine into my bloodstream in silence. Trina is already typing away on her phone, though I can't imagine to whom, until she releases a soft sigh and drops her phone into her handbag. "My wife. I've spoiled her. She doesn't like alarm clocks, and since I'm an early riser by nature, I always wake her up with coffee and a kiss. You got the coffee, she gets the long-distance kiss."

I don't know what to say. I can't even imagine a world

where Trina would be so sweet. A ballbuster who gets shit done, sure. But sweet?

Instead, I take another sip of my coffee and say thank you.

Once we hit the lobby of *TGMS*, we're met by a harried assistant whose name tag reads JACKIE P. She escorts us up an elevator and down three bustling hallways before knocking on a dressing room door that has my name scrawled across the plaque. The door swings open and my jacket is removed by one set of friendly hands while I'm pressed into a chair in front of a mirror by another set. The chatter is lively and kind, and within short order, my skin glows, my hair shines, and my eyes stand out. I'm passed a smart pair of black trousers in my size along with a sleeveless white chiffon blouse and red pumps. I dress and everyone gushes. Well, except Trina, who looks up over her phone and nods approvingly. Honestly, I prefer it to the gushing.

I'm told I'm to go on in fifteen minutes; then everyone leaves. I settle on the small formal couch and pick up my guitar, idly tuning it and warming up my vocals for no reason other than plain old nerves. It's been years since I went in front of a camera, and I'm a lot older now. Wiser. Bruised and shaped by the world. For a hot second, I wonder if any of my students will see me on the show today. The thought sobers me in a good way. Directs me. Solidifies my purpose.

I'm here to play music and I'm here to use the attention to help others who can't help themselves.

· · ·

Amy Anderson is tiny in real life. Petite to the extreme, she maybe meets the tip of my nose, and that's in sky-high heels.

But her stature doesn't make her any less intimidating, and in the moments before she reaches out to shake my hand and tell me what a fan she is, I about piss my new black boss-bitch pants. She hasn't lost her drawl in all her years on television, and I have to assume it's on purpose. Her blond hair sits right above her shoulders and gives off the perfectly mussed vibe. My slippery straight blue-black locks could never. We settle across from each other in stylish sofa chairs and a props person makes sure to let me know my guitar is waiting for me, just as I left it, on a small stage over my shoulder.

Amy makes small talk while people fuss with our hair and buttons and the way our clothes lie after mic'ing us. Her smile is genuine, and while she doesn't gush, she does tell me she has a niece in Texas who attended a school that unfortunately had a shooting. Thankfully, her niece was at a doctor's appointment that day, but the niece did lose a friend and the trauma was so awful that many families had to relocate and the school was bulldozed to the ground. Amy Anderson couldn't give two shits about the Second Amendment, but, she tells me, she sure likes that song I wrote last year about Cameron and Shelby Riggs.

The interview goes off, as they say, without a hitch.

Amy artfully leads me through a discussion of my career, surprising me with "embarrassing" early childhood footage of a county fair where I belted out Shania Twain's "Any Man of Mine" and some cringey photos of teen me in my cheerleader uniform singing "The Star-Spangled Banner" at a high school talent show. When she gets to the story about "Ohio," she doesn't even play the footage, claiming, "Everyone's already seen it."

"What's more important is what happened afterwards. What can you tell us about the days that followed? You were engaged, if I recall? To fellow musician Drake Colter?"

Without dwelling too long on the details, I explain how Drake broke off our engagement unexpectedly, followed by the disintegration of my band, my record contract, and my career.

"So there you were, left without a friend in the world."

I smile, thinking of Huck. "Well, not totally. But it was definitely time for me to reprioritize and start at square one. So I moved to Michigan, where I found myself back in the classroom."

"And where you met your close friend Shelby Springfield, now Shelby Riggs."

I nod, warming up to the subject. "Yup. I had a first-row seat to watching her and Cameron fall head over butt for each other."

Amy laughs and segues into "What They Have," the song I wrote for my friends.

"Here you are singing it at their wedding a few months ago."

"I was so nervous," I admit, glimpsing the footage on the large screen over my shoulder. "I practiced it a hundred times with my producer Craig, convinced I'd mess it up."

"And by Craig, you mean Craig Boseman, right? Rumor around Nashville is that you are longtime friends with the up-and-coming indie record producer."

"I've known Craig since back when I was touring with Drake Colter. He played bass for Drake."

"Craig's recently come into the spotlight after releasing a viral video singing 'Jonesin',' causing some to speculate that maybe *he* wrote it all along. Can you confirm that?"

I press my lips together, hesitating. "I can only confirm that the mystery bridge—that's my favorite part."

"Interesting." Amy's eyes glitter. "What about the rumors that the song is about you?"

I feel my face flush despite the cool stage, and I'm kicking myself for not presuming Craig and/or "Jonesin'" might come up.

"I can't say for sure. I've never straight-up asked! You'll have to get Craig on here and drill him about it."

Amy chuckles like I've just said the most hilarious thing and swiftly moves on to what I'm doing now. I tell her about my upcoming album *Avalanche*, produced by Craig and Arlo, and we chat about the duet debuting at number one on the *Billboard* Top 100. I easily settle into raving about Jefferson Coolidge and what a dream it has been to work together.

At which Amy breaks character and actually does gush. I don't blame her. I've been teasing Shelby about her Jefferson Coolidge crush for years. He has that effect on women of all ages. The man sings like Elvis, and I can't wait for the world to fall even more in love with this new and improved version of him.

"Well, I don't want to spend all our time with you talking. I hear you brought your guitar and are prepared to sing something for us. Is this another brand-new hit we're about to hear?"

"Yes, ma'am. This is just a taste off my new album *Avalanche*."

We go to commercial and I transition to the small stage to sing in front of the small live studio audience.

"This is about a man," I say with a wink, "but at the end of the day, it ain't about Drake Colter."

I strum the opening chords and sing for everything I'm worth.

Because I figure if I'm gonna put my whole-ass self out on a limb to dangle, I might as well put my heart out there, too.

32

CRAIG

SHAMELESS

According to Arlo, I've just missed Lorelai when I get back into town late on Sunday evening after dropping a newly clean and marshmallow-free Dustin at his mama's house. I should feel refreshed after a long weekend away at the cabin, and with regards to my business, I do, but I'm also crawling-out-of-my-skin ready to see Lorelai. We need to talk. Or I need to talk, anyway, and just lay it all out there, consequences be damned.

And at least I'll have told her the truth, right? Even if she doesn't feel the same, she deserves to know someone fell in love with her. To know she's that special to someone, even if it's just me.

Or at least that's what I was thinking before Arlo stormed into my office way earlier than he's usually in, let alone awake, startling me so badly I shoot hot coffee from my nose and all over the stack of paperwork that's collected on my desk while I was out of town. Not that I'd done anything more than shove the papers out of my way before picking up my phone, staring at it and arguing with myself about how early is too early to text Lorelai.

I'd just settled on sending her "Thank You" by Led Zeppelin as a sort of softball icebreaker text that wouldn't matter what time of day or night I'd sent it (because the song game doesn't play by normal rules of engagement) when my partner—in no fedora, mind you—slams open my office door.

Arlo's red hair is usually cut so short, I'll forget how curly it is, but this morning, he's got a halo of fiery frizz and wild eyes. He marches over to where a small flat-screen smart-TV monitor hangs against the wall and flips it on.

"Good morning?" I say to him, grabbing a bunch of takeout napkins out of my drawer and mopping up my desk.

"Morning, boss," he sings. "Sorry, I overslept."

"Um. For what?"

He gives me a look over my shoulder that clearly translates as "obviously to do this," which is not at all obvious, but I don't argue.

"How's baby watch going?"

"Her cervix is two to three centimeters dilated, and she thinks she shed her mucus plug this morning."

I choke on a fresh sip of coffee. "I'm sorry, did you just say . . ." I trail off, not daring to repeat what I thought I heard him say. Instead, I put the coffee down. Maybe later.

Arlo finds whatever channel he's been looking for and it's on a commercial. He fluffs his hair out of his eyes and swipes a bead of sweat trailing over his eyebrow.

"Mucus plug. Yes. Don't ask me, but Josh made excited

doctor noises when she told us that, so I'm going on a limb to say it's a good thing."

"Awesome, man. I'm so excited for you guys."

"Oh, I know. We got the Johnny Cash onesies."

"Hey! That was a surprise!"

"I know that, too." Arlo shrugs unapologetically. "But I want the baby to wear it home. Start them off right, you know? Nothing better than dressed in something Uncle Craig picked out special."

I swallow, my face feeling hot. "Hell, Arlo."

"I know," he repeats, his eyes brimming with meaning. "Anyway . . ."—he flaps his hands and sniffs loudly—"shush, it's about to start." He turns up the volume on the TV and settles across from me in a chair, turning it to face the screen.

"What is—"

"Shh!" he insists and gestures for me to watch.

And there she is. Holy fuck, Trina got her on *The Good Morning Show*? I surge to my feet, my chair forgotten, and in three steps I'm standing directly in front of the screen, hands on hips, jaw unhinged.

She's so beautiful, my chest aches just looking at her. Lorelai crosses her long legs and laughs out loud at something the host says and it makes the hair on my arms stick up. They're showing footage of her as a kid, and I'm overwhelmed with how powerful this moment is. How she's come full circle through the grief and bullshit and now she's on top of it all. On fucking national television, telling her story.

The interviewer asks about what went down after Lorelai played "Ohio," and Lorelai doesn't hold back. She talks about being abandoned by her label, her bandmates, and yeah, fucking Drake. But then something happens.

The interviewer, Amy something or other, reflects on how Lorelai was left without a friend in the world and there's this look. Lorelai smiles. It's small and familiar and I can feel it in my chest. "Well," she says, "not totally."

Because she wasn't alone. She had me. She's always had me. My heart is thumping now, racing, even, which is crazy because I'm just standing here. But my mind is spinning. Lorelai always knew she could count on me.

I might not have told her I love her, but she's always known.

I just have to explain it to her, is all.

I'm so distracted, having revelations and making plans, that I miss a lot of what's being said until my ears perk up at a name. *My* name. Shit, apparently they're discussing me and I didn't even realize it.

"Craig's recently come into the spotlight after releasing a viral video singing 'Jonesin',''" Amy is saying, "causing some to speculate that maybe *he* wrote it all along. Can you confirm that?"

Lorelai presses her lips together, clearly hesitating, and I want to shout at her, "It's fine! I don't give a fuck anymore!" But obviously I can't, and it doesn't matter because she's already speaking.

"I can only confirm that the mystery bridge—that's my favorite part."

"Interesting." Amy's eyes brighten with understanding. "What about the rumors that the song is about you?"

I swallow hard. Lorelai should know the truth, but does

she know it in the same way she knows I love her? Christ on a cracker, I need to communicate better.

"I can't say for sure. I've never straight-up asked! You'll have to get Craig on here and drill him about it."

I hear a snicker coming from behind me and whirl around to face Arlo, who is rocking side to side in his chair and smirking at his manicure.

"What?"

"Oh, nothing," he says, undeterred in his rocking. "Just imagining you facing down that itty-bitty host while she tries to worm out all your secrets."

"Lorelai's killing it."

"She is," he admits, proudly. "But we've always known our girl was meant for the national stage."

And suddenly I'm just *so fucking over* hiding everything. Keeping things locked up so long I'm just *asking* someone to swoop in and steal her out from underneath me. "I wrote 'Jonesin'' about Lorelai. Years ago. After we hooked up the first and only time—well, until recently," I tell him.

To his credit, he stops rocking, but doesn't look judgmental or even surprised. "How long has it really been?" he asks softly.

I grab a hank of my hair, making a face. "Since the first time she called me Huckleberry, probably. I don't know."

Arlo nods to himself, rising from his chair and leading me to it, placing his hands on my shoulders to sit me down. He looks me square in the eye. Communicating a hell of a lot of unsaid things that likely start with "it's about time you manned up" and ends somewhere around "get your head out of your ass and focus."

Out loud, however, he says, "She's gonna perform after the commercial. You should watch."

And so I do. I'm expecting her to play "What They Have," since Amy brought it up earlier and it's the song most familiar to her newer fans. It's also got that fantastic tie-in with Cameron and Shelby Riggs, who are still the media's darlings since *HomeMade* wrapped on their second season. If I was Trina, it's what I would have her do in lieu of the duet sans Coolidge.

But she doesn't play "What They Have" or any of the other songs from her album. Instead, she looks right at the camera—right at *me*—and says in the most beautiful voice I've ever had the pleasure of hearing, "This is about a man, but at the end of the day, it ain't about Drake Colter."

It's the song from the other night. The one she played on the balcony, and my stomach turns, uncomfortably. This is exactly what I'd imagined would happen. I don't want to listen, but I know I need to. She said it herself. This isn't about Drake. It's about me and what I did. I owe her this.

She finishes the first stanza and despite the sinking feeling in my gut, I'm proud of her. Proud to know her and be whatever it is I get to be for her from here on out. To do better than the man from this song.

She's still singing, and I'm mesmerized.

You told me no
*   More like you told me "screw your dreams, mine*
*   mean more"*
*   And ripped away your hand*
*   Wiping it clear of mine*
*   And canceling all our plans*

Her voice is a breathless near whisper, but the words pierce me and I shut my eyes, taking them to heart.

> *Of a wedding*

My eyes shoot open. What? We never—

> *Of a band*
> *Of a family*

What is she talking . . .

> *Of some land*
> *With our names on it—side by side*
> *You let me go*
> *And he was there instead*
> *Bet you wish he wasn't now.*

I can barely hear her over the thrumming of my heartbeat in my ears, but I swallow hard and focus as she presses forward toward the mic with a smile.

> *He held me close*
> > *Touching knees and half-drunk smiles, magic*
> > > *words passed between us like breaths*
> > *He picked up the phone*
> > *And opened his door*
> > *And cherished my dreams as his own*
> > > *Of singing*
> > > *Of sharing*

Of loving
Of home
With our names in it—side by side—
I let you go
And found someone better
And I
Bet you wish I didn't.

. . .

As soon as the song wraps, I sprint out of my office to locate Arlo and end up practically tripping over him in the hallway, where he's been waiting, giving me space.

"This was prerecorded?" I ask, sounding more strangled than I would like, but that's something I can fix on my way to wherever Lorelai is.

"Three days ago. She was taking her friend Maren to the airport this morning but should be on her way back by . . ."— he looks at his wrist, completely absent of any watch—"now."

"I have to go."

"You have to go," he agrees.

"I won't be back in today."

"Thank you Lord sweet baby Jesus for that."

33
. . . .
CRAIG

MY FAVORITE MEMORY

It's raining, because of course it fucking is. Therefore, by the time I'm pulling up in front of the duplex and hopping off my bike, I'm soaked through. The downpour doesn't let up as I jog up the front walk, and it doesn't occur to me I haven't had the chance to calm down one bit before I'm knocking on that absurd lavender front door. Which is the only explanation I have for the projectile word vomit after she opens the door and takes in my sopping-wet appearance.

"I took my bike to work," I say, the words stumbling over one another to get out. "I've taken it every day ever since you told me how much you like it. Because maybe you'll want to ride on the back of it again. In short, I'm pathetic," I finish.

Lorelai tugs me in by the collar of my jacket.

"I saw your song," I say, following her in. Still purging. "That was for me, right? You said a man, but not Drake."

ERIN HAHN

"Do you want it to be about you?" she asks softly, carefully, reaching for a small hand towel and blotting at my forehead.

I shake my head. "Don't do that. Not this time. We always fucking do that, you know? We hedge. We skirt the truth with more palatable versions, and I can't anymore." I take a deep breath, tugging the towel from her hands and throwing it to the side. I step closer and take her slim shoulders in my hands. "I love you. I have for years. You don't have to—I don't expect you to say the same, but if there's even a small chance, if that song *was* for me—then you need to know I love you and I want you." I finish on a near whisper as if maybe I can take the last part back. Her mouth is open, her luscious lips full and ready to kiss as soon as she tells me I'm not making a huge miscalculation . . . but she's silent.

Her silence carries on for a long painful moment before her eyes dart between mine and she sucks in a breath and holds up a finger. "I know you're spiraling. I can see it all over your face. Stop spiraling, Huckleberry. Of course I love you. I'm just . . . this isn't easy to say. Maybe it's easier to sing. I don't know. Hell, didn't Arlo show you the album? He was supposed to." She shakes her head. "Know what? Doesn't matter." She takes a deep breath and her dark eyes glue themselves to mine.

"I do love you, Craig Boseman. Head over ass, 'Maybe I'm Amazed' Paul McCartney in love with you, which you know is the best love song of all time."

Despite the way I feel like I could literally jump off tall buildings right now, I make a face. Lorelai raises a single brow, her expression challenging, reaching for my soaking leather coat and pulling it down my shoulders. I take a half step even closer to her, and in a low voice I say, "Well, I'm 'My Favorite Memory' Merle Haggard in love with you."

Lorelai's hands freeze in their ministrations, allowing my coat to fall to the ground with a wet thwap. "Damn," she whispers. And she closes in, pressing soft kisses along my jaw. "I love you always, but you should know that when you throw Merle at me, I just want to strip you down and drop to my knees and start—"

"Talking things through so we can start our relationship off more emotionally stable?"

Lorelai immediately stops her kissing and I wince, taking a tentative step back. "Did I fuck it up already?" I ask with a groan.

She bursts out laughing and pulls me farther into the apartment, picking up the towel I threw away earlier and tossing it back to me again. "You did not. You may have a point, actually. But," she continues with a sexy grin, "I'm gonna stay over on this side of the room while you stay on that side of the room for the talking portion. Better for all involved."

"Okay," I agree. I stall for a few seconds, drying myself off with the little towel and trying to collect the thoughts leapfrogging over each other in my brain. "I guess to start, I wrote 'Jonesin'' about you. I know you knew I wrote it, and everyone in the world seems to know it's about you, so ergo or whatever, but . . ."—I pull my hand out of my hair and let it fall to my side before meeting her eyes—"I wrote it after we slept together. And before you say anything, I know that was always supposed to be a onetime thing and I swear I never expected more from you. I wasn't even honest with myself back then, but I wrote the song, obviously, in a rare vulnerable moment. And I never meant for Drake to get it, but it was in this notebook of lyrics I threw at him when I left and anyway . . ." I exhale. "Now you know for sure."

"I meant what I said," she tells me. "In the interview. The bridge is my favorite. Probably because I hoped it was about me, and it felt like a little piece that was untainted by Drake and everyone else. Just a secret message from you to me."

I grimace. "That I put on social media."

She shrugs one shoulder, seemingly unbothered. "We're artists and musicians, Huck. We're constantly figuring out how to walk the fine line between privacy and publicity. Besides, I did you one better and played my confession on national television."

"Yes, thank you for that. I nearly had a stroke, followed by a spontaneous ejaculation. Arlo's lost all respect for me."

"I was trying to get your attention."

"It worked. In the interest of clearing the air, I should also probably admit that I accidentally heard the first part of that song a week ago." Her eyes widen and I nod. "Yeah. You were playing on the balcony when I walked up. You didn't see me. It was dark out. I left before I heard the rest. Or maybe you hadn't even finished it yet. In my defense," I say in a soft voice, "I could never resist listening to you sing."

Lorelai blinks and I can tell she's running it through in her head, making quick work of the lyrics, because her eyes grow impossibly wider before she cuts off with a frustrated groan. "Huckleberry, no."

"Yeah," I repeat. "So that was my bad. I should have stuck around. But look how much more dramatic this has all been . . ." She bites her lip, her eyes dancing. "Also, that song is definitely being added to your album."

"Jesus, we're hopeless," she says. "Maren did say something about people in love acting like idiots. I can't wait to throw it back in her face one day. So is that why you ran off to the cabin. Some kind of self-loathing exercise?"

I sigh. "Something like that. But Dustin asked for some man-to-man time at the cabin, too. It wasn't all self-loathing."

"Convenient." Lorelai smirks.

I grin, folding the towel in my hands. "He's my favorite nephew for a reason."

"Well, you know I wrote the song for you, but I guess I should concede, in the interest of clearing the air . . ."— she mimics my man-drawl in a falsely deep voice, and it's so fucking snarky—"and confess to loving you a lot longer than I wanted to admit to myself. It's just—I don't know. You've been a friend for a long time, and in the beginning, even if I might've found you attractive, I *was* with Drake."

My "What?!" strangles in my throat.

Lorelai blushes and it takes all my strength to force myself to stay in place. The talking portion isn't over yet.

"Yeah. Well, I mean. I was young. I didn't understand what I really wanted—what really did it for me, you know? I thought it was . . . him . . . and I was committed, but once things fell apart, it didn't take long to realize you and I fit." She sighs. "I relived that night for years, Huck. I never dreamed I'd see you again, but even so, I knew, deep down, he wasn't ever gonna be enough for me. I was yours."

"All this time," I say weakly, still reeling over the idea she might have chosen me over Colter years ago.

"You didn't miss much. Things have largely been a shit show up until very recently."

"I missed *all of it*," I insist. "But I refuse to miss another minute."

Lorelai presses her lips together, her eyes dark with want, and I feel my pulse kick up a notch in response. "Petition to table the talking portion for now?"

"You love me?" I can't keep from checking.

She beams. "More every second."

"Good. One day you might even catch up to me, if you're lucky."

I don't know who moves first. All I know is one moment we're across the room from each other, and the next, Lorelai is pulling off my damp T-shirt and I'm slipping my hands under her waistband. Her tongue dances with mine and I'm unhooking her bra. It falls to the floor and she's reaching for my button fly. I kick off my boots and step out of my sopping jeans before her hands are gripping and stroking me, lighting me on fire. I dip my head and suck one perfect dark pink nipple between my lips and swirl my tongue around her tip. She cries out and my cock strains in response.

"Bedroom," she pants, her fingers buried in my hair. "I want you to make love to me, Huck."

34

LORELAI

TO HELL AND BACK

Huck follows me to my bedroom and I thank all the stars that I stress-cleaned after taking Maren to the airport.

Sure, we've just confessed years-long feelings and he told me he loves me, but that doesn't mean I let him make love to me on dirty sheets.

I'm not that far gone.

Confession: I'm pretty far gone.

Head over ass doesn't quite cover it.

Huck makes quick work of my underwear and his and is kissing his way between my aching breasts toward the place where dreams come true when he freezes.

"Fuck. I don't have a condom. I was in such a hurry and . . ."

"I have an IUD," I tell him in between panting breaths. "It's okay. I've been tested, and it's been ages since I was with anyone besides you."

"Me too," he says, his blue eyes clear and tinged with

something like awe. Whatever it is makes my heart squeeze. I love him so much.

"I want to feel you. *Just* you. Is that okay?"

His Adam's apple bobs. "Are you sure? I can run out. We have all the time in the world."

I shake my head, feeling overwhelmed and . . . cherished. And I know I probably shouldn't ask him to marry me right now. We just confessed our love. Proposals should wait for tomorrow.

But I'm mightily tempted to snatch up this man and make it official.

I buck against him, closing my eyes and muffling my moan against his shoulder when his cock rubs just right against my clit. Hopefully that's answer enough.

"Fuck, Lorelai. Not yet. I want to make you come on my tongue first."

God.

Would it be weird if I asked him to put on his glasses first? You're right. Next time.

I'm scooting along the bed and rolling to my back when Huck grins and shakes his head slowly, stopping me. "Not like that, baby. I want you on top."

Hell. I don't usually blush. I'm not a bashful person, especially when it comes to sex, but I've never done *that* before.

"Oh, you don't have to—"

"Please," he insists, with those eyes, before settling himself on his back, his head on my pillow, and gently tugging me over him.

Oh my god, I'm doing this.

I straddle his face and am barely given half a second to

feel embarrassed before his hands grip my thighs and tug me close enough to feel his breath on my center, his tongue slowly curling along the length of my slit and circling my clit over and over.

Instinct takes over, seeking whatever feels the best, and my hips roll against his mouth, where he's intent on devouring me. His blessed tongue, lips, teeth, and even his scruff have me trembling from head to toe. I reach for the bed frame to steady myself and roll again, setting a rhythm and riding his mouth.

"Lorelai. Oh my god. You taste . . . I can feel you . . . It's . . . I love you."

"Oh god, right there. Your fucking tongue—I swear. I can't . . . I can't—"

I'm coming apart, gripping the bed frame so hard it creaks, my clit throbbing and my insides clenching. Suddenly his fingers are thrusting in and up and curling around that magical spot and everything shatters at once. Shivers and waves vibrate and burst again and again and I'm crying out, my voice hoarse and my heart wild.

Eventually I clumsily slip down his body and curl into his side, taking care to avoid his proud cock, and press a kiss to his neck. "I think I need a moment."

"To recover?"

I grin against his warm skin, tracing patterns on his chest. "To compose a song, more like."

"'Ode to Huck's Tongue,'" he teases.

"'The Night I Rode Huckleberry's Face,' more like. It'll be one of those epically long ballads."

Huck flips us so that I'm underneath this time, and his

erection presses against my hip in a way so delicious, my legs fall right open of their own accord.

"Look at that," I whisper around a smirk. "All recovered."

Huck doesn't wait, but he doesn't rush, either. We've had sex real fast, real hard, and real hot, but we've never had sex like this. He rocks into me achingly slow, his cock stretching me, filling me. Fitting me perfectly. I feel every ridge and flex of him as I come alive all over again. He thrusts in, all the way in, and slips out before doing it again, and quicker than I ever dreamed, I'm gasping and climbing once more.

I spread my legs as far as I can, taking him in, and then wrap them around him, holding him close. So close I can see the little flecks of navy in his irises. So close I can feel the thudding of his heart against me. And then I'm flying. Soaring. My orgasm sneaks up on me, ripping through me so hard I can't even move, but it's okay because Huck is moving, still driving powerfully until he seizes with a long, low groan, and I feel him spill inside me.

We stay like that, twined together, for a long time after that. My legs wrapped around him, his head buried against my neck, our bodies connected in the most impossibly intimate way. I should get up. Clean myself and use the bathroom. And I will. But wild fucking broncos couldn't drag me from this man, yet. This is one of *those* moments. The ones that flash before your eyes when all's said and done. The ones that you look back on and go, "Yep. Right there. That was when I knew."

This man is my forever.

"I love you," he tells me tiredly, this time muffled against my skin. "So much."

And even though I want to joke, because it's what I do, I find I can't. Not this time. I'm altered.

Instead I tell him, "I love you, too, Huckleberry."

. . .

We spend two whole days and a night in bed and out of it. First, we make good use of all the surfaces in my apartment, and then we head up to Huck's loft, which, let me tell you, is really convenient. Need fresh pair of undies, run downstairs. Need that phone number for the new Thai place around the corner? Run back upstairs. Want to rehydrate on the balcony? Need a shower and then a second shower because apparently the love of your life has a thing about unwrapping you from terry cloth? Can't find your phone charger and realize you've missed approximately thirty calls in the last twenty-four hours?

Okay, so that last one wasn't that great, but you get what I mean. Apparently, while Huck and I were busy christening every sexually viable surface in the duplex, Arlo and Josh's baby was born (no, they still won't tell me the gender until I actually arrive at the hospital) and the duet between Coolidge and me hit number one for the second week in a row.

So it's time to put some real clothes on and rejoin the world, is what I'm saying.

First, the hospital to meet our newest niece or nephew. I'll be perfectly honest: despite being one hell of a teacher, I've never really given much thought to kids. As in having my own one day. Maren and I fully anticipate Shelby will be knocked up before Season 3 of *HomeMade* kicks off. She's always wanted a family of her own, and everyone knows she and Cameron would make the best parents. But I wasn't sure being a country singer, recording albums, and eventually, hopefully, going on tour made for good parenting.

Anyway, that was *before* I ever saw Huck hold a baby. Before I caught a glimpse of the happy smile spreading across his lips and heard him sing under his breath, a lullaby he wrote just for brand-new little baby Jasper.

To paraphrase the late, great, ethically iffy Dr. Seuss, my uterus grew three sizes that day.

Or my heart. Whatever. I'm convinced they sprinkle crack cocaine pixie dust in baby hair so everyone who sniffs them will want their own.

Note to self: Make an appointment to have IUD double-checked.

The labor went as smoothly as possible, so the surrogate was able to be discharged after the first twenty-four hours and baby Jasper was ready to leave this afternoon, since they've apparently finished monitoring his bilirubin or something else that sounds like a sandwich (Arlo's words, not mine). So after eating the lunch we smuggled in of cheeseburgers for Mr. and Mr. Bishop and veggie burgers on gluten-free buns for me and Huck, we left them to get one final nap before they take home their baby and presumably never sleep again.

We're holding hands across the center console of Craig's Outback when he asks to stop in the studio.

"No appointments," he reassures me. "We purposely scheduled this month light because we knew Arlo might be called away at any moment."

"Do you want kids?" I ask suddenly.

Craig lifts a shoulder. "I think so. One day, anyway. Not like . . . you said you have an IUD, right?"

I squeeze his hand. "Yeah. I do. We're in no danger at the moment. Just one day? If you'd asked me before . . ."

Craig nods. "I know. Me too. I thought music was it for me. And then I thought the studio was it for me. And then *you* were it for me . . ."

"Your circle keeps getting bigger."

"Yeah."

"Mine too."

We pull into the small alleyway parking lot behind the studio and Craig keys in the security code to let us in. The halls are cool and quiet, mostly dark but lit with small motion-sensored runners along the floor. We get to his office and he opens the door, flipping on the light, and jumps back, swinging wildly when he's attacked by several floating helium balloons. I pull back his arm, stilling him before he pops one and sets off who knows what other kinds of alarms.

"What the? These must be for Arlo. Everyone knows I hate balloons."

"I don't think so," I say, reading one. "This one says, 'You did it!,' which Arlo and Josh did not."

"Maybe they were trying to be PC. 'Good job ejaculating in a cup, it worked!' is a lot to put on a balloon."

"'Comeback kid'?"

Craig's eyes narrow and he pulls on one of the strings, reading the tag attached to a plastic weight.

"'Congrats on debuting at number ten on the country charts! Love, Annie Mathers.'" Craig's head slowly raises, shock evident on his face. "What?"

All the blood slips from my face. "What?"

"Holy shit, Lorelai," he mutters, beating against the balloons and shoving his way to his chair. "Holy shit." His phone beeps with a notification and mine does, too. And another and another. I swipe the screen and open the first text from Arlo.

> ARLO: I know you hate balloons, boss, but it's hard to say no to Annie Mathers. Congrats, you two! Coolidge's been in touch, but he knew you needed some space, so give him a call back if you're done sexing it up all over town.

I snort, tapping out a response in the group chat.

> LORELAI: Just need to hit up your soundboard and we should be all set.

Craig laughs next to me, reading over my shoulder. "Serves him right. Remind me to tell you about the time they found out about my poetry account."

We call up Jefferson and make plans to meet at a nice bar downtown. Despite living close, we're the last to arrive because hello, celebratory "we debuted at number ten on the country charts" sex.

Yeah, we've been number one everywhere else and that's a big freaking deal, but we knew that. We celebrated that.

This, though? Country music has let us back in. Maybe begrudgingly, and it's very unlikely to be universal, but there's no taking it back now.

Craig pulls a record producer move, covering the entire

tab for the evening, and seeing him acting the professional turns me on way more than I dreamed, which leads to me giving him a surprise blow job in the far less dingy and far more tucked-away employees-only bathroom.

I know what you might be thinking: *Look at Lorelai climbing industry ladders by dropping to her knees in dimly lit bathrooms.* To which I might say, "Fuck you, I got my record deal way before he let me ride his face."

The scoop, according to Trina, is that country radio was being predictably stubborn about playing the duet, but whether it's due to my national appearance last week or the very public support of Annie Mathers and our "Toxic" performance, or maybe that Jefferson is so damn good-looking and everyone loves a good comeback story, not to mention that our song is being played *everywhere* else Top 40 hits are being played—well, some of them gave in. Spotify wants to do an artist highlight on both of us, which would extend to our upcoming solo albums, and Cameron Riggs is on deck to make a music video.

And Arlo just texted Craig that he refuses to come back into the studio until they hire a receptionist to answer the phone that's been ringing off the hook with agents and managers looking to get their clients in to work with the duo.

We close down the bar, which I haven't done in at least five years, but that's what you get for hanging out with twenty-somethings. Trina left hours ago, and Kacey and Fitz snuck out, very possibly to the same employee bathroom we used earlier, and then texted Jefferson that Kacey was starving and wanted waffles.

"Want to join us for breakfast?" Jefferson asks, Annie on

his back piggyback style, her arms wrapped tight around his neck. He loosens her grip with a patient grimace followed by an apologetic kiss to her forearm.

"I'm good," I say, squeezing Huck's hand. He squeezes back, his expression relieved.

"Me too. Another time, maybe."

We say goodbye and I tilt my head onto Huck's shoulder. "Wanna walk? I'm exhausted but still a little wired."

"Sure."

We walk intertwined like that, up and down neon block after neon block, people still spilling out into the streets from late-night diners and music filling the air.

"I used to do this when I first came to Nashville," he tells me. "I'd walk the streets late into the night, just listening to music and absorbing the culture into my bones." He looks up at the sky, as if talking to the stars, hidden away, but still watching it all play out beneath them. "In fact, I was feeling nostalgic and doing it again the night I heard you singing on the balcony. Even then I never really thought I'd have someone to walk with."

There's something in his tone. A longing. And gratitude. It fills me right up and nearly cuts off the breath in my chest.

"I never thought I'd be back," I admit. "But I always hoped. I thought I wanted back to Nashville. Back to country. I think . . ." I pause, everything crystallizing in my brain at once, overwhelming me. "I think," I repeat, my throat thick, "I just wanted back to *you* all along. I guess I knew deep down we weren't done with each other."

Huck pulls me in, his lips capturing mine and his arms circling my waist in one smooth movement. Easy. We've always been so easy together. His mouth is gentle and soft. Savoring. And when he pulls back, I sigh against his lips, melting all the way into him.

"I'll never be done with you," he admits.

And I know just what he means.

"I love you, too, Huckleberry."

EPILOGUE

CRAIG

I might be a sought-after multimillionaire record label executive, but I still feel like a complete fraud in a tux. I blame the pointy shoes. They have to be kidding me with these.

"They have to be kidding me with these," I tell my wife, petulant.

Lorelai spins me, taking in my expression and smoothing my bow tie. I glimpse the barely concealed laughter in her eyes as she pushes her lips to one side, considering.

"Okay. Obviously, you look hot. No question about that."

"But . . ."

She steps back, one hand on her robe-clad hip, the other resting on the tiny round bump of her growing belly. What I would really like to do is pull the tied knot nuzzled under her glorious breasts and peel back her silky robe, letting it slip to the floor. Then I'd smooth my hands over every sweet inch of her, followed by my tongue, and carry her back to bed, where I can devour her all night . . .

My wife's sly lips break into a knowing smirk. "Don't even think about it."

I step closer, reaching for the sash. "Too late."

She smacks my hand away with a laugh. "This morning wasn't enough for you? Besides, I already showered, and if you mess up my hair, Maren will murder us."

"I can't help it. You look ravishing."

"I'm not even dressed yet."

"All the better . . ."

She rolls her eyes lightly, leaning forward and pressing a soft kiss to my cheek before whispering in my ear, "You aren't getting out of this, so deal with it, Mr. Boseman."

"Knock knock!" Arlo shouts from the open door of the suite.

I huff out a laugh. "You don't have to shout. The door was open."

My partner makes a skeptical face. "That's never stopped you two before."

Lorelai waves him over. "Arlo, c'mere. We need a professional opinion." She waves in my direction. "What's missing?"

Arlo rubs his chin with one hand, examining me from head to toe. "I feel like cattle at the auction," I whine.

"That makes two of us," Lorelai says, gesturing to her belly. "Is it the shoes?" she asks Arlo.

"Hmm. Maybe? I think we need another opinion. Annie was just outside a minute ago . . ."

"Oh god, we don't have to call in more—"

"Annie Mathers! Get in here, woman!"

A moment later, the door opens again, this time with a line of people filing in. Annie, Jefferson, Shelby, Cameron with a drooling baby strapped to his broad chest, and Maren, toting a box filled with makeup for Lorelai. Presumably.

Hopefully.

"What's missing?" Lorelai says, gesturing to me.

"His Vans."

"His glasses."

"Johnny Cash T-shirt?"

"You're never fully dressed without a smile," Cameron says, bouncing his very wet daughter, Gracie.

"Maybe he shouldn't have shaved today?" Arlo suggests, his head still tilted to the side.

I give Lorelai an imploring look over all their heads and she winks. "All right, everyone out. I know what he needs."

"We'll see you there," Annie chirps, dragging out a smirking Coolidge by his tie. Despite the bouncing, baby Gracie is starting to fuss.

"I think she needs to eat," Shelby says. "We'll be in our suite. Good luck!" She presses a kiss to both my and Lorelai's cheeks before she and Cameron head back across the hall. They aren't coming tonight, but we'll catch up with them after at the small party being hosted by On the Floor Records at a nearby craft brewery.

"I'll give you guys a few minutes and be back to get you in your dress, Lore," Maren says. She turns to me and in a low voice says, "You were right to shave. No regrets, Boseman."

"Thanks, Maren."

Lorelai shoos Arlo out and closes the door, locking it. "Sorry. I should have known they'd be no help."

"No, they're right. This is a disaster. I look like a penguin."

"You look like an executive worthy of being honored. But you're right. You don't look like yourself. And honestly, why the fuck not?" Lorelai tugs on my bow tie. "Strip."

"That's what I've been trying to tell you—"

Lorelai isn't listening, though. She's inside the closet and I can hear the rustling of bags and boxes.

A moment later she comes out, her arms full. "Lose the pants, and for Christ's sake, get out of those shoes."

I follow her command and she hands me a pair of pressed dark-wash jeans. "Put those on." They fit perfectly and I raise my eyebrow as I button the fly.

"These just happened to be in the hotel closet, huh?"

She waves me off with a grin. "Now the boots." She passes me a pair of shined-up black Luccheses.

"My size, I'm guessing?"

"Can't have them pinching on your big night."

"I could have just worn my Vans."

She snorts. "Save them for the after-party."

The boots fit perfectly, and I stand up, walking up to the mirror. I still look like me, but a cleaned-up version. Business on top, different kind of business on bottom. The good-time guy from Tennessee who's gone and made something of himself.

"Better?" Lorelai asks.

"It's perfect."

She wraps her arms around my neck and presses her soft lips to mine, her tongue darting out to taste mine briefly. I place my hands on her belly before sliding them to her hips and squeezing gently. "I love you," I tell her.

314

"Love you, too." She kisses me again and again before pulling back. "Now, if you're done being a prima donna, I need to get dressed. We're cutting it close."

"You know we could still just skip—"

"Fuck off, Boseman. You're going to the Grammys and you're gonna like it."

· · ·

Two hours later, Lorelai shifts uncomfortably in her seat.

"Nervous?" I ask her.

She narrows her eyes and lowers her voice. "No, but your child has the hiccups and decided to perch on my bladder. It's not great."

I bite back a laugh at her expression and instead try for contrite. "That's unfortunate."

"Laugh it up, Boseman. As soon as we're done here, I'm gonna order you one of those carrier things Cam's got."

I shut my mouth and turn back to the show. They're announcing our category next.

Song of the Year.

I've been nominated twice this evening. Once alone, and once as a cowriter with Lorelai. On the one hand, to be nominated is an honor in itself and we're both thrilled for the recognition.

On the other, there's a high-stakes bet on the line depending on whether I can win alone or with my wife or not at all.

Our category is announced, and a fresh-faced sitcom actress reads the teleprompter, introducing the songs up for Song of the Year. I can feel the moment the camera pans to Lorelai and me, and she reaches for my hand, squeezing. My eyes are drawn to her, my brain memorizing this moment. Her long, flowing shiny black hair and dark, laughing eyes. My ring on her finger, our child growing to the sound of her steady heartbeat. I'm gone for her and suspect I always will be.

In the next moment, both our names are called to massive applause. She reaches her hand to me and I take it, pulling her gently to her feet. I give her my arm and escort her up the steps, her ethereal white gown glittering and wrapping around her legs, stealing every ounce of my concentration.

I don't know if it's hormones or the moment, but when Lorelai reaches the mic, glittering tears spill onto her cheeks.

"Hell," she says, "I never thought I'd be here." She swipes her face and looks to me, her watery gaze beaming. "But you knew it, didn't you?" She turns to the mic, her voice clear. "He always knew. Thank you for giving me this chance to come back. I promise I don't take it for granted. Huck?" She shifts aside, and suddenly I'm there in front of the mic. In front of my peers.

I take a deep breath. "She's wrong. I didn't always know. But I hoped. Which is sometimes the same thing, I guess. I hoped to one day make it up here in front of y'all. Way back when it was just Lorelai and me, trading lyrics back and forth and whispering daydreams on the floor of my tiny apartment. And then there was a time I was afraid it never would." I look at my wife and she's pressed her lips together, but it does nothing to diminish her happy smile.

"But one day three years ago, Lorelai called me up out of the blue and told me she was coming back to Nashville. 'I might have something,' she'd said. 'Can you listen and let me know what you think?'"

I look out to the audience, feel something warm inside me at the familiar faces. "*That's* when I knew. Alone, I'm all right, but together?" I reach for Lorelai's hand and kiss her knuckles. "We're unstoppable."

"Together we're unstoppable," my wife repeats in a whisper, her fingers squeezing mine tight.

ACKNOWLEDGMENTS

If you've gotten to this point, you might be thinking to yourself, "Hmm, the premise of this story felt familiar, but I can't quite put my finger on it. . . . I wonder if anyone specific inspired Erin to write this?" And you would be correct. So first, I want to shout out my lifelong adoration and love for Natalie Maines and The Chicks. If you don't know Ms. Maines's story, you should close this book and hit the internet to do some research and then download all of the band's albums. Unfortunately, I can't give everyone their happily ever afters, even if they really deserve it, but if I could, I'd like to think they would look a little like the one Lorelai and Huck got.

All right, so now for my thank-yous, and I've got a mighty list. First, my agent, Kate McKean, who I figure is about as fierce as Trina Hamilton, just with better hair. Thanks for always being in my corner, Boss. I couldn't ask for anyone better. Also my editor, Vicki Lame, who has been my favorite partner in writing-crime since the very beginning through

YA and now adult romance. This one was really for the both of us. As I said from the start, Lorelai's story is exactly our shit. Vanessa Aguirre was the editorial assistant on this story, and thank goodness she was . . . everything runs real smooth with Vanessa around. I appreciate her so. The jacket and cover design came from the brilliant brain of Kerri Resnick, who barely batted an eye at my twelve emails of *"Craig's beard is really not there, but is more mossy, but also he can't look nineteen but also skip the beard and just try the glasses"* and *"OH NO, Lorelai is celiac that bread will kill her!"* The end result is a dream. Kerri is why.

Now my list (unfolds paper, leans into the mic, and speed-reads as the music plays her out): publisher Anne Marie Tallberg, designer Michelle McMillian, managing editor Chrisinda Lynch, production editor Ginny Perrin, champion copy editor Nancy Inglis, production manager Jeremy Haiting, marketing geniuses Alexis Neuville and Brant Janeway, and, finally, the publicity team, which was the brilliant combo of Kelly South, Tracey Guest, and Mary Moates.

Early beta readers and dearest, talented friends Kelly Coon, Lillian Clark, and Laura Namey rock my world. Vegas misses us. My oldest besties who, in truth, claimed Craig Boseman as their collective book boyfriend in our group chat months before anyone else laid eyes on him: Cate Unruh, Megan Turton, Jessica Steenlage, and Angela Swope. Thank you for cheering me on, keeping me sane, and throwing the best book bash signing slash friends' Thanksgiving a girl could ask for.

Thanks to Karen McManus and Kathleen Glasgow. Regular chats with you two keep me sane. I hope I do the same for you!

ACKNOWLEDGMENTS

Brittany Bunzey, Mike Lasagna, and Addie Yoder, every book needs fairy godparents. Lorelai and I are so lucky to have you three.

To my relentlessly supportive mom, Deb; my fierce mother-in-law, Karen; my younger, smarter, wiser, more beautiful, more awesome sister, Cassie; and my Tom: Thank you for being just as excited for me after five books as you were with the first. I wouldn't be here if it weren't for all of you. Even if you don't read the sexy scenes (Mom!), I still write better knowing you all will be on the other end of the pages. To the rest of the Vrtis, Jenkins, and Hahn family, thank you for showing up over and over for my books. Special shout-out to my cousin Annie Werner and my great-aunt Charlotte Bobbitt, who make my day on a regular basis with their constant cheer and support. You may be far away, but I feel your love like warm long-distance hugs.

Finally, to my hot husband, Mike, and our two awesome kids. I don't know how I managed to be the only one in our household who loves reading, but in this case it's likely for the best. You three probably won't ever read this book, but others who know you will. For that, I am both sorry and not sorry. Love you, Family.

To my readers, you're the very best. A thousand erotic poems and song-sexts to every one of you! Catch you in Maren's book next!

ABOUT THE AUTHOR

Erin Hahn

Erin Hahn is the author of the young adult novels *You'd Be Mine, More Than Maybe,* and *Never Saw You Coming* as well as the adult romance *Built to Last.* Romance is her vibe, grunge is her soundtrack, and fall is her signature color. She fell for her flannel-clad college sweetheart the very first day of school, and together they have two hilarious kids who keep her humble. She lives outside Ann Arbor, Michigan, and has a cat named Gus who plays fetch and a dog named June who doesn't.